Catch
A
Falling Star

LAUREL HEIDTMAN

DEDICATION

My earliest memory is my mother reading me stories while I cuddled against her. This, my first novel, is dedicated to you, Mom, with thanks for instilling in me a love of fiction. I wish you were here.

ACKNOWLEDGMENTS

A special thanks to my friends—especially Pat, Kathy, Tony, and Bernie—who helped by reading an earlier draft of this book. The feedback was much appreciated.

Chapter 1

People strolling down the Chicago street that cool spring morning didn't give the nondescript tan Chevrolet or the two men in it a second look. The street was home to office buildings housing therapists and lawyers, and the two men weren't the only people sitting in cars. The difference was the other people were waiting for family members who had appointments in those buildings, and the two men in the tan Chevy were waiting for a fortune to roll their way.

Wendell Halsey, the man behind the wheel, was jazzed. He never felt more alive than just before a job, the adrenaline flowing, the anticipation building, and when the action started—well, it was almost better than sex. It was certainly more profitable, and this job would be the most profitable of all if everything went according to plan. Take out the armored car drivers at the back door of the Drayer Museum before they had a chance to make their delivery and disappear with the package. Simple and clean.

Wendell jumped when his cell buzzed and saw Leonard Nowles, his passenger, shoot a disapproving glance his way. Leonard never got jazzed. The closer it got to a job, the quieter he became. He'd just sit, hands folded, for hours, barely moving a muscle. Then, when the time was right, he'd strike, and someone would die. Like a damn snake, Wendell thought. The guy gave him the creeps, but he had Baby's ear.

"It's the Professor," he said and pressed Accept. "Yeah?"

"About forty minutes. She talked to them less than five minutes ago, and they were just leaving the airport."

"We're in place," Wendell said. "We'll pick 'em up and follow 'em on in."

"The sooner, the better!"

Wendell laughed. "Whatsa' matter? Tired of that rich pussy already?"

"Fuck you."

"Man up, Professor." Wendell had nicknamed him "Professor" back in the joint after learning he had a college degree. "Keep her happy a little bit longer."

"Yeah, yeah. I hear you. Gotta go before she comes looking for me."

"Goddamn Professor!" Wendell was laughing as he disconnected the call. "Shoulda heard him bitchin'! Ain't no one ever told him even bad pussy is good?"

"Maybe if the Professor knew it was his last piece, he'd relax and enjoy it more."

"Yeah." Wendell stopped laughing.

It was the one thing he hated about this job. The Professor had saved his ass—literally—less than a week after he got to Big Muddy. Wendell squirmed just thinking about what could have happened. The Professor was no cherry when it came to doing time, and he'd learned to take care of himself. It wasn't that he was tougher than the other inmates. He just had a knack for learning a person's weak spot. Wendell had seen some flat out monsters give the Professor respect, guys who would just as soon slit their own mother's throat as look at her. He had talent, Wendell thought, a true gift. He hated that Leonard had orders to do the Professor, but he knew better than to argue with Baby. If it was between the Professor and him—well, it was gonna be the Professor. But he didn't have to like it.

***

What I wouldn't give for a brown paper bag right about now, Mick thought as he left the washroom down the hall from Frances's office. Put one over her head, stick a clamp on my nose to block out that damned perfume, and doing her just might be bearable.

Frances Drayer claimed to be forty-five years old. Her hair was fashionably short and a deep rich brown, thanks to the best colorist in Chicago. The nice hairstyle did nothing to offset her dog-ugly face, however, which was long and narrow with a beak nose and huge teeth. Why the hell she'd never had her nose and teeth fixed was beyond him. Her old man certainly had the money to pay for it.

She was naked when he opened the door. One thing he could say about her—she had a nice body. No excess pounds, a flat stomach, a nicely rounded butt, and decent tits, not huge, but nice and only sagging a little. Now if I just had that bag, he thought as he dropped his pants, turned her, and bent her over the desk.

He'd met Frances through a lucky accident. They were walking down intersecting streets, both in a hurry, not watching where they were going, turned the same corner at exactly the same time, and collided. Frances had staggered on her three-inch heels and would have fallen if Mick hadn't grabbed her. He'd watched as her initial anger faded within seconds of looking into his blue eyes.

He pegged her in two seconds—expensive clothes, expensive haircut, ugly face. He saw an opportunity, and he took it. Women like her were easy marks. Turn on the charm, add a little flattery, mix in some hot sex, and they'd open their wallets and checkbooks as fast as they dropped their drawers. When they finally wised up, it was usually possible to make an exit with a few of their valuables. He invited her to lunch as an apology for crashing into her.

Taking her for whatever he could get had been his plan before he'd found out her family owned a museum. He'd used the Mick Donovan ID with her from the start, describing himself as a man down on his luck, and she'd suggested a position with the Drayer before the waitress brought their sandwiches. The idea of working in a museum had started his mind whirring with possibilities. On the one hand, he'd have a lonely, rich woman he could twist around his little finger; on the other hand, he'd have access to a building full of valuable items. He'd smiled, lowered his eyes humbly, and told her he'd be ever so grateful, and if there was ever anything he could do for her....

There were times over the past couple months he'd considered sticking with Frances for the long haul. He wasn't getting any younger, and she was perfect for someone looking to marry money. Only child, so no siblings watching over their inheritance, and a senile daddy who had trouble remembering what day it was. There was an attorney, but he was used to jumping when Frances said frog. If Frances decided she wanted to marry a security guard, the attorney would offer to be best man if it would make her happy.

But during the post-coital cuddling after their third fuck, she told him about the Shooting Star. He'd tried to figure out a way to work the job alone, but he had no idea how to fence something that big. He'd gone to Wendell because he knew Wendell's brother-in-law had connections. So he wouldn't be getting as rich as he'd like now that he had partners, but he'd get enough money to buy some time. He figured he'd head for Vegas, see what he could get into there, or maybe Europe. There were rich women over there same as here, and he had a few good years left. Besides, marrying Frances under an assumed identity was asking for trouble. There was bound to be someone who would recognize him when their picture appeared in the society pages, as it was sure to do.

Frances let out a wail that sounded more like a stray cat having an orgasm than a human. Mick wondered if Sam could hear her down at the security desk. He pulled out of her and used one hand to wipe his dick with a couple of the paper towels he'd brought from the washroom. She turned to him and practically collapsed into his arms, panting for breath.

"Oh, Mick, that was amazing!"

"It sure was." Amazing that I'm able to get it up with an ugly bitch like you, he thought. Not that looks or age ever stopped Mr. Happy from doing his job. His dick was a tool, and it never failed him.

"Mick—I—well, you must know how I feel about you."

"Yeah, you just made that pretty clear." He chuckled and kissed her on top of the head then pulled up his pants.

"Be serious. I mean, yes, you know how much I enjoy our time together, but it's more than that. More than just sex. Mick—I love you."

He stared into her brown eyes that looked back at him expectantly. If he wasn't mistaken, she was holding her breath, waiting for him to say "I love you" back. He could do that, just to keep up appearances. He'd be gone in a couple of days anyway. Before he could decide whether to say the words she wanted to hear or tell her he needed more time to know how he felt, her cell rang.

Saved by the bell, he thought, trying to hide his relief.

"That must be the delivery," he said, buttoning his uniform shirt and tucking it into his pants. He gave her a quick peck on the cheek. "We'll talk later. Okay?"

Frances nodded, disappointment evident in her eyes, and pressed Accept on her phone.

"Yes, okay, I'll be right down. Thank you."

He finished buttoning his uniform shirt and tucked it in his pants.

"Are you ready, sweetie?" Frances said now.

"Oh, yeah." Mick held the door for her. "I've never been more ready."

***

Sam Jankowski didn't mind working Memorial Day weekend. Being a security guard for a museum didn't pay all that well, so the time and a half for the weekend and the double time for the holiday itself was a welcome addition to his paycheck. Besides, he'd worked a lot of holidays and holiday weekends when he was on the force. Wasn't anything he wasn't used to.

Not that he needed the money. His police pension was decent, enough to cover his and Faith's living expenses and leave a little for a nice vacation once a year. But they were both getting old. If one of them got sick or had to go in a home, what savings they had would be wiped out. So he figured he'd make hay while the sun shone.

His only complaint was his partner. In Sam's opinion, Mick Donovan's problem was he'd been born too pretty, and he'd learned to get by on those looks instead of hard work. He was still what Sam supposed women would call handsome, but the signs of too much alcohol and hard living were starting to show. Sam had seen plenty of that on the force, both on people he'd arrested and fellow officers. Sam wasn't the only guard who'd complained about him. Donovan was still in his probationary period, and he'd already been written up twice. Three strikes and he was out.

Maybe.

Sam had seen Donovan using his charm on Frances Drayer, old man Drayer's daughter and the museum director. Using his dick on her, too, Sam thought. Figures he'll screw her silly and catch himself a rich wife—and it just might work. Poor Frances was a homely middle-aged woman who probably didn't have much experience with men. Be like leading a lamb to slaughter.

Ah, well, Sam thought, Donovan's getting old, too. Can't blame a guy for shooting for some security for his old age any more than Frances could be blamed for shooting for some companionship in hers.

Guess that's what they're doing up in that office right now, Sam thought. Shooting for security and companionship. Or maybe just plain screwing. He chuckled and turned back to his newspaper just as the phone hanging on the wall by the security desk buzzed for an inside call. He answered and listened for a moment. "Be right there," he said and hung up the phone.

Well, he thought, here's a surprise. Frances wanted him to meet her and Donovan at the rear door for a delivery. Usually guards scheduled to work a particular shift were made aware of deliveries in advance, but this was the first he'd heard of it. Must be something special to be delivered on a holiday weekend, he thought, and for it to be so hush-hush.

Ah, well, pays the same, he thought. He stood up and started to adjust his nonexistent gun belt. He wondered if he'd ever get used to being without a gun. The Drayer believed armed guards looked bad to the public so the only weapon they were permitted to carry was mace. He'd worked for the museum for a couple of years now and hadn't needed the mace, much less a gun. God forbid I ever do, he thought, as he headed down the hall. Bringing mace to a gunfight would be a real bad idea.

***

"Goddamnit!" Wendell beat the palms of his hand against the steering wheel. He'd barely slammed the brakes on in time to avoid the fire truck. As the light turned red on his side, he saw the armored car signaling the turn into an alley a half block on the other side of the intersection. The Drayer's back door opened onto that alley. The plan had been to take the armored car guards by surprise and grab the Star before it ever got inside. Now there was no way that was going to happen.

"Calm down before you start attracting attention." Leonard sat, unmoving, a faint smile on his thin lips. "It's not like we don't know where they're heading."

"How the fuck does that help? By the time the goddamn light changes, they'll have passed the thing off to the Drayer bitch, and she'll have shut the door."

"And the Professor will open it again. He won't know not to."

Wendell stopped mid-hit and rested his hands on the wheel. "Hey, yeah. You're right. Sorry. I got carried away there."

Leonard stared straight ahead. Wendell glanced around at the other cars stopped at the light, but no one seemed to have noticed his outburst.

"But," he ventured, "what about the Drayer broad, and anybody else who might be there when he opens it?

Leonard didn't reply.

"Oh," Wendell said.

It seemed to take forever for the light to change, and Wendell had to force himself to move through the intersection at a normal speed. As they turned into the alley, he saw the armored car pulling away from the Drayer's rear door.

"Shit!" he muttered. Even though he'd known the chances were slim, he'd hoped they might be in time to stick to the original plan. Doing a couple of rent-a-cops was one thing. Doing a woman was another.

Leonard calmly pressed a button on his cell. "We had a problem. We're in the alley now. You need to open the door."

***

As he disconnected the call, Mick started to sweat. He didn't like it when things didn't go according to plan. The box should never have made it inside, yet here he was holding it, Frances and Sam waiting to accompany him to the vault.

"Sorry." He held up the phone. "Misfire. Nobody there."

Frances accepted the explanation, but Sam looked at him funny. The fucker had cop instincts. Sam asked too many questions every time they worked together. Mick had always heard a cop could smell a con, just like a con could smell a cop. After being around Sam, he believed it.

The rear entrance bell rang. Frances had already taken another step toward the vault. She turned, surprised.

"Must be Vic and the other guy," Mick said. "Probably something else to sign."

Frances nodded. Recently the armored car company had instituted new measures involving extra paperwork. Just as she turned the lock and started to pull the door open, Sam moved forward, drawing his mace from his belt.

"Wait!" he said, but it was too late. Frances was pulling the door inward when Leonard and Wendell hit it hard from the outside.

Frances stumbled, slipped, and fell backward. As she went down, Mick saw Leonard bring a gun up, aim it at Sam, and fire, striking him in the chest. Sam went down, the useless can of mace dropping from his hand. In slow motion, Mick saw Sam hit the floor and roll to his side, his hand on his chest, blood running between his fingers. As if from a distance, he heard Frances scream and saw Leonard swing the gun toward her while Wendell kicked the door shut behind them.

"No!" he shouted. "Don't hurt her!"

Leonard stopped, stared at him for what seemed like a long time but couldn't have been more than a second or two, and moved the gun away from Frances and toward him. No one had been supposed to get hurt, much less killed. That had been part of the deal. Now Mick knew the terms of the deal had changed.

Slow motion clicked back to real time. Mick started back-pedaling away from Leonard and Wendell, but he knew it was no good. He was at least thirty feet from an intersecting corridor. There was no way he could beat a bullet.

"Sorry, Professor." Leonard's trigger finger began its pull. "Just how it is."

Frances lunged, screaming and growling, like some half-mad cougar protecting her cub. She grabbed Leonard's right leg with her left arm and swung her other fist into his groin. He screamed and doubled over but maintained enough control to swing the gun at her head. He hit her hard on her right temple, and she crumpled to the floor. Still doubled over, he aimed the gun at her head and pulled the trigger.

Mick only heard the shot. He didn't see the bullet hit its target because by that time he had rounded the corner of the intersecting corridor. It ran about fifty feet before dead-ending into another corridor. Two doors opened off it on the right, one to a supply closet, the other to the basement. Still holding the box containing the Star, Mick quickly slipped through the basement door and locked it behind him.

He had one advantage. He knew the museum, and they didn't. He held his breath as he heard them tear around the corner into the corridor where he hid and run its full length, feet pounding on the tile floor. He was counting on them thinking he'd made it to the next corridor, which went a short distance in both directions before it ended in another corridor on the right side and a display room on the left. They wouldn't know which way he had gone and would have to split up. It would be a couple of minutes before they figured out they had passed him.

He flipped the lock and opened the door quietly. He could still hear one of them running in the direction of the corridor to the right. The other was probably searching the display room. There were a few display cases stationed around the room but looking for him behind those wouldn't occupy Leonard or Wendell, whichever one it was, for long. He didn't have much time.

He quickly moved back the way he had come, toward the rear entrance. Even though he knew what to expect, he groaned as he came around the corner and saw Frances lying in her own blood and brains, the bullet's entrance wound just above her right temple. Her eyes were open, staring at the ceiling. She'd saved his life, Mick realized, feeling a sudden rush of affection for the fallen woman.

Sam was on his side, facing toward Frances, bleeding and breathing, Mick saw, although he probably wouldn't be for long. As Mick moved toward the rear door, Sam moved his right hand toward him, as if trying to grab his leg.

"Hey, Sam, I'm sorry." Mick shifted the box under his left arm and bent over the man, whispering. "This wasn't supposed to happen. You gotta play dead, understand? Those fuckers need to think they finished you. Okay?"

Sam stared at him, tried to form a word, gave up and moved his head in what passed for a nod.

"You see him?" Mick heard Leonard shout, and a moment later, Wendell responded from the direction of the display room with a "No, man. He's gone."

"He's not gone," Leonard called back. He sounded almost amused.

"Dead, remember? Look dead," Mick said to Sam.

He opened the door then stopped. The keypad beside the door had a panic button that would set off a silent alarm at the monitoring station. He pressed it down and held it for the requisite three seconds before slipping into the alley.

A tan Chevy was parked in the delivery pull-off. Mick almost laughed when he saw the keys dangling from the ignition. Wendell had been driving. As he slipped behind the wheel, started the car, and peeled out of the alley, he wondered what Leonard would say when he realized his boss's dipshit brother-in-law had been dumb enough to jump out without the keys.

He was three blocks from the museum when he started shaking. Jesus H. Christ! They had never intended to let him live. He'd gone to them with a plan, a chance to get rich, and they'd played him along, knowing they'd never have to share the money with him. Treacherous sons-of-bitches! They'd killed Frances, probably killed Sam, and now he was in it up to his neck. It wasn't just an art museum robbery anymore. If he were caught, he'd be as guilty as they were of murder because he was part of a felony crime where somebody died.

He glanced over at the box on the seat beside him. There was at least fifteen million bucks in gems and gold in that box, more to a collector, and no way to get at it. The only reason he'd gone to Wendell in the first place was because he had no idea how to move something like the Star. He had enough money to get out of town, maybe hole up for a couple weeks, but he needed more than that to completely disappear.

It was a good thing he knew where he could get it.

CHAPTER 2

"It's so good to have you home, Katherine," Bette Rawlings said for the third time in the last twenty minutes. "How long will you be staying?"

"At least for the summer, Mom," Kate answered, also for the third time. "I'm teaching a summer writing class at the university."

"Oh, that's nice."

In the living room, the television volume went up a notch. Steven looked at her and shrugged as if to say "I told you so."

The three of them were seated around Steven's cherry dining table. Harry Rawlings was sprawled in a recliner in the living room, watching television and making himself as invisible as possible. Deja vu all over again, thought Kate.

"Mom, I'm going to go check in at the Holly and unload my stuff. After I get cleaned up, I'll be back. Steven has promised us a good home-cooked meal."

"Oh, that will be nice."

Her mother's voice faded as if she were thinking of something else. Kate stood and went around to her mother's side of the table. She hugged the petite woman from behind and kissed the top of her head. Bette automatically reached up to smooth her thinning gray hair. She had always been a stickler for good grooming, and that part of her personality hadn't disappeared. Kate found that reassuring, but she knew it was a case of grasping at straws.

"I love you, Mom," she whispered.

"I love you, too, honey."

Kate blinked back the tears that threatened to spill and turned to Steven. "So what time do you want me back here?"

"Six should do it," her brother said.

"See you at six then, Mom."

Bette smiled, nodded, and went back to patting her hair.

As Kate moved through the living room, she glanced at her father. His long bony frame was stretched back in the recliner. Kate had always thought her father would have looked at home wearing a Stetson and seated on a horse, even though he'd never ridden one as far as she knew. He just looked like the stereotypical cowboy, all alone atop his horse, a solitary figure with no ties to home and family. The image fit him in more ways than just physical appearance.

When she'd arrived, he'd given her a perfunctory hug and a peck on the cheek before flopping back down in the recliner, his gray eyes focused on the television screen. Never mind that they hadn't seen one another for months. He was more interested in the loud political discussion on the FoxNews channel.

"See you at supper, Daddy."

"Sure thing, Katydid." He glanced at her and turned back to the set.

"I'll walk you out," Steven said.

At her car, she hugged her twin hard. "God, Stevie, how do you do it?"

"Day to day." Steven stepped back, running his hand through his thinning brown hair as was his habit when he was agitated or anxious. "What else is there to do? Dad's no help—no big news flash there. If it were up to him, he'd have Mom in a dementia wing at some cheap nursing home. That's not happening as long as I have anything to say about it."

"I'm so sorry you've had to handle all this alone."

"Hey, you're here now, aren't you? Not the best homecoming, but I'm glad you're here." He opened her driver's door. "Go get checked in, fix your face, and get back here. I'll make sure Dad stays for supper."

"What do you mean?" Kate was surprised. "Why wouldn't he be here?"

"He's the original invisible man, remember? Ever since I moved them in with me, he's spent the nights at their house. Or at least that's where he says he is. For all I know, he's got a girlfriend somewhere. Claims if the house is empty, somebody will break in and clean them out."

"Isn't everything moved out?"

"Not quite. There wasn't room for the furniture here, and Carla advised us to leave it furnished when we listed it with her. Apparently people like to see a house with furniture in it. So Dad has a place to sleep and a chair to sit in, and he keeps moving his clothes back a little at a time. To tell the truth, I don't think he'll sell the place. I think he'll just leave Mom here with me, and he'll stay there."

His thin lips pulled back in a humorless smile, his blue eyes cold behind his wire-rimmed glasses. "And that's fine with me."

Guilt threatened to suffocate Kate as she drove the two blocks to Holly House. Using the excuse of her career, she had put as many miles as she could between herself and her father, but in so doing, she had lost time with her mother. Now Bette Rawlings had Alzheimer's, and she was disappearing fast. She had needed her children, and one of them had deserted her.

***

Holly House had been built in 1900 by one of Samuel Eden's sons-in-law as a wedding gift to his new bride, Holly. Judging by a portrait displayed in the University's history department, Holly was a beauty but unfortunately a frail one. She died less than a year after their marriage while giving birth to a son.

Holly House changed hands three times, sitting empty for over twenty years after the third owner lost it during the Depression. Then John and Edna Hill came to town when John accepted the post of vice-president at Raven University. Their infant daughter, Ann, was four months old when they moved into Holly House, living at first in the three rooms least in need of work. Both John and Edna had been born with the proverbial silver spoons in their mouths so, money being no object, all twenty rooms and twelve baths were soon restored to their former glory. Two years later, a son, Edgar, was added to the family.

Kate had known of the Hills, but living in a neighboring town, she hadn't known the Hill children. The paths of the two families crossed and became intertwined when Edgar Hill met Steven Rawlings, and the two fell in love.

Kate had long known Steven was gay, but they had kept it from their parents. When he fell in love with Edgar, he told them. Bette accepted her son's predilection with barely a blink, but Harry

Rawlings did not take the news well. Surprisingly, he actually screamed and shouted and threatened to kill his son instead of simply disappearing like he usually did when faced with something he didn't wish to face. He refused to speak to or even acknowledge Steven for nearly three years but gradually returned to his usual grunt or nod when his son came to visit. Steven once told Kate that he kind of wished he could see the violent Harry again because negative emotion was better than no emotion.

Edgar had passed away five years previously from pancreatic cancer, but the Hill women had remained part of Steven's extended family. Edna and Ann had turned Holly House into a bed and breakfast a few years after John died. They both loved to cook, and the sumptuous breakfasts and lavish rooms quickly moved Holly House into the award-winning category of bed and breakfast inns. As impressive as the house, the grounds occupied the six acres of an entire city block. Edna now lived in what had been the servants quarters, the three rooms and bath having been remodeled into a private apartment, while Ann had her own place above the six-car garage. Ten bedrooms with private baths in the main house and another four in the guesthouse were available to the public. Whenever Kate came home for visits, she usually rented a room at the Holly.

"Honey, it's *so* good to see you!" Edna threw her arms around Kate and squeezed. At six feet, Edna was taller than Kate by four inches and still strong at seventy-nine. When Edna hugged a person, that person knew she'd been hugged.

"Let up, Edna, before you squash her!" Ann admonished her mother.

As Edna reluctantly let go, Ann pecked Kate on the cheek. "It really is good to see you, Kate. Especially since you'll be staying for a while this time."

An inch or so taller than her mother and just as strong, Ann presented as more controlled. Edna's mother had passed her Swedish genes down to her daughter and granddaughter, and Kate could easily picture the two as Viking matriarchs. They wore their multi-shaded gray hair short in similar cuts, their eyes were the same piercing shade of blue, and their facial features and solid muscular builds were so similar that a stranger would know them instantly for mother and daughter.

"It's wonderful to be here," Kate said. "Thank you for finding me a room. Based on the cars in the lot, it looks like you're full."

"It's Raven's Welcome Week for new students entering in the fall," Edna said. "The parents stay here and other places around town, and the kids stay on campus. But you don't have to thank us. We wouldn't want Eden's only mystery novelist staying at the Shady Nook."

Kate laughed. The Shady Nook was a no-tell motel at the south edge of town with the reputation of renting its rooms by the hour. Locals called it the "Shady Nookie."

"You never know. I might get some good ideas for a book."

Edna snorted. "You'd probably get bedbugs and a few other things as well."

"We reserved the Bluebell for you," Ann said. "As usual."

All bedrooms at Holly House were named after flowers and had floral themes in their decor. The Bluebell's walls were covered with paper imprinted with the small bluish purple flowers. On the walls hung several paintings of bluebells done by Ann. On her first visit to the Holly, Kate had noticed small figures peering out from among the bluebell stalks. She'd asked Ann if they were fairies.

"As I imagined them to be," Ann had replied. "Fairy lore has it that bluebells are rung to call fairies to secret meetings. Only fairies can hear them. If a human does, it puts them in danger."

Kate had stayed in the Bluebell on every visit since, charmed by the magical paintings and the beautiful room.

"Have you seen Bette yet?" Edna said.

Kate nodded. "I stopped at Steven's before I came here."

"How was she?"

Kate thought for a second or two. How *was* her mother? What was the best way to describe a woman who was gradually fading away like a human Cheshire cat? "Vague, I guess I'd say. Confused. I mean, it was nothing she said that was off. It was just that she said the same thing several times."

"Steven says he's seen some improvement with the new drugs the doctor has her on," Edna said. "And who knows what medicine will come up with in the next few years."

"Make the best of today, right?" Kate managed a weak smile. "Well, I'd better get my stuff unloaded. Steven wants me back at six for dinner."

"I'll help you," Ann said.

It took the two of them three trips to empty Kate's car of her luggage and boxes of books and papers. Kate loved the room with its mix of antiques and good replicas, the overstuffed chair, and the comfortable bed. She felt the tension that had been with her since seeing her mother and father begin to lift. As with every other visit home, the Bluebell would be her escape.

"I might never leave this room." She turned in a full circle, her eyes devouring the room's beauty. "I'll just stay in bed or cuddle up in that chair and forget about everything in this world. Just dream of fairies and flowers."

"I can understand you feeling that way," Ann said. "I'm so sorry for what you and Steven are going through."

"Funny how you never expect anything to happen to your parents, isn't it?" Kate shook her head. "You know better, but you never expect it."

Ann nodded.

"Edna seems as young as ever. You're very lucky, you know."

"I do know," Ann agreed. "Sometimes I think she's in better shape than I am. She certainly has more energy!"

Kate smiled.

"Well, I'll let you get settled." Ann stopped in the doorway. "Since you'll be here for at least the summer, I'd love to introduce you to some lady friends of mine, Ginger Ray and Nan Davis. Ginger works the Friday and Saturday breakfast shift at the Main Street Diner downtown, and Monday through Thursday she works here, helping with whatever needs doing. Nan owns the local paper. We get together every week or two for coffee or brunch, usually at the diner. We're meeting this Friday, so if you're not too busy getting settled in at the University, please join us."

"It sounds wonderful," Kate said. "Thank you for asking me."

***

Steven fixed a delicious vegetable lasagna for dinner, accompanied by salad and garlic bread, and followed by fresh fruit for dessert. He made enough for four. Kate and Steven split their father's portion when he didn't show.

Chapter 3

Jo had lost track of how many coffees she'd had since arriving at the station, but whatever the count, it wasn't enough. All she had to show for the caffeine were jittery nerves and an acidic stomach, although some of both could be an aftereffect of fighting with Nick half the night. What irritated her most was that he'd expected her to be pleased when he announced he'd been offered a supervisory position with a private security firm headquartered in D.C. She hadn't even known he was looking for a different job, much less being considered for one.

The company had government contracts in war zones, and with private companies and wealthy individuals around the globe. He had informed her breathlessly his starting salary would be mid-six figures, and they would be relocating to Washington within the month. She told him he was out of his mind if he thought she was moving. Things went downhill from there.

The Eden Police Department was housed in the basement of a nearly 150-year old building that held a place of distinction on the local Historic Register. What the building lacked in modern upgrades and space, it made up for in charm, and that mattered most to the city council. It was pointed out to parents of prospective Raven students and visiting businessmen to Eden Steel alike as evidence that Eden valued tradition and American values. Made of stone quarried from the surrounding area, it consisted of a full basement, two floors, an attic and a clock tower. City offices were located on the first floor, while the second floor was home to a courtroom, an office suite used by the visiting circuit court judge, and another belonging to David Priest, who held the dual roles of city attorney and prosecutor. Both floors sported gleaming oak woodwork, brass light fixtures, charming oil paintings, and black and white photographs of Eden's early days.

Charm wasn't an issue in the basement since businessmen seldom had reason to visit the police department and parents didn't until their already enrolled offspring misbehaved. The Eden Police Department's detective section was barely fifteen feet wide and twenty feet long. It was jammed with six desks sitting in pairs with fronts touching, chairs for each of the six detectives and one chair for civilians to the side of each desk, five four-drawer vertical file cabinets, a cabinet holding a printer and fax machine, and a small counter with a bar sink and coffee maker.

The walls were what Sticks called puke-pink, scuffed and scratched between the bulletin boards holding outdated BOLO alerts, For Sales posted by officers, and law-enforcement related cartoons. The floor was covered with equally scuffed and scratched beige vinyl. Sunlight hadn't invaded the premises since 1953 when the windows were bricked up for safety after a prisoner who had just made bail took a potshot at the detective who had charged him. He'd missed, but the bullet hole was still visible two feet from the floor on the inside wall. One fluorescent light had a constant flicker, and the smell of burnt coffee and stale sweat permeated the room.

Looking at it objectively, Jo figured most women would consider her nuts to choose this room and what it represented over a husband who brought home an annual paycheck bigger than what she earned in a decade, but that's exactly what she was considering doing.

"You're in early." Donnie Lewis had a Starbucks in one hand, a croissant in the other. His gray pinstripe suit and carefully styled blond hair made him look more like a hotshot attorney than a cop.

"Couldn't sleep," she said.

"It shows."

"Thanks a lot." She stood and stretched. "Anything new on the break-ins?"

Lewis and Rick Samuels had been working a string of office burglaries and car break-ins, both on and off campus. Initially the Raven University Police had handled the campus incidents, but once it was determined the off-campus incidents were likely the work of the same people, Eden P.D. had shouldered most of the work.

"Nada," Lewis said. "Rick and I have talked to every douche bag in the county, but so far nobody looks good for it."

"They've got douche bags in the neighboring counties, too."

"It must be one who knows how to keep his mouth shut," Lewis said. "Our usual blabbermouths swear they haven't heard anything."

"Sooner or later some of the stuff will turn up."

"From your mouth to God's ears." Lewis sighed. "I miss the old days when all a guy had to do to find stolen property was keep a watch on the pawnshops. Today it's eBay and Craigslist and flea markets."

Jo's phone rang, and Lewis turned to his desk.

"Detective Valentine."

"Hey, Jo." It was Vera Carter, the day dispatcher. "I've got a Chicago detective on the line. Says a guy he's looking for might be in Eden. He asked for the chief, but when I told him Leffitt wasn't in yet, he asked for a detective."

Chief Brody Daniels had left Saturday morning for a conference in Arizona sponsored by the International Association of Chiefs of Police. Daniels had taken his wife, Gloria, along, and the two of them were flying on to Hawaii for a week's vacation before coming home.

The department was unusual in that the ratio of brass to officers and detectives was weighted in favor of the peons. Under the chief was one deputy chief, a lieutenant in charge of patrol, and four sergeants to cover all patrol shifts. Detectives answered directly to Daniels, and in his absence, Deputy Chief Leffitt.

"Put him through," Jo said, putting Nick and Washington out of her mind.

CHAPTER 4

As Kate dug into the generous stack of blueberry pancakes, she began to see the downside of staying at Holly House. If she indulged in these breakfasts every morning, she would soon be buying clothing a couple sizes larger than the size ten she was wearing.

Slipping on her reading glasses, she turned to the Lexington paper. When Ann dropped it off at the table, she had pulled the Arts and Leisure section out and pointed to the front-page article about Jackson and his book.

Jackson Price, her friend and grad school advisor, was the reason Kate had a job in Eden. When she first met him, he had been only three years out of his doctoral program and a shining star in the literary world with a novel based on his Vietnam experience. Jackson had enlisted in the Army within weeks of graduating from college, and after officer's training, deployed to Vietnam. He survived a year in-country and spent the remainder of his enlistment in Germany before returning home and continuing his studies. He hadn't been physically injured in the war, but he'd been profoundly changed, and he wrote about that change beautifully.

Raven University hadn't been the only school to offer him a position, but the Prices were an established Eden family and Jackson was homesick. He'd once told Kate he hadn't expected to stay more than a couple of years, but those years had stretched into decades. Now he was chair of the English department.

The article was about Jackson's latest book, *Dogwood Days*. The years between the novel that made Jackson a rising star and this one had not been kind to him as far as successful published works went. He had written a half dozen more novels, each one worse than the last. Now, at sixty-five, he'd hit the jackpot again. *Dogwood Days* had not only garnered glowing critical reviews from the intelligentsia, it had shot to the top of bestseller lists all over the United States, Canada, and Europe. The article was about a movie deal, reportedly for a seven-figure amount. Kate wondered how Jackson, the intellectual, felt about becoming Jackson, the popular author. He hadn't even owned a television in the "old days."

"Isn't that wonderful about Dr. Price?" Edna refreshed Kate's coffee.

"It certainly is. I'm so happy for him."

"Great publicity for Eden and Raven, too," Edna said. "Enrollment has dropped lately. This should give it a boost, at least in the English department."

Except for the fact that Jackson is leaving, Kate thought. During their phone conversations about the summer position, he'd told her he'd made the decision to retire. Still, she supposed, the publicity and prestige probably would help enrollment for a year or so, and Jackson would likely teach the occasional graduate seminar in his retirement.

Edna patted Kate's shoulder. "And getting you should give it another boost."

Kate smiled as Edna moved off to another table. Edna assumed she was in Eden permanently, and maybe she was. Alzheimer's tended not to kill its victims for many years. She'd already lost too much time that could have been spent with her mother, plus she owed it to her brother to stick around.

Turning to the front section, she noticed an article in the lower right corner, an update on the Memorial Day weekend theft from the Drayer Museum. She had visited the Drayer when she was in Chicago signing with Dolly's agency six—no, seven—years ago. She remembered the Drayer as a small, but impressive, family-owned museum, a rarity in and of itself.

Two people had been shot. The owner's daughter and museum director, Frances Drayer, had died at the scene. A retired Chicago police officer who worked as a security guard for the museum had also been shot but had hung on to life since the incident. Today's article reported the man, Samuel Jankowski, had passed away without ever regaining consciousness. A second security guard was missing and was "being sought for questioning."

Only one item had been stolen, a valuable artifact from the Indus Valley civilization, which flourished in India as long ago as 3000 B.C. It was believed to be the centerpiece of a tiara-like headgear, although the rest of the tiara had long since been lost. A grainy photo accompanied the article, and a sidebar described the artifact as consisting of a 60-carat deep-red star ruby. A star ruby, the sidebar explained, was a rare stone that, due to its internal structure, reflected light in a six-pointed star pattern. Diamonds trailed out in a fan above the stone, as if the ruby were a shooting star coming straight at the viewer. The gems were set in gold and several diamonds larger than those in the trails were set at random intervals around the ruby and the other diamonds as if they were stars still in the firmament. The artifact was called the Shooting Star, with an estimated value of fifteen million dollars based on the gems and gold alone but as much as twice that to a collector.

"Maybe an idea for your next novel?" Ann had noticed the headline as she bussed Kate's empty plate and silverware.

"It might be. I'm always on the lookout for ideas." She glanced at her watch. "But it will have to wait. Duty—and a department meeting—calls."

***

Raven University was named after Holly Eden's younger sister, Isabelle. Unlike the blond and frail Holly, Isabelle was dark and strong. Her nickname from childhood was Raven, given to her for her black curls and her sharp intelligence like that of her namesake bird. The university consisted of dark red brick buildings sprawled over the hillside leading down to a retaining wall that kept the river in its place during rainy periods. Between the buildings were mature deciduous and evergreen trees, and green spaces dotted with benches and pebbled walkways. From the air, Kate imagined the university might look like a verdant ground cover blooming with red flowers. Or maybe that was just the effect of spending the night at Holly House. She'd have to watch that she didn't start using too many floral metaphors in her mysteries. She wasn't sure she could get away with describing a spreading pool of blood from a knife wound as a "blood-red rose opening its petals."

Grabbing the packet of papers Jackson had mailed her, she locked her car and cut across campus to the personnel office, enjoying the warm June morning and the quiet. Summer school was always that way. Fewer students, therefore quieter and more laid back than the fall and winter semesters, with their hordes of students, football games, and frat parties. She dropped off her papers, signed a few forms, and headed back to Hanover. As she rounded the corner, she saw a man exit the front door and turn in the other direction. There was something familiar about him. It looked like…but, no, that couldn't be.

As she entered the building, the smell of formaldehyde struck her nostrils. Hanover's basement level and first floor were the Zoology department's bailiwick, while the second and third floors belonged to English. No one had ever been able to explain this illogical pairing. Jackson liked to postulate that some past administrator had wanted to keep the lovers of literature firmly grounded in reality by exposing them to the odors emanating from the labs in the basement.

"Welcome home!" Mary Dunn, the department secretary, smiled and gave her a quick hug. Mary had started at Raven as a floater office worker shortly before Kate finished her master's. A couple of years younger than Kate, she was a short, pudgy woman, with hair as white as snow and a cheerful ruddy face. "You look wonderful. As usual. Loved your last book, by the way."

"That makes you, my brother, my mom, and a half dozen acquaintances."

"Hardly! Next to Jackson, you're our most famous person around here."

"Doesn't say much for Raven."

"Enough with the false modesty, Dr. Rawlings." Mary smacked her hand on the counter before turning and going to a cabinet on the back wall. Unlocking it with a key from a chain around her neck, she selected a key ring from a hook inside.

"The keys to the kingdom," she said. "One for the front door, one for the door to the parking lot, and your office key. You're in 307, by the way. They're marked, but after you get used to them, remove the labels, please. In case you lose them, we'd rather they weren't easily identified.

"Not that the crooks need keys," she added. "I don't know if anyone's told you, but we've had a rash of break-ins on campus over the last couple of months, both cars and offices. Campus police have been advising everyone not to leave valuables in either place."

"I'll remember that." Kate slipped the keys into her pocket. "Is Jackson in?"

"He was, but he stepped out right after one of his fans stopped by to see him." Mary glanced at the clock on the wall. "Since it's only fifteen minutes until the staff meeting, I don't expect him back."

"I'll see him then," Kate said. "After I check out my new digs."

"Freshly painted and we even cleaned the carpet—very carefully, of course, since it's pretty thin in places. It was probably here when you were."

Mary might not have exaggerated, Kate thought, as she stood in the doorway of her office. The carpet did look pretty thin, but the walls were a nice eggshell color, the ancient wooden desk and bookcases dust-free, and she even had an old brown leather love seat against one wall. Not bad, she thought. A few prints, a plant, some books, and it will be downright homey.

The message light on her phone was blinking. She followed the message-retrieval instructions taped to the phone, surprised to find it was a message meant for her. She had expected it to be for the office's previous occupant. She was even more surprised when she found the call was from Ann's friend.

"Dr. Rawlings," a woman's voice said. "This is Nannette Davis from the Eden Chronicle. I would love to interview you about your books and your return to your alma mater. I'll check back with you, or you can call me."

The woman repeated a phone number twice and disconnected.

Kate was embarrassed to feel flattered, but flattered she was. She had gotten some attention from the press after each book came out, but Dolly, her agent, and the publisher played a part in that. She doubted the biweekly Chronicle was on Dolly's radar. She guessed she would agree to the interview. Dolly would throw a hissy if she didn't, especially since *Flee* had been on the shelves less than a month.

Well, so much for that. She quickly unpacked the papers and few office items she'd brought in her briefcase. It was time to meet the rest of the faculty.

CHAPTER 5

As he shifted in the chair, trying to find a comfortable position for his back, Cal wondered—not for the first time—why anyone in their right mind would pay big bucks for chairs that could be used for enhanced interrogation at Guantanamo. He had no doubt that Gallagher Holdings had paid big bucks. All the offices looked like something out of a high-class decorating magazine, but only the bosses had chairs that looked comfortable. Probably a method to their madness. Keep the subordinate off his game, like sawing an inch or two off the front legs of chairs in the interrogation rooms back at the precinct to keep the suspect uncomfortable and off balance—literally and mentally—during questioning.

Then again, maybe it had more to do with his almost sixty-year-old back and the extra forty pounds he was packing.

"He can't have disappeared into thin air!" Foreman's voice was inching higher with every sentence. It did that when he was upset. "Even if his accomplices murdered him, the police should have found a body by now or picked up some intel from snitches."

George Foreman, Managing Director of Investigations for Gallagher Holdings and Cal Becker's boss, didn't look anything like his namesake. He looked thin, balding, white, and worried. Understandably worried, since it wasn't every day Gallagher Holdings faced a fifteen-million-dollar payout. Hell, more than fifteen by the time you added in compensation to the families of the two murder victims, damage to the museum's reputation, and who knows what else. Cal figured if he was the man in charge of the men tracking down the doers and the Star, he'd look worried, too. Sometimes it was good to be a peon.

"Are you sure the cops don't have any leads?"

"Not a hundred percent sure," Cal said. "But I've got pretty good sources inside the department. So do Mike and Andy."

Mike Watson and Andy Miles were two investigators working the Star case with Cal, the three of them retired from the Chicago Police Department. Mike was the first to land the Gallagher gig, going to work the day after his retirement party. He'd courted Andy and Cal for Gallagher as their retirement dates approached. At first Cal had resisted, but after a month long "vacation," he'd found he was bored to tears and took Mike up on the offer. Two years later he was still bored most of the time—insurance investigation was not the same thing as police work—but his bank account looked better than it had three years ago after Virginia decided a divorce was the answer to her midlife crisis and cleaned him out.

"Our sources are happy to share," Cal continued. "They know we'll do the same. Sam was one of us, and we want his killers. Mabry's record indicates he's not the violent type, so we get him, there's a good chance he'll give up his pals."

Sam had been more than a fellow police officer. He had been Cal's friend since they'd survived the academy together. Over the years, they drank their share of beers in each other's backyards, watched ball games together while Virginia and Faith went shopping, called each other "dickhead" and "asshole," which in man-speak means "I love you." Cal spent many sleepless nights in the two weeks following the robbery, haunted by the image of his friend lying in the hospital bed, tubes stuck in every orifice, mouth hanging slack, lips peeling from lack of moisture, eyelids floating half-open. "Lights on, nobody home" persisted in repeating itself in Cal's mind like a sick chant whenever he looked at those eyes.

Well, the lights weren't on anymore. The doctors had told Faith that Sam was brain dead and that there was nothing they could do for him, but she'd been unable to bring herself to pull the plug. Sam spared her the agony of having to make that decision. His heart had stopped the day before—just over two weeks after he'd been shot—while the fluids still flowed into his veins and his chest still rose and fell, thanks to the respirator pumping air into his body.

The Chicago Police Department had over 12,000 sworn officers—a big enough organization that everyone didn't know everyone else's business. Even Andy and Mike weren't aware that Cal and Sam went way back. Unless Cal told him, Foreman wasn't likely to learn of their friendship, and Cal wasn't going to tell him. He knew Foreman would pull him off the case because he would be afraid Cal was too personally involved in finding Sam's killers to be focused on finding the Star. He couldn't and wouldn't be robbed of the chance to get the lowlifes responsible for his friend's death.

"The Star is our priority here. You need to remember that."

"The way I see it, find the man, find the Star." Cal tried to hide his irritation at Foreman's obtuseness. He shifted in the chair. "We did find something, but it's a long shot."

"What is it?" Foreman's voice continued its climb. Cal figured the atoms in the crystal vase on Foreman's bookcase were starting to quiver.

"The detectives working the case found four books in Mabry's room. Three were written by the same woman and the other by a man. They were the only four books in the place, and it looked like they'd been read and reread."

"So?"

Cal nodded toward the file in front of Foreman, "As you know from our reports, once the cops got Mabry's real name from the fingerprint check, they did a background on him. Went to college in Kentucky."

"Yes, yes, I know. Bachelor's in English from Western Kentucky University, started a graduate program in creative writing at Raven University in Eden, Kentucky, dropped out before finishing. That was what, over thirty years ago? How is it relevant to this investigation?"

"The male author is Mabry's old professor, Jackson Price. The book is on the bestseller list. He just sold the movie rights to it as well. The other three books are all mysteries, written by a woman named Katherine Rawlings."

Cal handed Foreman the latest novel in Rawlings's lineup face down so he could see the author's photo on the back. An attractive woman smiled at the camera. Cal knew from googling her that she was in her mid-fifties, but she looked younger—a hint of matching lines from her nose to the corners of her mouth, a little crow's feet at the eyes, but overall not bad. Her honey-colored hair was straight and worn chin length, her green eyes flecked with blue, her smile wide and welcoming.

"I did a little digging on her. Turns out she was in grad school at Raven at the same time as Mabry and just took a summer teaching position there. So these are two old friends of Mabry's, both with money and both in the same place."

"You think he'd go to them for help?"

"I don't know, but it might be worth checking out."

"What do the Chicago police think about it?"

"Not much," Cal admitted. "But they don't have the resources or time to spend chasing down thin leads. Guy working the case said they'd phoned the police down there and gave them the information, but he didn't expect anything would come of it."

"But you think it might?"

"Who knows? But if you okay it, I can catch a flight into Lexington, get a rental, and be there by evening. Andy and Mike can keep looking here."

Foreman thought for a minute. When he spoke again, his voice had dropped back a notch. Maybe the crystal vase had a chance after all. "What about his accomplices? Any new leads there?"

"Nothing more than what's in the reports already. The cops think Dominick Duda's organization is involved. Wendell Halsey is married to Duda's sister, and he and Mabry were on the same block at Big Muddy. Word from the guards is they were pretty tight. Guy I talked to says his snitches act all nervous when he pumps them—like maybe they've heard something, but are afraid to talk. They tailed Halsey for a few days, but when nothing came of it, they had to pull it off."

Cal shifted his body and something popped. Damn back.

"The more things change, the more they stay the same. Duda scared the crap out of everyone on the street when I was on the job, and he still does. His nickname is Baby, because he's got a fat babyish face, but there's nothing baby-like about him. He'd gut his own mom on Mother's Day if she interfered with business and everyone knows it. That's why nothing ever sticks on him. No one will talk."

"Okay," Foreman's voice was almost back to normal. Guess having some new possibility to check out gave him hope. At the least, he'd have something new to spin to *his* boss. "It's not much, but let's give Kentucky a look."

He hit the intercom to his secretary's desk. "Linda, book Cal on the next flight to Lexington."

"Round trip?"

Foreman looked at Cal, eyebrows raised in question.

"Better make it one way," Cal said. "If there's something there, I don't want the hassle of rescheduling. I'll have a rental anyway, so I can drive back. It's less than eight hours."

"One way." Foreman told his secretary and disconnected. "Get the times and airline from Linda before you leave. I want this checked as soon as possible then get back here."

"Shouldn't take more than a couple days, I wouldn't think. Unless we get lucky."

Chapter 6

In addition to Jackson, Raven's English Department boasted fifteen full-time associate and full professors and three part-timers. A skeleton crew worked summers. Only six people besides Jackson and herself occupied chairs at the large conference table. Kate had met three of the six at a dinner party hosted by Jackson during one of her visits home. Linza Collett was a thin, fortyish linguistics professor. She had attended with her partner, Alice something, who worked in student aid. Bill Herrick, who taught eighteenth- and nineteenth-century American lit, had been there with his wife. Kate remembered them all as genuinely nice people.

Chris Irons, who taught nineteenth-century British literature, had been Kate's male counterpart at the dinner party. He'd been recently divorced, and Kate suspected Jackson had been trying to play Cupid. In his fifties, he was one of those men who get better looking with age. Tan and muscular with a full head of dark hair liberally streaked with gray, he had been a pleasant dinner partner. She glanced at his ring finger. Nothing there. When she looked up, he was watching her, an amused smile on his rugged face. She smiled back, feeling like a silly coed caught checking out the boys.

She knew one other at the table by reputation, both good and bad. Paul Holland taught twentieth-century American literature and poetry writing classes. In his early forties, he was an accomplished poet, with several major awards. About six months ago, Kate had seen a notice in the journal *Wordsmith* about the release of his fifth book of poetry. Mary was wrong about Kate being Eden's most famous person after Jackson. Paul held that distinction, at least among the intelligentsia. She'd heard he also held the distinction of being a pompous jerk. Blonde, blue-eyed and good-looking almost to the point of being pretty, he was rumored to have problems keeping his hands off female students.

Jackson stood and nodded a welcome. He wasn't a tall man, well under six feet, but his commanding presence made him seem larger. His still thick hair was silver gray with darker gray streaks, his blue eyes broadcast his intelligence to any who looked into them, and his skin had the healthy glow of a younger man. While the others at the table were dressed in office casual, Jackson wore a light gray three-piece suit with a white shirt and blue and gray necktie.

"I don't know how many of you like to curl up with a good mystery on a rainy day, but if you do, you may already be familiar with the works of our visiting professor," he said, gesturing to Kate. "May I introduce Katherine Rawlings, a former student of mine and an excellent spinner of tales of murder and mayhem."

Kate smiled at each person around the table. All smiled back except Paul Holland who simply stared at her without expression. Guess he doesn't like mysteries, she thought.

"Katherine, I believe you've met Linza, Bill, and Chris," Jackson gestured to Paul. "This is Paul Holland, a distinguished poet and a fine professor. Paul's got five books of poetry under his belt, and I've lost track of how many awards."

"It's an honor to meet you," Kate said. "I have *Rainbow Lives* and *Crossings* on my shelf at home—well worn from repeated readings."

Paul honored her with a flicker of a smile and a slight nod of his head.

"Georgia O'Connor has been teaching Rhetoric and Composition with us part-time for, what, five years now, Georgia?" Jackson turned to the pretty brunette in her mid-thirties sitting directly across from Kate. "Georgia is also a freelance publicist. I've tried to get her to teach full-time, but she says she can't afford to live on what we pay."

"Ask me again when you can offer more than minimum wage," Georgia said, getting a laugh from the people around the table.

"And last, but not least," Jackson said, turning to the slender, fit-looking man on his right. The man, who appeared to be in his forties, had long brown hair pulled back in a ponytail at the back of his neck, a mustache and goatee, and a stud in his left ear. "Mark Harrison. Mark teaches Drama and Play Writing part-time when he's not working on Chicago stages or running marathons."

"Summers only," Mark said. "When it's too hot for running."

"It's nice to meet you all." Kate nodded at Mark, Georgia, and Paul. "And to see the rest of you again. It's nice to be back home."

"So you're from here?" Georgia said.

"Not Eden. One town over—Mayfield. I left after graduate school and only came back for the occasional visit. Things have changed quite a bit, I'm sure."

"Maybe not," Georgia said. "My husband and I moved here five years ago from Cincinnati, and I haven't seen anything change since."

"Why mess with perfection?" Jackson said. "Now, before we start planning how we're going to introduce malleable young minds to the wonders of the written word this summer, I'd like to make an announcement."

There was a shifting of bodies in the chairs. Announcement or not, Kate guessed the news of Jackson's impending retirement was already known by or guessed at by everyone at the table.

"I'm stepping down from the chair," Jackson said. "I've thought about it for some time, but now that I have a successful novel and the demands that go with it, I've made the decision. I'll stay on in an advisory capacity throughout the fall semester to help with the transition, of course."

"I think I can speak for all of us, Jackson, when I say you will be missed," Linza said. "But I certainly can understand you choosing to leave now."

"Go out in a blaze of glory." Georgia smiled at Jackson, who smiled back.

"Exactly right," he said. Several people chuckled. "Now that was the first part of my announcement. The second is that the university search committee has asked me to submit up to three potential candidates from within the faculty as possible replacements."

The body shifting started again. Kate looked around the table, trying to pinpoint the chair wannabes. Not Georgia, she decided, or Mark. They both seemed content to keep one foot in the academic world and the other firmly planted in the "real" one. No question that Paul Holland wanted the position. He was practically salivating. The others were harder to judge.

"I have made my choices," Jackson said. "And you're all sitting here at this table. I've talked to the four of you I suspected weren't interested, so I'm going to tell you whom I've nominated even though I haven't talked to any of you privately. I will, of course, to address any concerns you might have."

Kate swallowed. Jackson said he had talked to the four who weren't interested. Besides Jackson, there were seven at the table, and he hadn't talked to her. Her eyes locked with Paul's, and she realized he had done the math as well.

"Bill, I couldn't ask for a better replacement than yourself," Jackson said. "You've been with Raven eighteen years and have done an excellent job. You know the ins and outs of this department and the university, which leads me to believe you would be an excellent administrator."

"Thank you, Jackson," Bill said. "I'm honored you would offer my name."

"Paul, you also are on my list. You're an excellent professor, and your success as a poet has been a selling point for the department when recruiting students. That success would be an even greater advantage with you as chair."

Kate noticed Jackson hadn't said he thought Paul would be an excellent administrator. Based on the expressions that flickered across the faces of the others, no one thought so.

Jackson turned to Kate. "I've nominated you as well, Katherine."

He held up a hand as she started to protest. "Yes, you're a visiting professor, but we both know you will stay in Eden. You were acting chair for nearly two years at Nebraska, while Joe Flynn was on family medical leave, and from what I've heard, you did an excellent job. So you have experience, and like Paul, your publishing success would be a selling point for the department."

Kate could feel the hate emanating from Paul's direction.

"Jackson, really, I don't think…" she began, but he hushed her with a wave of his hand.

"I will talk with you later." He looked around the table. "And with you, Paul, and you, Bill. Remember, my nomination doesn't mean the committee will pick one of you. They also are looking outside the university for viable candidates."

"Now, lest I forget, let me extend a personal invitation to each of you to my Summer Kickoff this Saturday. You'll find your printed invitation in your box."

Jackson started what became his Summer Kickoff tradition his first year as an associate professor. When he returned to Eden, he moved into his family home, a spacious Tudor on a three-acre lot. That first summer he hosted a simple cookout in his backyard for the English faculty and grad assistants. Over time, he expanded the guest list to include faculty, staff and graduate students from any of the Humanities, along with friends and neighbors with no connection to the university.

"Please don't tell us this will be the last Kickoff now that you've gone Hollywood," Georgia said, again eliciting a laugh from several around the table.

"I don't expect that to happen. But just in case, be sure to attend this one." He picked up a stack of printouts and handed them to Mark, who took the top one and passed them to Georgia. "Now let's talk about how we're going to open minds to the wonders of literature and writing this summer."

***

"I wish you hadn't blindsided me with this," Kate said, barely waiting until the door to Jackson's office had clicked shut.

"I didn't talk to you first because I knew you would decline." Jackson motioned to the chair in front of his desk. "Have a seat."

"I still decline!" Kate ignored the chair. "I'm more than willing to consider a part-time teaching position here, like I told you. If I stay. But the chair?"

"Katherine, we both know you will stay as long as your mother needs you."

"Okay," she admitted. "I've already come to that conclusion myself. But that's even more reason for me not to accept the responsibilities that go with being chair. I want to spend as much time with her as I can, and I have my writing. I wouldn't even want to teach full-time."

"I understand your concerns," Jackson said. "But, in truth, being chair is less demanding than teaching even part-time. Thanks to Mary, the department nearly runs itself. She tells me what papers I need to sign and chooses the dinner and cocktail parties I need to attend. I just follow her orders."

Knowing Mary, Jackson probably wasn't exaggerating much. "Okay, maybe you are just a figurehead. I still don't want to replace you on the prow of this ship."

"You can always say no. If and when the committee offers you the position."

"Jackson, you saw Paul Holland when you said you had nominated me! He resents me, and I can understand that. Bill probably does, too, but he's too nice to be so obvious about it. No one likes an outsider to waltz in and steal something they've spent years working toward."

"As I said in the meeting, the committee is considering bringing in someone from the outside. You know that has its advantages. An outsider doesn't already have relationships—positive or negative—with the people he or she is supervising. You would be a good compromise. You attended here so you're familiar with Raven, and you'll have this summer's experience teaching here, but you don't know any of the faculty so well that you would be encumbered by that baggage."

Kate tried to think of an objection, but she had to admit Jackson was making a good argument. Except for the fact she wasn't interested.

"Not to mention," Jackson continued, "you are the only one I've nominated who has administrative experience."

"That wasn't the same. It was a temporary thing, and everyone knew it."

"Did they? Might not Joe have decided to retire after the stress of his wife's illness?"

Kate didn't answer. When she'd been acting chair at Nebraska, it had indeed been known that it wasn't a certainty Joe would return. And even though the chair hadn't been guaranteed to go to her, it likely would have. Things had run smoothly during those two years, and she was well liked by the university's powers-that-be.

"Just give it some consideration, Katherine. That's all I ask. Please."

She glared at him for a few moments before letting out the breath she'd been holding. "All right. I'll think about it. But I know what my answer will be."

"Thank you," Jackson said, with a satisfied smile. He reached for the phone and moved it closer to his chair. "Now I don't want to seem to be brushing you off, but I have some calls I need to make. To Hollywood—as much as it pains me to say that."

He was already punching numbers as she left his office.

Paul was standing at the counter. He glared at her openly, not bothering to hide his resentment. "You move fast."

She opened her mouth to explain that she hadn't known anything about the nomination and that she didn't want it but stopped. What right did this pompous jerk have to be angry with her anyway? If the committee members had any sense, they'd never offer the position to Paul Holland. With him as chair, the department would be in turmoil within one semester.

"Jackson is busy now," she said. "He's making some phone calls. They're important so you might have to wait a while." She emphasized the "you." Judging from the color that rose in Paul's cheeks, she knew he'd gotten the message about the relative order of his own importance.

**

That evening, as Kate walked to her office to get her purse, she decided she was going to enjoy the biweekly evening writing class in spite of the monkey wrench Jackson had thrown into the works. The three men and four women weren't stereotypical college students, dividing time between grudgingly attending classes and happily attending beer bashes. All seven worked during the day, five were married and three had children. They were here because they wanted to be.

She unlocked her office door, pushed it open, and let out a yelp of surprise as a man sitting in her desk chair, back to the door, swung around.

"Hey, Kat," he said, his voice low and caressing.

Michael Mabry, the man she had loved thirty years ago with every fiber of her young being, had somehow materialized in her locked office and was sitting at her desk. And she thought Jackson had blindsided her!

Chapter 7

"What!" Lou sprayed a mouthful of coffee onto the table.

"Sorry." Grabbing a napkin, Kate mopped the spilled coffee. "Guess I shouldn't have told you about Michael while you had a mouthful."

Louise Hall, now Pelfrey, had been Kate's best friend since fifth grade. Lou had been an extroverted tomboy, Kate a shy studious girl, but the two of them had somehow fit together. Inseparable throughout childhood and adolescence, they enrolled at Raven at the same time, Kate pursuing a degree in English and Lou pursuing one in sociology with an emphasis on criminal justice. After graduation, Lou took a job with the Raven University Campus Police. Climbing through the ranks, she was now a Deputy Chief and serving as Acting Chief until a replacement could be found for her newly retired boss. Although the university search committee was going through the motions and interviewing outside applicants, the word according to Jackson was that Lou was the current favorite for the job.

Funny, Kate thought as she watched her friend gather her wits, even with all the miles I put between us these past years, it seems as if we've always been together. They had emailed, texted, or chatted nearly every day and talked by phone at least every couple of weeks. Kate was Lou's maid of honor when she married Roger and the designated godmother at Drew's and Ethan's christenings. From time to time over the years, they met somewhere for a long weekend version of a girls' night out. She guessed the two of them were what her younger students called BFFs—Best Friends Forever.

But lifelong friend or not, could she tell her everything? When she'd called Lou to meet for coffee at the University food court, she'd already decided to tell her Michael was in town. There was too much chance of them running into each other. But as far as Lou knew, last night was the first time she'd seen Michael in thirty years. Kate didn't want to think how Lou would react if she knew the truth.

"Okay." Lou took a deep breath. "Tell me. And don't leave out a thing."

"Kat," Michael had said. "Long time, no see."

And so it had been. She and Michael met in grad school, and she was lost from the first minute she laid eyes on him. A shy girl, she'd had few dates in high school and college. She had a serious inferiority complex back then, especially when it came to boys. In her mind she was too tall, too skinny, too flat-chested, too clumsy, even too smart.

Michael was out of her league. He was the most handsome man she'd ever seen, with thick dark hair, twinkling Paul Newman-blue eyes, and a body that could have graced a Playgirl centerfold. He was intelligent, and even better, he was a writer. He was everything she had ever fantasized about on those Friday and Saturday nights when she didn't have a date, but she knew she didn't stand a chance. With all the pretty, popular girls at Raven, he wouldn't notice she existed.

But he had noticed. That first day he chose a seat next to her at Jackson's round table graduate seminar even though other seats were empty. He smiled and introduced himself, and when they shook hands, he didn't let go right away. She was still unclear how she made it through that seminar. No one seemed to notice the effect Michael had on her—except for Michael himself. She knew from the way he smiled conspiratorially at her and brushed against her during class that he was very aware of it.

That evening she and Lou were having hamburgers at an off-campus student hangout, and suddenly Michael was there, sliding into the booth beside her. He was polite and friendly to Lou, but reserved his charm for Kate. She'd been aware of other women in the cafe casting glances his way, but his full attention was focused on her. She had never felt so beautiful and desirable in her life. Being the good friend Lou was, she read the signs and excused herself as soon as she finished her burger. Kate and Michael stayed, talking, laughing, and getting to know each other.

An only child, Michael was raised from the age of twelve by his grandmother in southeastern Kentucky after his father was killed in a coal mining accident. His mother had died the year before from cancer. Although he didn't say so then, Kate got the impression that the grandmother did not fit the loving grandma stereotype. One night after they moved in together—and after a few too many beers—Michael told her about the beatings. He said it explained why his father had been so mean, although he had reserved his belt for his wife and not his child.

At fourteen, Michael put a stop to the beatings. He'd grown tall and strong in the two years he'd lived with his grandmother, and one day he simply yanked the belt from her hands. No more, he'd said. You ever touch me again, I'll wrap this belt around your scrawny old neck. She laughed at him, but the beatings stopped. It was a good thing, he told Kate that night. Otherwise I'd be in prison for murder instead of in this bed with you.

Although she was young, Kate had recognized how amazing it was he'd come out of that background and made it as far as he had. When she asked if he'd ever thought about dropping out of school, he shook his head emphatically.

"Not once," he'd said. "Guys who drop out of school in Perry County end up in the mines or in jail. I wanted out of that county and that life. Getting educated was the best way to do it."

He'd always done well in school, he said. In his senior year, he filled out every scholarship and student aid application he could get his hands on, landing both at Western Kentucky, and matriculated four years later with a Bachelor of Arts in English. Thinking he might want to teach college if he didn't make it as a writer, he'd applied to Raven's graduate program in creative writing and was accepted. He'd also landed a teaching assistantship, providing him enough money to live on.

"I expected to get a good education here," he'd said, nuzzling her neck. "But I sure didn't expect to find you."

There hadn't been any more conversation after that.

Later, after Michael left town with an undergrad, Lou told Kate she'd liked Michael at first. Like her, Lou was impressed with all he'd accomplished. But after the cheating started, she no longer trusted anything he said. She did some checking and discovered he had a sealed juvenile record, but considering his background, that wasn't surprising. She kept digging.

Lou had cousins in Perry County, and she made some calls. Michael had told the truth about his parents and grandmother but not about how well he'd done in school. Oh, he was smart, all right, just not book-smart. He'd been an average student until his junior year when he suddenly started making A's and B's in nearly every class taught by a woman. Since there were only two or three male teachers in the high school, he sailed through on his charisma. The one exception was his English class. The teacher was a man and definitely a heterosexual one, so Michael couldn't use his charm there. But in English classes, he didn't need to. It was the one subject he excelled in, especially when it came to writing.

Lou's cousin told her he wasn't sure he blamed Michael for doing whatever he could to get through school. There was no question he'd had a tough home life. In his place, he said, and with Michael's looks and appeal, he might have done the same. Only thing he did blame him for was a girl named Lucy Crouch.

Lucy was a sophomore, Michael a senior, when he got her pregnant. She told him she was expecting a few days after he'd gotten his acceptance letter from Western. He promptly dumped her and told anyone who would listen she'd been screwing around and the baby wasn't his. He'd already left for Bowling Green when Lucy killed herself and their unborn child.

"I think Mike was so desperate to get out, he didn't think about Lucy," Lou's cousin said. "Her daddy swore he'd kill him if he ever saw him. Johnny just got hired at that steel company you got up there. Family's moving there this month. You might warn Mike to keep a low profile, or he's liable to get his ass kicked."

Lou never warned Michael that Lucy's irate father was coming to Eden. A part of her, she admitted, wanted him to get his ass kicked for what he was doing to her friend. Kate and Michael had been on again, off again during that time. She'd discover he'd been cheating, he'd swear it would never happen again, he loved only her, she would forgive him, and then it would happen again with someone else. The third time he left town with his new friend, leaving only a short note saying he wasn't ready to settle down, and he needed "life experience to write." That was when Lou told her the rest. Lou knew all of that because she'd been there when it happened. What she didn't know was what came after.

"Tell me," Lou urged again, when Kate hesitated.

"Not much to tell. When I went back to my office after class, he was sitting in my desk chair."

"How did he get in? Surely your door was locked."

"It was. Robbie Applegate let him in."

"The maintenance guy?" Lou scowled. "He knows better than to let people into offices where they've got no reason to be, especially with all the break-ins and thefts we've had on campus."

"Don't say anything to anyone, please. I'll talk to Robbie about it today. Remember, he knows Michael from back when. I really don't want to get him in trouble."

"Well...okay." Kate could see Lou wasn't happy with it. "He's a nice old fellow, so I won't cause him any problems. He's got enough with that son and grandson of his."

"What's wrong with them?" Kate was glad for the change of subject.

"Meth heads, both of them. Using, manufacturing, selling, the whole shebang. Been arrested so many times I've lost count. It's a real shame. Robbie is as honest and trustworthy as they come. Guess the apple can fall far from the tree. Anyway," she said, dragging out the word, "let's get back to the topic at hand. Why was Michael in your office? For that matter, why is he in Eden?"

"He said he was just passing through and wanted to congratulate Jackson and me on our books."

"How *considerate* of him." Lou turned serious. "Are you okay?"

"Of course." Kate kept her expression neutral. "Why wouldn't I be?"

"Honey, you can't tell me seeing Michael didn't throw you for a loop."

"Well, of course, I was surprised that he's in Eden. But that's all."

"Did he say how long he was staying?"

"No, but I don't think he'll be here long. He said he's on the way to a job in Florida, but who knows? I don't think he's doing too well financially. He asked if he could leave his suitcase in my office. He's got a room at the Shady Nook and doesn't want to leave anything there other than his overnight bag."

"Well, he's not totally brain dead at least." Lou signaled the waitress for a refill on her coffee. "Did you let him leave the bag?"

"I couldn't think of a good reason not to."

"What's in it?"

"A change of underwear, as far as I know. I didn't ask and he didn't offer."

"You didn't look inside after he left?"

"No, Lou, I didn't. I have no interest in violating his privacy."

Lou snorted. "Like he deserves that kind of consideration. For all you know, you might have a suitcase full of drugs in your possession."

"He wouldn't do that."

"What? Do drugs, transport drugs, leave drugs in your possession, screw over you with God knows how many women?"

"Lou!" Kate held up her hand. "That was a lot of years ago. Michael was a kid, and so was I. Just because he was a shit back then doesn't logically lead to him involving me in a criminal enterprise."

"We need to be sure." Lou signaled for the check.

"It might be locked."

"If it is, I'll take possession of it, and you can tell him to see me when he wants it."

The bag wasn't locked. It took just a few minutes to verify that the contents contained nothing more exciting than clothing, a sheaf of papers wrapped in a plastic grocery bag and a worn photo album. Kate held her breath while Lou flipped through the first few pages of the photo album before passing it to her.

"Old family photos, from the look of it. Have you seen these before?"

Kate nodded and pointed to a picture of a pretty dark-haired woman with her arm around an equally pretty dark-haired toddler. "That's Michael and his mother, Jeannette. I don't think he ever got over her death."

Kate closed the album, hoping Lou wouldn't decide to look at the rest of the pictures. Lou would expect there to be photos of Michael and her from their grad school days, but she wouldn't expect the ones that came later.

Lou pulled the sheaf of papers from the grocery bag and leafed through them. "Huh! These look like short stories — *old* short stories, I'd say. Done on a typewriter, not a computer. Wonder if he did these back in grad school?"

She passed the stories to Kate.

"I remember two of these," Kate said, looking through them. "He used them as class assignments. I don't recognize the others. Either he did them later or he just didn't show them to me. He could be pretty secretive about his writing."

"He hid stuff from you? Gee, what a surprise."

"Michael was funny that way," Kate said. "He had plenty of confidence when it came to his looks, but he was insecure about his writing. He never wanted anyone to look at it until he was ready."

"Well, you've got your chance now."

"No." Kate put the papers back in the bag and placed it and the photo album under the clothing where they had found them. "I won't intrude on his privacy that way. Unlike certain other people I might mention."

"Hazards of being a cop." Lou shrugged. "We poke around in everything. So what are you going to do with the bag? Leave it here or take it back to Holly?"

"I guess I'll leave it here. Why?"

"The burglary epidemic," Lou said. "We've been advising everyone to be careful what they leave in their offices."

"Mary Dunn mentioned it."

"So far none of the English Department offices have been hit, but I wouldn't count on them being safe. I could care less if Michael gets his drawers ripped off, but I'd hate to see him lose the pics of his mom."

"Why, Lou! I do believe a heart beats under that badge after all!"

"Hah, hah." Lou stuck her tongue out at Kate and then turned serious. "You know, I never would have pegged Michael as sentimental enough to keep pictures and stuff he'd written, much less hang on to them for this long."

"He isn't all bad, Lou. He's not perfect, but he's not a bad person."

"I wouldn't go that far," Lou said. "Sentimental or not, he's still an asshole."

Kate decided not to argue the point. If she did, she might have to explain how she knew Michael had a good side. "I'll take the bag to Holly House," she said. "It should be safe there."

Kate locked up. They walked to their cars, Kate carrying Michael's bag.

"How's your mom?" Lou said after Kate stowed the bag in her trunk. "I haven't seen her in a month or so."

"You know." Kate shrugged. "Sometimes bad, sometimes not so bad. But never good. It's like pieces of her are being chipped away a little at a time."

"It's an awful disease. And not just for the person with it. How are you and Steve doing?"

"Steve is amazing!" Kate smiled. "He's so good with her. When we had dinner Sunday night, he would hand her the dishes and tell her to take some lasagna or bread or salad and pass it on to me. He was telling her what she needed to do, but it seemed normal, if you know what I mean. She'd eat a little and then seem to forget what she was doing. He'd remind her to eat but in such a way that it was part of the conversation. Like, 'isn't the lasagna good, Mom?' That sort of thing. She'd look at the lasagna like she'd noticed it for the first time and take another bite."

"Bless his heart! He guides her but preserves her dignity at the same time."

"Exactly," Kate said. "I knew my brother was a good man, but I don't think I realized just how good until that dinner."

"And how are you doing?"

How *was* she doing, Kate wondered now. Before Alzheimer's had reared its ugly head, her life had been a comfortable routine of teaching, writing, household chores, lunches with friends, the occasional dinner date, and phone calls home. Now she was trying to deal with a family tragedy, a new job, and co-worker hostility from at least one source. Not to mention the complication of Michael.

"Can I get back to you on that when I figure it out?"

Lou laughed and hugged her. "You're crazy, girlfriend, you know that? But I love you." She turned serious. "Anything you need, Kate. Anything."

"I know. And I love you for it."

"I'd like to stop by and see Bette," Lou said. "When's a good time?"

"What about on your way home this afternoon? I'm heading back to Holly now to work on some ideas I have for my next book, but I'm going to Steve's later for supper. I'll probably head over around 3:30. Give me a call, and if Mom's doing okay, come by and eat with us."

"Sounds good to me." Lou pecked her on the cheek. "Now I've got to get to work and keep the dark powers of evil at bay."

Kate watched her friend drive off, wondering if there was any feeling lower than knowing you had been lying to your BFF for thirty years?

CATCH A FALLING STAR

Chapter 8

Cal wasn't sure what he'd expected of a female detective in a
small town department, but Jo Valentine wasn't it. The woman
who stood to shake his hand when he approached her desk was a
tiny thing, probably no more than a couple of inches over five feet,
if that. He guessed her to be in her late forties. Her brown hair was
cut short in what they called a pixie style back when he was in
school. No gray visible, but that didn't mean much what with all
the chemicals women could choose from for coloring hair. She had
a slender build to match her petite frame, but in spite of the
business-like slacks and jacket, he could see she had curves where
she should have curves. She kind of reminded him of a middle-
aged Barbie doll with short brown hair—all cutesie and feminine
with nice boobs and hips.

That is, until you looked into her brown eyes. They were cop
eyes, and unless he was very much mistaken, they were not the
eyes of a Barbie cop. Cal guessed Detective Valentine was not a
woman to be trifled with.

"Have a seat, Mr. Becker." She motioned to the chair at the
side of her desk.

The accent explains a lot, Cal thought, as he took a seat.

"You don't sound like you grew up in Kentucky, Detective
Valentine," he said. "New York City would be my guess, although
I can't guess which borough."

"Brooklyn. Bensonhurst. What can I do for you, Mr. Becker?"

That's New Yorkers for you, Cal thought. No time for chit-
chat. Guess Kentucky's laid-back ways haven't rubbed off on her.
He'd had lengthy conversations this morning with the waitress, the
cashier, and a couple of customers at the Shoney's where he'd
stopped for breakfast. The topics had ranged from where he was

from to the weather to how UK had done in the last football and basketball season and how they were expected to do come fall. Cal had enjoyed the friendly chitchat.

"I do private investigations for Gallagher Holdings in Chicago." Cal proffered his company identification. "Gallagher is an insurance company that deals primarily in insuring valuable art. Our customers include both private collectors and art museums. Chicago's Drayer Museum is one of our clients."

"And it recently got hit," she said. "Two people killed. Read about it in the papers, and we had a call the other day from a detective up there."

Cal nodded. "Right. Don Braxton. I'm retired from the Chicago P.D., by the way. I asked Don to send your department the information on the suspect we're looking for. He told me he'd spoken to you, which is why I asked to do the same."

Detective Valentine turned to her computer, tapped a few keys, and looked at the information on the screen.

"Michael Mabry," she said. "White male, 55 years of age, 5'11", 170, dark brown and blue. Security guard at the museum under an assumed name. Five convictions for theft and fraud, two stints in prison, rest in county jails. Student at Raven back in his younger days."

She swiveled back to stare at Cal. Damn, those eyes could cut glass, he thought. Bet she is hell in interrogations.

"And you think he is in Eden, why?"

"It's a long shot," he admitted. "But we're having no luck locating him in Chicago. The detectives working the case believe he was in it with a hard case up there named Dominick Duda. Duda's brother-in-law and Mabry were in prison together and reportedly became friends. The thinking is that Mabry double-crossed Duda or maybe Duda double-crossed him. Mabry is a lowlife, but he doesn't have a history of violence, unlike Duda. It's possible Mabry didn't know anybody was going to get killed, and it's also possible they intended to kill him."

"Maybe they did."

"Could be. But no body has turned up. I think Mabry's running scared, and I think he's got the Star. When I checked his background, I found out about the Raven connection. He was in the graduate creative writing program here, although he dropped out before finishing. His old professor is Jackson Price."

"Our local celebrity."

"Right. Another student in the program at the time Mabry was here was Katherine Rawlings. Turns out she's teaching at Raven this summer."

"The mystery writer?" Valentine looked surprised. "I wasn't aware she was in town."

"Anyway, like I said, it's a long shot, but Mabry had just four books in the room he rented in Chicago. One was Price's, and the other three were written by Rawlings. Could be he skedaddled down here to hit his old friends up for a loan."

Valentine stared at him.

"Mr. Becker, let me explain the way things are in Eden. Trust me, it's not the Garden here. Between meth, pills, and synthetics, we're up to our asses in crime—adult and juvenile. And heroin's making a comeback, believe it or not. We've had six drug-related murders in this county so far this year, four of them in the city limits. And there's been a string of recent burglaries and car break-ins both in town and on campus. This department has 22 full-time officers, with a few on vacation, sick leave, or in training at any given time."

"And running down leads, particularly weak ones, for other departments isn't high priority," Cal said. "I get it. Which is why I'm here. Gallagher wants me to follow up on this, but I don't want to step on any toes. Figured I'd check in, see what you found out—if anything—and okay it with you to snoop around."

"I gave the info on Mabry to the shift commanders. They passed it on to their patrol officers. If Mabry gets stopped for a traffic violation or arrested for public intox, we'll haul him in. I also had our secretary call the local motels and hotels, but no Mabry registered anywhere. Not that I'd expect him to use his own name. Didn't and don't have time to run his picture around to the desk clerks, but feel free to do so."

"Thanks." Cal stood and stretched, hearing his back pop. "What can you tell me about Dr. Price or Ms. Rawlings?"

"Nothing about Rawlings, other than what I know from her book jacket bio. Like I said, I wasn't aware she's in town. I was introduced to Price at a city function last year, but that and his reputation as writer and chair of the English department is the extent of my knowledge about him." She smiled a tight smile. "I'm afraid I'm so busy getting to know the law-breaking citizens that I don't have a lot of time to get to know the law-abiding ones."

Definitely not a climber, Cal thought. From what he'd read about Jackson Price, he was an important person in Eden, not just because of his recent bestseller but also because of his family money and connections. If Jo Valentine had her sights set on higher office, she'd be more interested in knowing Eden's movers and shakers.

"I'll want to talk with them, of course," he said. "Not just to find out if they've heard from him but also to warn them about him. I doubt they'd risk their reputations and careers to help Mabry, but he could get money out of them before they knew why he needed it."

"That's fine," she said. "Just don't cause me any headaches. I don't want any complaints coming across my desk about a hard-ass Chicago investigator browbeating our celebrities."

Cal thought he detected a note of sarcasm. He took out one of his business cards, turned it over and scribbled his cell phone number on the back, along with his room number at the Holiday Inn. He passed it across the desk to Valentine.

"My cell number and room number's on the back. I'm at the Holiday Inn out by the interstate."

She took it, glanced at the information, and placed it in a plastic card tray on her desk. She stood, and Cal knew he was being dismissed. He stood as well and shook her hand.

"Thank you for your time, Detective."

"One more thing, Mr. Becker," she said, as she released his hand. Those eyes bored into him. "You come across Mabry's location, you call me."

"No problem," Cal said. "I'm an insurance investigator. I'll leave arresting people to you."

Chapter 9

Wendell Halsey often wished he had never met his wife. He loved Gabby, sure, it wasn't that. She was a great cook and a good housekeeper, and if they ever had kids, he had no doubt she'd be a great mom. And in bed? No woman he'd ever known could hold a candle to her in *that* department! No, it wasn't Gabby herself that made him wish they'd never met. It was her brother. Sure, Wendell knew most guys bitched about their in-laws. But most guys didn't have a brother-in-law who was a stone cold killer.

Dominick "Baby" Duda owned numerous businesses in Chicago. While their main purpose was providing a legal front for his shadier enterprises, each was successful in its own right, the main reason being that in the neighborhoods around each one, the locals were afraid to patronize anyone else.

He'd been summoned to Baby's office at the rear of Quick Clean Dry Cleaning. The place was warm on the coldest winter day, thanks to the steam and heat emitting machines, but it was unbearable during the other three seasons. At least it was unbearable from Wendell's point of view. He was sweating so much, he'd probably have to toss the shirt he was wearing. He didn't think Gabby could run it through the washer enough times to get the stink out. Baby seemed to thrive in the heat, not a drop of moisture on his face, sprawled back in his desk chair like some fat damn lizard. Not for the first time, Wendell wondered if his brother-in-law had been fathered by a reptile.

"I got some information I want you to check out," Baby said. "A place the Professor might be."

"Sure." Wendell nodded. "No problem. Where?"

"Kentucky. A town called Eden."

"Kentucky?" Wendell was surprised. He'd been expecting a location in Chicago or close by, not another state—well, maybe Indiana, that wasn't that far away. But Kentucky?

"The cops found some books in his room," Baby said. "One was by some professor named Price, the rest by some broad named Rawlings. They're both in Eden. My source told me the insurance company thinks the Professor might try to hit them up for money or a place to hide out. Said they're old friends of his."

"Rawlings." Wendell shifted from one foot to the other and back again, feeling a new trickle of sweat run down the middle of his back. "Yeah, I know that name, I think. The Professor always talked about how he'd met the love of his life when he was in college. That kind of shit. Said he fucked it up because he couldn't keep his dick in his pants. I know the broad wrote books because he wrote her at least once while he was in the joint, right after she got a book published. Said he wanted to congratulate her. Probably figured she was gonna get rich writing books, and he could get back in tight with her."

Baby leaned forward, the chair creaking under his weight. "Any reason you didn't mention her before now?"

"Hey, I didn't remember until just now." Another trickle of sweat ran down Wendell's back and into his shorts. "I mean, who woulda thought he'd go back there? I swear I never even thought of the broad until you said her name."

Baby closed his eyes. Wendell knew that meant he was thinking. Probably deciding whether he should send me down to hillbilly country to look for the Professor or just gut me where I stand for not telling him about Rawlings.

When he and Leonard had told Baby about the fuck-up at the museum, he'd thought Baby was going to stroke out on the spot. For the past two weeks, Wendell and Leonard had been scouring Chicago for any sign of the Professor. Each evening, they'd had to report to Baby that they'd come up empty-handed. After the first week, Wendell thought even Leonard looked like he dreaded evening's arrival.

"Probably a wild goose chase." Baby opened his eyes. "But I'm gonna send you down to check it out. Kentucky ain't that far away."

Wendell thought he had a pretty good idea what a man on death row felt like when the phone rang and the governor said he could keep breathing for another few days. Only downside was a road trip with the creepy fuck.

"Leonard can keep looking here."

Thank you, sweet Jesus, Wendell thought.

"You find the Professor, you do nothing, understand? Just keep an eye on him till Leonard gets there. And don't let him see you and fuck things up anymore than you already have. Got it?"

Wendell nodded. It pissed him off that Baby was blaming him for the museum screw-up, but he didn't intend to tell him so.

"Take Gabby with you."

"Gabby? You want her in this?"

"Be good for the two of you to get away for a few days," Baby said. "She's been bitchin' about how much I got you workin'. Besides, she's got good eyes and good instincts. Be a big help to you."

Big help, my ass, Wendell thought, although he nodded in agreement. Gabby had good eyes, but they were extensions of her brother's eyes. He knew Baby was sending her along to use those eyes to keep a watch on him. Nothing he could do to stop it, though. And it would be nice to get out of town for a few days with Gabby. Find some nice motel with soft sheets and....

"Get outa here."

Wendell got.

Chapter 10

"She's asleep," Steven said when Kate arrived to find their mother was still in bed. "She didn't sleep well last night. Set off the front door alarm twice—once at midnight and again at four—and the back door one around two-thirty."

Steven had installed alarms on all the doors at his house when he'd moved their parents in. The alarms sounded when someone tried to open the doors from the inside, and the alarm rang through a device he kept by his bed.

"She was so good yesterday evening! She was like her old self, Steve! Knew Lou and was glad to see her, no fogginess, laughing. She was Mom!"

"It happens," Steven said. "But just when you think the doctors are wrong, and everything is going to be okay, the fog creeps back in. When she has a good day, it's almost always followed by a bad night. Maybe it wears her out or something. I don't know."

"Maybe she just wanted to walk outside for some air." Kate knew as she said it that her mother would never go outside by herself in the middle of the night unless the house was on fire.

"She didn't know where she was, sis."

"So the alarms are necessary." Kate crossed her arms, hugging herself. "My God!"

When Steven had first told her about the door alarms, she thought he was overreacting. She had done the research, of course, and knew that people with Alzheimer's sometimes wandered away from their homes, but surely their mother wasn't *that* far along in the disease process.

"Unfortunately." Steven said. "I didn't tell you, but the second night after I brought her here, and before I had the alarms installed, she got out in the middle of the night. Something woke me, maybe the door shutting, I don't know. By the time I got awake enough to think to check her room, she was a block down the street wearing only her nightgown and no shoes. Thank God it *was* the middle of the night, and traffic was practically nonexistent."

"I take it Dad wasn't sleeping in the same bed?"

"Same bed? Hell, he wasn't sleeping in the same house! Just like last night. We haven't seen him since the night you got here. For all I know, he's died in the old house and stinking it up as we speak."

He snorted. "Not that we could get *that* lucky!"

"Steve…."

"I know, I know." He waved a hand at her. "I shouldn't say such awful things. Of course, I don't mean it. It would make selling the house harder."

Kate chose not to belabor the issue.

"I'll be back later," she said. "I want to stop by the university and have a word with Jackson and then go back to Holly House and do some things. I'll check with you after I leave Jackson's office to see if Mom is up yet."

In her car on the way to the university, Kate thought back to the phone call that ultimately changed the direction her life was heading. She'd just had her second novel published, her first was still selling well, and on the heels of her stint as acting chair at Nebraska, her academic career was flourishing. She'd been at home that Saturday afternoon, working on an outline for what was to become her third novel. It was a lovely fall day, warm, but with a brisk breeze that caused cascades of red and gold leaves to periodically shower past her open window. In the distance, she could hear the sounds of the Nebraska band practicing, and somewhere closer by she could smell food from a neighbor's grill. If asked to offer one word to describe the day, she would have chosen "peaceful." Then the telephone rang.

"Hey, sis," Steven had said. "Are you busy?"

"Never too busy to talk to my brother," Kate had replied. "How are you?"

"I'm doing okay," he said, but he didn't *sound* okay, and Kate felt the first flutter of apprehension.

"Mom?" she'd said. "Is she okay?"

That's when he told her that their mother had been diagnosed with mild Alzheimer's. That was nearly two years ago now, two years during which the disease had made steady inroads into their mother's brain. Her diagnosis was now moderate Alzheimer's, but so far the newer drugs the doctor had prescribed seemed to be holding her steady at the moderate stage. That was good news, if one considered extended bouts of confusion interspersed with all too short periods of clarity a desirable state of existence.

It had taken Kate nearly a year to come to grips with her mother's diagnosis and finally admit the doctors had not been mistaken. It was at that point she started making plans for the move back to Eden. She knew she was lucky in that she had the beginnings of a reasonably successful career as a novelist. It was even possible that without her mother becoming ill, she would have turned her back on climbing further in academia in order to devote herself to writing. Not that it mattered one way or the other. Once she accepted that her mother was really and truly sick, all she wanted was to spend what time she could with her. That time was limited and far more important than an academic career.

Still, if the search committee decided to go with Jackson's nomination of her for chair of the English department, she wouldn't have to choose between her mother and her profession. But would she have enough time in her day for three demanding roles—novelist, English chair, *and* dutiful daughter? Jackson swore that the chair position didn't require much time or effort. Maybe it didn't after you'd done it as long as Jackson had, but Kate knew from experience that the first year or so in any new position was time-consuming while a person learned how things were done. Just dealing with resentful co-workers like Paul Holland could probably fill the better part of the average day.

And time wasn't the only consideration. There was mental stress involved with any new job, stress that could rob her of the desire to sit down with her laptop and create stories. Could she handle the stress of a new position in addition to the stress of watching her mother slowly disappear, and still meet publisher deadlines?

"I am woman, hear me roar," she muttered, as she pulled into Hanover Hall's lot. "More like, I am woman, hear me whimper!"

***

When Kate entered the office, Mary was on the phone but waved her on through. She knocked lightly and opened Jackson's door. He was at his desk, looking over some papers.

"Is this a good time?"

"Certainly!" He laid the papers aside. "I'm thoroughly sick of looking through movie contracts!"

"Don't you have an attorney for that?"

"I do." He nodded. "But he prefers I look at the contracts first and note changes or questions I have, pass them to him, he notes more changes and questions, and then it goes back to the studio and *their* attorneys before coming back to me and the cycle begins again. The worst part is the writing! It's so damn dull!"

Kate laughed. "Makes me glad none of my books have been bought for film."

"Your time will come, Katherine, I have no doubt. I feel sorry for you when it does! Now, what can I do for you, or did you just stop by to hear me grouse?"

Kate moved to the chair in front of his desk and perched on the edge.

"I don't know if you're aware that Michael is back in town," she said, watching his face carefully.

He looked at her, his face betraying nothing of what he was thinking. After several seconds, he leaned back in his chair, sighing deeply.

"I did know," he said. "I wasn't sure if you did. Michael stopped by here Monday morning, not long before our staff meeting."

Kate flashed back to the familiar figure she had seen leaving Hanover Hall Monday as she was coming in. So it had been Michael. She had thought for a second that it looked like him but had dismissed the idea as ridiculous. Michael's life had moved on from Eden. She'd never expected him to come back.

"Oh," she said. "I didn't know you'd seen him."

"I'm sorry I didn't say anything Monday, Katherine. I debated with myself whether I should or not. I didn't know if Michael was aware you were here."

"You wanted to spare me in case he didn't know. I understand. But apparently he did know. He was waiting in my office Monday night after my class. Robbie Applegate let him in."

"I'll speak to Mr. Applegate immediately. Under no circumstances should the maintenance staff be letting people into offices."

"I've already spoken to him," Kate said. "I'm sure he won't do it again."

"Michael was vague about why he's in Eden. Did he say anything to you?"

"He claims he just stopped by for a visit on his way to a job in Florida. Said he wanted to congratulate you and me on our latest books."

"You don't sound convinced."

She shrugged. "I don't know. Maybe that is part of his visit. I just never expected him to come back here."

"Maybe he's here because of you."

"Me?" Kate felt her face flush. "Why would you think that?"

"It makes sense," Jackson said. "Michael's getting older and probably having regrets. This is where you two were in love. Now you're back and he's back. He's probably kept tabs on you over the years and knows you've had success in academia and in publishing. It wouldn't have been that difficult for him to find out you're teaching here this summer, so maybe he thinks he can pick up where the two of you left off. It doesn't seem to me that Michael's had much success with his life, and you would be"—Jackson made finger quotes—"a good catch."

"Thanks a lot," she said, trying to hide her relief. Jackson was perceptive, but not as perceptive as she'd feared. "It's good to know I'm so desirable."

"I didn't intend that as an insult to you, Katherine, but rather as a reflection on Michael's morals. We both know his ethics weren't praiseworthy in his younger days, and based on how he appeared Monday, I doubt they've improved over the years. I suspect he wouldn't be above trying to use you for his own personal gain."

"I don't think he would ask me for money."

"Don't put it past him. I know men's clothing, and trust me, his were off the rack and a cheap rack at that."

Kate smiled. Jackson's fondness for bespoke suits was well known in Eden. She wouldn't have been surprised to learn that he had his pajamas tailor-made.

"And he could have more in mind than just money. Michael hasn't done well. You have. Maybe he hopes to charm you into taking him back." Jackson leaned forward, resting his elbows on the desk. "And he likely still has feelings for you. One thing doesn't necessarily preclude the other."

"Well, all he's asked me for so far is permission to leave his bag with me. He's staying at the Shady Nook and said he doesn't trust the locks."

"He always was an intelligent boy."

"It might be," Kate said, "that it's *you* he's here to get money from."

"Why do you say that?" Jackson straightened in his chair.

"Your success is well known—a bestseller and a movie? The news has been out there for some time. He did come to see you first."

"Only to say hello. He never brought up the subject of money." Jackson shuffled the papers on his desk, glancing at them and then at her in a way that indicated he wanted to end the conversation and get back to work. Kate took the hint.

"We're probably both reading too much into this visit." Kate rose from the chair. "Maybe he does just want to wish us well."

As she closed the door to Jackson's office, she glanced back. He was staring at the papers on the desk, but it was obvious he wasn't seeing them. She'd been trying to deflect attention from herself when she suggested Michael was there to get money from Jackson, but he had seemed eager to end the conversation when the focus switched to him. What, she wondered now as old suspicions began to rear their ugly little heads, did Michael have on Jackson?

Jackson had never married, and as far as anyone knew, he'd never been in a relationship with a woman. She didn't know of relationships with men either, but she had often wondered if Jackson was in the closet. Back in the old days, Michael and Jackson had been close, maybe closer than normal for a student and an advisor. She'd teased Michael about it once after a late evening with Jackson. He had winked and said he couldn't help it if people found him charming.

After he walked out on her, and Lou told her what she had discovered about his past and the way he used his high school teachers, she wondered if his and Jackson's relationship had been even closer than she thought. She still couldn't picture—or didn't *want* to picture—the two of them in a sexual relationship, but she wouldn't put it past Michael to have tantalized Jackson with hints of more. Michael always had ready cash for evenings out, maybe more than he should have had from his teaching assistant duties. Maybe some of that cash had come from Jackson.

She was so engrossed in her thoughts that she didn't see Paul Holland as she exited the English office, nearly colliding with him in the doorway.

"Visiting Dr. Price again, I see?" he said.

Irritated, she smiled sweetly at him. "Yes, actually," she said. "We had a nice conversation. Your name never came up."

She heard Mary Dunn choke down a laugh as she stepped past him.

Chapter 11

"Damn, it feels good to sit down!" Ginger flopped into the chair next to Kate. "I only had one pee break since five-thirty this morning! This keeps up, Walt's gonna have to make bladder pads an employee benefit!"

The three other women at the table burst out laughing. Nan Davis had been taking a sip of coffee and sprayed it out her nose, causing them all to laugh harder.

"Christ!" Nan mopped her chin with her napkin. "If you keep this up, Ginger, I'm going to need one of those pads!"

Kate had seen Ginger through the open door of one of the Holly's rooms the day before. The thin blonde woman had her back to the door, running the vacuum, so Kate had not had a chance to introduce herself. The diner had been busy when Kate and Nan arrived just before ten that morning, but Ann had made quick introductions when Ginger brought coffee to the table.

Ginger was like a surge of energy in a room. She was average height and slender build, with shoulder-length straight blonde hair held at the back of her neck by a black scrunchie. Her eyes were a piercing shade of blue behind wire rim glasses, her features sharp and birdlike, her smile wide and welcoming. In the past half hour, she had watched Ginger flit from table to table, taking orders, delivering orders, cleaning tables, and ringing customers out at the register. Yet somehow she still found time to lend a hand at the grill, joke with regulars, and smile at everyone.

"It's been busy this morning," Ann observed.

"No shit! The parents of those little darlins' that will be coming to school this fall are packing up and going home, and they all want their breakfast yesterday. The first bunch got here right after we opened—that's six, by the way," she said, looking at Kate, "and they just kept coming!"

"Think of all that tip money," Nan said.

"Yeah, right! Half the tables didn't have a dime on them. Guess they figure I'll forget their faces by the time they come back to visit their babies in the fall."

She turned to Kate. "Nice to meet you, honey. Glad you could join us. I absolutely love your books!"

"Thank you." Kate felt her face redden. She had yet to get over feeling embarrassed when someone she didn't know praised her books. "I appreciate that."

"I appreciate a good story," Ginger said. "When's the next one out?"

"It might be a while. I'm still playing around with ideas at this point."

"Well, I'll be waiting for it. Nothing I like better after a hard day than curling up with a good book and a beer."

The man laboring over the grill behind the counter caught Ginger's eye and motioned to her.

"Looks like our food's ready," she said. "Be right back."

Nan exuded as much energy as Ginger, but it was a more controlled force. She was tall—Kate guessed 5'10" or so—with white-streaked wavy red hair worn to just below her ear lobes, pale green eyes, and lightly freckled skin. She was dressed in a simple beige seersucker shift and brown sandals. Ann had told her that Nan had been a foreign correspondent before returning home to take over the family newspaper. Kate suspected she chose clothing based on how easy it was to care for, a habit probably developed after decades of living out of suitcases.

When Kate returned Nan's call regarding the interview, she mentioned Ann's invitation to the Friday brunch. Nan suggested meeting at the Chronicle a half hour before, and Kate had agreed. The interview had gone smoothly. Nan gleaned the pertinent biographical facts, asked questions about Kate's creative process, her teaching career, and her ties to the area, wrapping the entire interview up in no more than fifteen minutes.

"Guess what I heard this morning," Ginger said after she'd brought their food and reclaimed her seat at the table.

"It's hard telling." Ann rolled her eyes.

"Hey, don't stop her flow," Nan said. "I get some of my best leads from Ginger's diner gossip."

Ginger stuck her tongue out at Ann and leaned forward, lowering her voice. "You know that jewel theft from that Chicago museum? The one that's been in all the papers?"

"You mean the artifact from ancient India?" Nan said.

"That's the one. Word around town is there's an insurance investigator in Eden looking for a man they want to question about it."

"In Eden?" Kate was surprised.

"Hard to believe there's a connection to our little town," Ann said.

"Who did you hear this from?" Nan said. Kate noticed she wasn't as quick as Ann to dismiss Ginger's news.

"From three different customers right after opening this morning," Ginger said. "Mary Jacobsen cleans at the Holiday Inn, said he showed her a picture and asked if she'd seen the man. She didn't know who he was, so wouldn't answer until she'd seen ID, and her manager said it was okay. Adam Wilson—George Wilson's kid—works day desk at the Best Western, said the same thing. Man came by showing the clerks and maids a picture of a man. Said he was a 'person of interest.' Adam's boss said to go ahead and answer. Told them all later who the guy was, and what it was about."

"And last but not least"—Ginger lowered her voice—"Vera Carter told me the guy stopped in to see Jo Valentine yesterday."

"No kidding!" Nan pulled out a pad and made a few notes. Ginger had definitely caught her interest.

"Jo Valentine is a detective with the Eden Police Department," Ann explained to Kate. "Vera is a dispatcher who talks too much."

"It's not exactly a state secret!" Ginger glared at Ann. "I mean, the guy's been talking to everybody. I expect he'll stop by here anytime now."

"Anyway"—Ginger turned back to Nan—"Vera said Jo had gotten a call from the Chicago police a couple days ago about this guy they're looking for. She passed it on to the street guys in case they stop him for something."

"Do you know his name?" Nan said. "Is he from here?"

"Vera said she didn't recognize the picture, and she's been here all her life. Customers started pouring in about then, and I never thought to ask for a name. She did say he was nice looking."

Nan made a few more scribbles on her notepad. "I'll run by the P.D.," she said. "See what else I can find out."

"Isn't it exciting?" Ginger squirmed in her chair. "Like one of your books, Kate!"

"The funny thing is, I *have* been following the story in the papers, thinking it might be the basis of an idea for my next book."

"See? It's like an omen!" Ginger said.

"You and your omens!" Ann said.

While the two squabbled, Kate looked around the crowded diner. What possible connection could Eden have to a Chicago theft and two murders, she wondered. Was the "person of interest" the missing security guard himself, or was the insurance investigator simply trying to find a relative or friend who might know his whereabouts? If that was the case, who might it be? The exhausted-looking suburban mom with the toddler two tables over, or maybe the big man in the rumpled suit seated at a table against the opposite wall, his nose buried in a newspaper? Maybe even one of the three young men in Raven tees texting at the counter between bites of food? That might explain an Eden connection. Maybe the missing security guard had a younger brother or son or nephew attending college here.

As her eyes scanned the restaurant, they locked with the eyes of a wiry man with slicked-back brown hair and a sparse mustache. He was seated with a woman at a table in the center of the room. The woman's back was to Kate, so all she could tell about her was that she had long curly brown hair and big hips. Kate guessed the man to be in his late thirties, not bad-looking, but he had a well-used look about him as if he'd lived a rough life. Not an unusual look in this area, since many of Eden's residents came from poorer areas of the state for work at the steel mill. This man looked different, though, maybe because of the cheap blue suit. Denim jeans and wife-beater tees were the summer uniform of choice for most of the mill workers. When he realized Kate was staring back at him, he hastily looked away as if he'd been caught at something.

The conversation turned to local news and upcoming events at the university. Kate didn't have anything to contribute but kept an ear tuned to the conversation as she finished her breakfast. Her three companions had work to get to, so they finished up quickly. As the four left the diner, Kate failed to notice the man with the mustache and his female companion get up from their table.

***

The man in the rumpled suit noticed. Interesting, Cal Becker thought to himself, as he laid a ten on the table to cover the food and tip, waited until the couple was out the door, and then stood up. The Halseys in the flesh!

Cal had spent the previous day making the rounds of motels and hotels in the area with an old booking photo of Mabry. He hadn't had any luck finding a match between the registered guests and Mabry, but the photo was old, and it was a booking photo. Nobody looked like themselves in booking photos, what with the usual rumpled hair and desperate stare. Add the changes that come with age, and Mabry's own mother might not recognize him from the picture. He needed to hit the motels and hotels again at different times of the day. He hadn't talked to every desk clerk, and maids didn't necessarily see the occupants of every room.

There was also the chance that Mabry had done something to change his looks, although in his experience Cal found most criminals never did. He'd never been able to figure that one out. If he were ever a wanted man, he'd damn sure be buying some hair dye at the drugstore and growing a beard. Of course, criminals were typically not the sharpest tools in the shed, although Mabry might be a little smarter than most. After all, he was still a free man, and the Star was still missing.

That Baby's sister and brother-in-law were in town was proof that Baby hadn't found him and that, like Cal, he thought Mabry's old friends might know where to find him. That could spell trouble for the old friends, since Baby wouldn't ask as politely as he would. Cal had told Jo Valentine that, if nothing else, he needed to warn Jackson Price and Katherine Rawlings against helping Michael. Now he also needed to warn them that they were on Baby Duda's radar.

Exiting the diner, Cal stopped short. Rawlings and the Halseys were standing two doors up at the corner, engaged in conversation.

Cal slipped his sunglasses on, took his cell phone from his pocket, and called his home number.

"Hey, there," he said, as his home phone rang on the other end. "Thought I'd check in with you and see how you're doing."

Continuing with the fake conversation, he watched as Rawlings and the Halseys talked for another minute, picking up a word now and then, but not enough to get an idea of what was being said. Rawlings didn't look spooked. What was her story, Cal wondered. She was the last person he'd have expected to have a connection with Baby Duda, but his years on the force had taught him the dangers of stereotyping people.

Maybe they had it all wrong. Maybe Halsey and Mabry were pulling a fast one on Baby, and their ladies were in on it as well. Mabry was hot so he'd be hiding out, but his old cellmate could easily be arranging a way out of the country for all of them. Rawlings would be the perfect go-between.

He decided it was time to check out of the Holiday Inn and get a room at the Holly House.

***

"Ms. Rawlings!"

Kate was just turning the corner on her way to her car when she heard her name. Turning, she saw the man in the cheap suit and his dark-haired companion.

"Yes?"

"I wonder if we could ask you to autograph this for us." The man extended a hardback copy of *Flee*.

"Well, yes, I guess," Kate said, embarrassed. Being recognized and asked for autographs happened occasionally but seldom enough that she had yet to grow accustomed to it.

"I gotta apologize for staring back there," the man said. "I recognized you but couldn't put a name to the face. It was only after you left that I realized I'd seen you on the back of the book my wife is reading."

"I'm such a fan," the woman said. "I've read your other books and just loved them."

"Thank you. That's always good to hear." She pulled a pen from her purse and opened the front cover of the book. "Is there anything in particular you'd like me to write?"

"Gee, I don't know," the woman said. "How about 'To my loyal fan?' "

"I can do that." She wrote the requested words, signed her name, and handed the book back to the woman.

"Thank you so much!"

"Wonder if you could give us some advice on where to stay," the man said. "We're taking a little road trip—just driving where the mood takes us. It's kinda pretty around here, though, so we thought we might stop for a day or two."

Behind them, Kate saw the rumpled man exit the diner. He glanced their way, put on his sunglasses, and stopped to make a phone call.

"I can highly recommend the Holly House," she said. "It's a very nice bed and breakfast just a few blocks over. There are also several motels out by the interstate—a Holiday Inn, a Best Western, and a couple others to choose from."

"We're kind of on a budget," the woman said. "I doubt the bed and breakfast would fit in it."

"It is a little pricier than the chains," Kate admitted. "Well worth it, if you can afford it, of course, but even the chains usually include breakfast. I can't say anything about them, though, since I've never stayed there.

"I would avoid," she added, "a place called The Shady Nook. It's a little farther outside of town and not any place you want to stay, believe me."

"Thanks for the warning," the man said. "We'll go to one of the chains."

"Thank you so much for the autograph!" the woman said. "I will treasure this book even more."

Kate found herself smiling as she walked on toward her car. Although it always embarrassed her, it was a good feeling to know people enjoyed reading what she enjoyed writing.

***

"I hope coming face-to-face with her that way was a good idea," Gabby muttered to Wendell, as they watched Kate walk away.

"It gave her a reason for me staring at her," Wendell said. "If she's in cahoots with the Professor, she's gonna be paranoid about anybody paying too much attention to her."

"And if he'd showed her a picture of you or described you, she'd be running to warn him right now."

"No way she recognized me," Wendell said. "She couldn't have hidden it that well. She bought that you just wanted her autograph."

"Too late to worry about it now. Guess we're heading to the Shady Nook?"

"You think that's where the Professor is staying?"

"Fleabags are a good place to hide out. No credit cards are required, and they don't get too interested in the guests."

"And just how do you know so much about fleabags?" Wendell put his arm around his wife's waist and gave her a squeeze.

"I'll never tell." Gabby kissed him on the cheek.

They didn't notice the man in the rumpled suit watching them as they got into their rental.

Chapter 12

Jackson's drive and both sides of the street were crammed with cars. Three blocks from the house, Kate spotted an opening on the opposite side of the street. She pulled into a driveway, turned around, and parallel parked in the space.

The walk back was pleasant. The day was warm, but not suffocatingly hot as it had been earlier. Jackson's neighborhood was an old moneyed one with no more than three houses per block. The homes sat well back from the sidewalk with established trees and flower beds colorful with early summer flowers. One wide lot was divided from the sidewalk by tall fragrant evergreen shrubs from which a cute bunny shot out as Kate approached. As she came closer to Jackson's home, the sound of people having a good time reached her. The perfect soundtrack for a perfect evening, she thought.

She made her way around the house to the large backyard. Even though she had been expecting a crowd, she was a little surprised at the milling throng she found there. It appeared Jackson's newfound fame had generated more interest in his party than usual. She spotted him near the gas grill overseeing two young men laboring over the sizzling burgers, brats, and chicken.

Three low stone walls enclosed the cooking area with cedar posts reaching up to a tiled roof. The prep counters were brown granite, with a deep stainless steel cleanup sink at one end, a double-bowled prep sink near the middle, and teak storage cabinets underneath. A rotisserie and an oven complemented the large, built-in grill. A semi-circular island between the cooking area and the house contained a bar sink, large under-counter fridge, ice maker and wine cooler. Seventy-five feet of slate patio connected the cooking area to the back of the house and the keg set up to one side of the patio doors. When winter came, Kate knew folding panels would be brought out of storage and attached to the roof and the cement floor to create protective walls around the cooking area and island.

"Glad you could make it, Kate." Jackson pecked her on the cheek in welcome. "Beer, wine, or something with more kick?"

"Jackson's got moonshine, do you believe it?" Mary Dunn was doing her best to appear indignant, but she was obviously charmed by Jackson's daring. "And with all these students here!"

"It's good stuff," Jackson said. "The man's supplied me for years. He hasn't killed or blinded anyone yet. Besides, the students know nothing about it. I save it for my adult friends."

"I think I'll stick with wine." Kate poured a paper cup of the supermarket Zinfandel that sat at one end of the bar island. Every inch of the countertop held bottles of wine and liquor, soft drinks and juice for mixed drinks, paper cups, drink stirs, and ice buckets.

Jackson turned back to shout a warning as the grill flared up, and Kate wandered into the yard. She sipped at her wine and stopped to speak to several of her students. Shirley Kramer, from the evening writing class, was there with her husband. Kate was exchanging pleasantries with the man when she felt someone grasp her arm.

"Excuse me, Shirley," Bill Herrick said, "Can I steal Kate for a moment?"

"So are you as thrilled as I am about Jackson's nominating us to be his replacement?" Bill said, as they moved out of Shirley's hearing. His tone was sarcastic.

Kate grinned. "Paul's been jabbing at you, too, has he?"

"Nonstop. You know, if we had any sense, we'd hire bodyguards. The man's liable to do anything to improve his chances."

"I told Jackson I'm not interested. Not that he paid any attention to me."

"What Jackson wants, Jackson gets. You should know that. But I agree with him. You'd be a great chair."

"So would you."

"Probably." Bill shrugged. "Certainly better than Holland, not that that's saying much. But I like what I'm doing. I'm a firm believer in the old saying, if it ain't broke, don't fix it."

"I like what I'm doing, too. I've even given some passing thought to giving up teaching altogether or at least only doing it part-time. I'd really like to have more time for my writing." She looked away. "And my mother."

"I've heard about her problem," Bill said. "I have some idea what you're going through. Alzheimer's killed my father."

"I'm so sorry," Kate said. "I didn't know."

"No reason you should. His came on early—in his late fifties. He died over ten years ago, two months before his sixty-fifth birthday." He sighed, his expression sad. "I know how tough it is on everyone concerned. If there's anything Susan or I can do to help, don't hesitate to ask. Or if you just want to talk, we're here."

"Thank you." Kate was surprised and moved by the offer. "I appreciate that."

Bill glanced past her and smiled. "Speaking of Holland, he's standing over there by the fence glaring at us."

Kate turned and saw Paul staring at them. No, Bill's choice of verb *was* more appropriate. He was glaring. Surrounded by a group of animated students who were chattering nonstop in their effort to impress him, he didn't look as if he even heard them.

"Now he knows we're conspiring against him," Bill whispered in her ear and waved at Paul. Holland looked away, his face reddening and his jaw clenching. Kate could almost see steam coming out of his ears.

"You're terrible, Bill!" Kate couldn't keep from laughing, even though she knew Paul was probably watching again and growing angrier by the second.

"He asks for it. Oh, will you excuse me, Kate? I see Henway from the Classics department. I've been wanting to talk to him about setting up an introductory course specifically for English majors."

Kate continued to mingle. Except for the vicious looks directed her way by Paul Holland, she was having a good time. She was pouring her second Zinfandel when someone nudged her hard, and she sloshed the wine on the counter.

"Oops," Lou said. "Sorry about that. Didn't mean to waste good wine."

"That's how I know you didn't do it on purpose. Hey, Roger. Good to see you."

"You, too, Kate." Roger gave her a quick peck on the cheek. "It's great to have you home."

Roger Pelfrey was a solidly built man with a round face, thinning gray hair and intense brown eyes—puppy dog eyes, Lou called them. He was the kind of man who, had he been an aspiring Hollywood actor, would have found himself typecast as a blue-collar worker, father, and husband. At one time in his life, all three roles had fit him.

Roger and Lou met in college. He was a few years older and working at Eden Steel while attending Raven part-time. After Drew was born, he almost dropped out to work more overtime, but Lou refused to allow it. Ethan came along two years later, and a year after that, Roger completed his teaching degree and landed a position at Mayfield High teaching history and social studies. He continued to work toward the state-required master's degree, but with an eye toward administration. Three years after completing his master's, he became assistant principal at Eden High, and five years later, he replaced the retiring principal.

"It's good to be back." Kate turned to Lou. "I thought you weren't coming."

"Changed my mind. I still don't like the idea of partying with students who'll be puking in my holding cell next weekend, but Roger pointed out that I should probably be more sociable with the admin bigwigs if I want to be chief. There's always one or two bigwigs at Jackson's parties."

"Roger always was smarter than you."

"And you thought I married him just for his body."

"I can't take all this girl talk," Roger said. "Especially when I'm the subject. Time for some cornhole." He moved off toward the left side of the yard where several of the guests were playing cornhole, cheered on by their supporters.

"Quite a turnout," Lou said, as they moved away from the bar.

"Guess everyone wants to celebrate Jackson's success with him."

"People seem to think luck rubs off."

"It wasn't luck," Kate objected. "Jackson has worked hard over the years and had more than his share of failure. He deserves this."

"I didn't say he didn't." Lou held up her hand. "Sometimes people look at it that way, though, and want to touch the magic."

Kate didn't reply. She was staring at Michael who had just walked through the gate. He glanced around, homed in on her, and headed their way.

"Uh-oh," she muttered, dreading Lou's reaction.

"Hey, Kat!" Michael gave her a quick hug. Letting her go, he turned to Lou and hugged her. "Lou, you look great. How many years has it been?"

"Wasn't counting," Lou said. "How have you been, Michael?"

"Oh, you know." He waggled his hand. "Ups and downs."

"I can only imagine."

Michael grinned. "I won't ask you to expand on *that* comment! So you're still a school cop, huh?"

"Lou's a deputy chief," Kate interrupted, "and in line to be the next chief."

"No kidding? Impressive."

"To what do we owe the honor of your presence, Michael?" Lou said.

"Was that an official inquiry?" Michael held up his hand. "Don't answer that. There's nothing for you to worry about, Lou. I just wanted to see old friends again. And Raven."

"A walk down memory lane?"

"It was a good time in my life," he said, his swagger disappearing. "I think about those times a lot."

"Yeah, it was a good time. Until you fucked it up."

"Lou," Kate protested, but Michael silenced her.

"It's okay. Lou's right. I fucked up the best thing that ever happened to me."

Kate stared into his eyes for a moment before looking away from the pain she saw there.

"I guess you could say I chose the wrong fork in that lane," he said, looking back at Lou.

"So how long are you in town for, Michael?" Lou's voice was as hard as before his admission of his mistake.

"Not long," he replied, his swagger returning. "I wouldn't want my presence to keep you up nights worrying what I'm up to."

"If you're up to anything, trust me, sweetie, I *will* find out."

Lou took a step toward Michael. He stood his ground. The two of them stared into each other's eyes for a few silent moments. He looked away first, grinning at Kate.

"Your girlfriend is even tougher than I remembered, Kat. I think she wants to kick my ass for breaking your heart."

"Nice to see you again, Michael," Lou said, steering Kate away while she was still trying to come up with a response. "We've got people we need to see."

"Damn him!" Lou's cool disappeared. She was furious. "Don't let him get to you, Kate. He's a loser, always was, and always will be."

"I think he was getting to you more than me," Kate said. "Actually I feel a little sorry for him."

"Sorry for him! What the fuck for? He made you love him and then treated you like shit! You ought to want to cut his balls off!"

"It's not that simple," Kate started. She might have continued, might have finally confessed the truth to Lou, but a voice interrupted them.

"Deputy Chief Pelfrey! There you are!" Kate recognized the man who took Lou's shoulder as someone in administration, although she couldn't put a name to the face. "Can I borrow this lady for a few minutes, Professor Rawlings? I have some people I'd like her to meet."

"Remember what I said, Kate," Lou said before allowing herself to be led off.

Kate took a deep drink of the wine she'd forgotten she was holding.

***

One minute he was gone from her life, if not her memory, although his reappearances in the latter were decreasing in frequency. The next he was leaning against her six-year old black Cutlass in the parking lot outside her office at The University of Toledo. Taken by surprise, she smiled, happy to see him, feeling her spirits lift at the love in his eyes. Then she remembered, the hurt flooded back, and her smile faded.

"Hey, Kat," he said, straightening, but not moving from the car.

She stopped several feet from him. He looked the same, she thought. Maybe a little thinner, but otherwise, the same. How could he look the same after what he had done? He should look like a monster who crushed hearts and hope, not like the man she had fallen in love with.

"What are you doing here, Michael?" she said, surprised that her voice sounded steady.

"I wanted to see you." He looked down at his feet, thrust his hands into his pockets like a penitent child. "To apologize."

That was all? He wanted to *apologize*? He didn't ache with missing her, didn't want to hold her, didn't want to kiss her and make all the bad disappear? She stood silent, dumbstruck at the shock of it.

"I miss you, Kat." His voice broke, and he swallowed hard before continuing. "I really screwed up, didn't I?"

"Yes," she managed. "You did."

He came to her then and wrapped his arms around her. At first, she simply stood woodenly while he pulled her to him, but then her arms snaked around him as if they had a mind of their own. She noticed first that his shirt was damp before she realized her tears were the cause.

When she found him in the parking lot, it was late afternoon on a Friday. They didn't leave her apartment until Sunday morning when they walked to a place on the lake for a late breakfast. Monday she called off, pleading a migraine, and they drove into the country, stopping at a small winery for lunch and in small towns for antique-store hopping.

She told him about her time at the University of Chicago, her part-time teaching job at a community college, a job that paid her living expenses while she completed her doctorate. She told him about her current job in Toledo, how her parents were doing, that Lou had gotten married, how she was thinking about getting a dog.

He told her very little. He confessed that the undergrad had run home to Louisville less than six months after they'd left Eden. They were in Reno at the time, their third landing after their flight from Eden. She'd been homesick, he said, missing her parents and sister.

"Decided she'd made the biggest mistake of her life by taking off with me," he told Kate. "I couldn't argue with her on that."

Kate knew if she opened her mouth, the poisonous hatred she felt for the girl would spew out like venom from a snake. So she stayed silent, feeling the poison churning in her gut.

"I just bummed around after that," he continued. "Here, there, nowhere important."

When she'd tried to find out more about what he had been doing in the years since he'd abandoned her, his answers were vague, and he quickly changed the subject. It wasn't until he was gone and she'd had time to think that she began to suspect he might have gotten into trouble. She remembered what he'd said about the men in his county who dropped out of school, how they'd all ended up in the mines or in jail. He had worked to keep that from happening to him but had he ended up in jail after all? Was that why he wouldn't tell her anything about his life after Reno?

He stayed a week. Or, more precisely, six days and eighteen hours. She hadn't taken notice of the minutes. She relaxed after the first day or so. Everyone deserved a second chance, didn't they? Michael realized he had messed up, and he missed her and loved her. That was what was important now. Over the week after she'd first found him in the lot, she grew to believe they still had a future together. He seemed to believe it, too, brainstorming with her on how they would build it.

"You could go back to school," she had told him the day before he left. "Or, if you don't want to do that, concentrate on your writing. I don't make a lot yet, but I make enough for us to live."

"I couldn't ask you to support me."

"It would only be until you wrote a bestseller," she said, only half joking. "Then I expect you to support me."

"You're amazing. You know that, don't you? I don't deserve you. Or more to the point, you don't deserve me."

"Silly man." She kissed him on the mouth, stopping the conversation.

The next day, a Friday, a week after he'd walked back into her life, he walked out again. As she kissed him goodbye on her way to work that morning, he held her tightly and told her again how much he loved her. Running late, she had squirmed out of his grasp, pecked him on the lips, and promised she'd be home for lunch. But he was gone when she came home at lunch time, his things cleared out, leaving only a brief note that said he couldn't screw up her life anymore by tying it to his. Her landlady, a sweet old woman who lived next door, told her Michael's car had left around ten that morning, and she hadn't seen it since.

She didn't leave her apartment that weekend, but by Monday she was ready to begin the business of forgetting Michael all over again.

***

Kate continued to mingle with the guests in Jackson's back yard, exchanging pleasantries with students and longer conversations with faculty. One of the student chefs offered her a paper plate with a chicken and vegetable kabob, telling her it was per Jackson's orders. She hadn't felt hungry, but it was surprisingly good and she devoured it along with the rest of her wine. She had just helped herself to a refill when Lou reappeared.

"Roger will be proud of me," Lou said. "I was charming to everyone. In other words, I wasn't my usual self. I don't think I used one swear word."

Kate laughed. "Have you had any food? The kabobs are wonderful."

Lou helped herself to a plate, Kate got seconds, and they moved through the crowd toward the back of Jackson's spacious yard to a small formal garden complete with brick paths and stone benches. They ate in silence for a few minutes until loud laughter and shouts erupted from the gathering around the beer keg on the patio where Michael was holding court. He had obviously just told a story the crowd found hilarious.

"Same as always," Lou muttered.

Kate watched Michael as he charmed the students around the keg. He looks like a silly boy, she thought. Older and dissolute, yes, but a boy all the same. A deep sadness came over her. Michael wasn't a total loser like Lou said. She knew from firsthand experience that he could be loving and kind. He was intelligent and he was talented, but he had wasted those gifts. Had he ever had a chance? Was a lousy family and childhood ever a good excuse for throwing your life away?

Michael broke off from the crowd and approached Jackson who had just emerged from the house. They moved off to the side. Michael had a beer in one hand; his free hand was around Jackson's shoulder. Michael leaned close, talking earnestly to Jackson, who was frowning and shaking his head.

"Aw, shit!" Lou said. "I should have guessed that's why he's here."

"What?"

"Money, what else?" Lou glanced at her. "Have you forgotten? When Michael left town, he took off with five thousand dollars of Jackson's money."

"What?" Kate was surprised. "I didn't know that."

"It was a loan. Michael told Jackson he would pay him back by teaching over the summer, but he left before the summer session started. He never paid Jackson back. You didn't know?"

"No. I didn't."

Jackson must have decided not to bother her with the details of Michael's disloyalty to him. He probably figured Michael's running off with another woman and leaving her heartbroken was enough.

Or maybe he was embarrassed to admit he'd been taken.

"He probably didn't want to upset you with any more proof of what a shit Michael is," Lou said, echoing Kate's thoughts. "He was really hurt. He trusted Michael—like we all did."

The conversation grew more animated. Jackson started to walk away, but Michael took hold of his arm and stopped him, still talking. The expression on Michael's face was one of determination—and something else. "Desperation" was the word that popped into Kate's mind. Michael looked desperate.

"My guess is Michael's trying to bum more money," Lou said. " I think it's time I interrupted his little party."

Lou started across the yard, Kate hurrying to catch up. As they approached, she caught Michael's insistent tone and the words, "I need it, Jackson, I really do."

"Is everything okay?" Kate interrupted. They both looked up, surprised. Neither had been aware of their approach. Michael pasted a smile on his face.

"Jackson and I were just catching up on old times, weren't we?" He squeezed Jackson's shoulder.

Jackson moved his head in what might have passed for a nod. "Hello, Lou. Glad you could make it."

"I wouldn't have missed it for anything," Lou lied. "I wanted to celebrate your success with you. And mooch some free food, of course."

Jackson laughed and took a few steps to the side, putting some distance between himself and Michael.

"Seriously, Jackson, congratulations," Lou said. "I should have called or stopped by and told you that before now. I know the success of this book has to be quite a thrill for you."

Jackson glanced at Michael and nodded. "Yes, it is. I've been fortunate."

"I'm sure you'll continue to be, Jackson." Michael squeezed Jackson's shoulder again and then released it. "I think I'll help myself to another beer and mingle a little. Anything I can get you, Kat?"

She shook her head, feeling Lou's and Jackson's eyes on her. Michael moved back to the keg. Lou turned to Jackson.

"Don't give in to him, Jackson. He wants money, doesn't he?"

"Lou, really—" Jackson started but Lou didn't let him finish.

"I can't believe he has the gall to ask for another so-called loan after he didn't pay you back the other money," Lou said. "God! Sometimes I wish this were some third-world dictatorship so I could throw shit heads like him in jail just because I want to!"

"Lou, my dear, thank you for being so protective of me, but I assure you everything is fine."

"I'm serious, Jackson. Don't you dare give Michael any more money."

"I promise I'm perfectly capable of handling Michael Mabry's requests. I was surprised at his appearance here, I admit, and saddened by the memories of his betrayal. But that's all, I assure you."

"You never told me, Jackson," Kate said.

"Didn't I? It's been so long, it's difficult to remember. But I suppose I probably didn't. You had enough on your plate back then. Michael had only taken money from me. He'd taken so much more from you."

"Thank *you* for being so protective of me," she said, echoing what he had said to Lou, and grinned at him.

He smiled and hugged her to his side.

"Jackson, if the asshole is bugging you, I can do my best to run him out of town," Lou said. "In fact, I'd enjoy making his sorry life even more miserable than it already is."

Jackson laughed. "Lou, you sound like you've been watching too many cowboy movies. 'This town isn't big enough for both of us' kind of shows."

Lou didn't smile. "I'm serious. I'm going to run some checks on our old friend and hope and pray I find something on him."

"Thank you both." Jackson looked from one to the other of them. "It's nice to know that some old friendships last. But don't worry about me. I doubt Michael will be in town very long."

"Let's hope not," Lou said.

Someone called Jackson's name from the grill area. He excused himself and moved off. Lou and Roger left soon after.

Dusk had fallen and the backyard lights flicked on automatically as they sensed the darkening sky. The crowd had grown louder as the alcohol flowed more freely and someone had propped a boom box on a chair. An Eagles CD began to play and Kate flash backed to high school parties. Where had the years gone?

Suddenly she felt old and tired.

Chapter 13

"Kat! Wait up!"

She had just reached her car when she heard Michael's voice. He was jogging to catch up with her. She waited at the passenger side of the car, keys in hand.

"I saw you leave, but I had a little trouble getting away from a drunk classics student who thinks I'm his new best friend." He motioned toward her car. "Can we sit and talk for a while? Away from the crowd?"

"Of course."

She hit the remote button twice to unlock both front doors, went around the rear of the car and got in the driver's side, while Michael got in the passenger seat. He leaned forward as if stretching his back and then leaned back, stretching his legs as far as the dash allowed.

"Damn, I'm stiff! Seems like a sore back is getting to be a regular thing with me. Guess we're getting old, huh?"

"The years will do that," she said.

"They've been kind to you. You look as good as ever."

"And you're the same smooth talker you always were."

He laughed. "Hey, it's about all I've got going for me anymore. But in this case, what I said is true."

"Seven years at our age is a long time. It shows on both of us."

"Has it been that long?" Michael seemed surprised.

The seven years since the last time she'd seen Michael had indeed left their mark on him. He was still trim and solid, but the lines in his face were deeper and his hair showed streaks of gray that hadn't been there before. Gravity—and hard living, she guessed—had begun to exert their pull on his cheeks and eyelids, and his chin had lost some of its firmness. His eyes, however, were still the same beautiful blue that had so mesmerized her that first day in Jackson's seminar.

She wished she could see herself through his eyes. Did he see the remnants of the girl who had been swept off her feet by him amongst the deterioration age had brought, or did he only see an aging spinster schoolteacher? On second thought, maybe some things were best left unknown.

"What have you been up to, Michael? Or dare I ask?"

"A little of this, a little of that. Nothing too exciting." He looked at her. "Unlike you. Three books—I'm really proud of you, Kat."

"I got your roses after *Escape* was published."

"I would have sent more after *Deadfall*, but I was out of the country. Didn't know you'd published it until I bought *Flee* and saw it mentioned on the jacket. I googled to see where you were teaching so I could send you more. That's how I found out you were here."

"So where are my flowers?"

He laughed. "I'll get you some, babe, I promise. But I wanted to congratulate you in person this time, not just FTD it."

"What were you doing out of the country?"

"Just a job." He shrugged. "Driving for a family that does a lot of traveling."

"Driving for a family or a woman?"

"A family!" He lightly punched her shoulder "I'm getting old, remember?"

"Not *that* old."

He laughed. "Well, no, maybe not. I don't need the little blue pill yet, if that's what you mean." He leaned closer. "I'll be glad to prove it if you want. We could drive over to Hanover and spend some time on the roof like we used to do."

The roof! That brings back memories, she thought. She and Michael had first made love on the roof of Hanover Hall one warm fall night while she was still living at home. Michael had been chatting with Robbie Applegate one day when he noticed the door at the back of the maintenance room. It was kept locked, but both the locks on the maintenance room and the lock on the door to the roof were simple ones for Michael to pry open with his driver's license, and he often did.

Even after they'd moved in together and until winter's cold stopped them, they often sneaked up to the roof to lie on the sleeping bag Michael had secreted in the old corrugated metal shed that was no longer used for storage. Sometimes he'd hide a gift in the sleeping bag, something inexpensive but sweet, like drugstore perfume or a romantic card. They'd drink wine and look at the stars and talk about the wondrous things they were going to accomplish with their lives. It always ended with them making love.

"Michael, you are incorrigible!" She shoved him away, laughing. "Get back on your side of the car! I am not going up on the roof with you."

"Can't blame a guy for trying." He leaned against the passenger window, facing her, and turned serious. "It really is good to see you, Kat. I mean that. You're the one good thing that's stayed constant in my life. I have no idea why you even talk to me. It's puzzled me for a long time."

"It's a puzzle to me, too."

He laughed again, pulled her to him, and kissed her quickly on the lips. He tasted of beer with a hint of barbecue sauce. "I love you, you know that?"

"Yeah, I know," she whispered. "I love you, too, Michael."

"But not *that* way, right? Not anymore."

She didn't respond. They stared into one another's eyes for a few seconds until he broke eye contact and sat back, closing his eyes.

"I screwed up back then, Kate," he said, "and I haven't stopped since."

She hesitated, not really wanting an answer to the question she was about to ask, and then went ahead anyway. "Are you in trouble, Michael?"

He didn't answer for a moment, but then he looked at her. His expression had changed. He looked like Michael, smelled like Michael, and his voice was Michael's, but the crooked smile and twinkling eyes belonged on a carnival huckster, not the man she knew first as a lover, now as a friend.

"Of course I'm not in trouble. No angry women or cuckolded husbands after me, and I don't owe anybody money." He pulled her to him and kissed her again, this time lingering. "I just wanted to see you, Kat." He gently smoothed her hair back from her face, gave her a quick peck on the forehead and released her. "Now I think I'll get back to the party and let you head home."

Opening the passenger door, he quickly got out of the car.

"Michael!" Kate just as quickly exited on the driver's side. "Michael, wait!"

"I'll give you a ring before I leave," he said, barely glancing at her. With a dismissive wave, he started down the sidewalk toward Jackson's.

As she turned to get back in her car, her eyes locked with Paul Holland's. He was standing next to a car on the opposite side of the street, along with three students, one female and two males. The students were whispering to one another. They had all been watching the exchange between Michael and her. How long had they been there, she wondered. Had they seen Michael and her kissing?

She was suddenly angry at the intrusion. So she had been "caught" kissing a man in a car! She was considerably over twenty-one, and so was Michael. There wasn't much Paul Holland could make out of *that* bit of gossip.

***

The locks on the Holly House guest rooms were embarrassingly easy to pick, but Cal supposed the Hill ladies didn't usually rent to thieves or nosy detectives. He shut the door quietly behind him and stood for a moment looking around Katherine Rawling's room.

She was tidy; he'd give her that. Unlike his own room two doors down, there were no clothes flung over chairs, no suitcases sitting out in the open, no dirty Styrofoam cups on the nightstand. Her bedspread was a little rumpled where she'd probably sat on it while dressing for Price's party, and her desk held a laptop and a couple stacks of papers, but everything else was neat or out of sight. He began a methodical search, first of her dresser and nightstand drawers—nothing incriminating or interesting in either unless you counted white cotton panties. He moved to the closet. She had hung her dresses, skirts, slacks, and tops by type, and arranged her five pairs of shoes neatly on the top shelf. On the floor were three matching suitcases and one bag that didn't match the others. Cal could tell by the weight it wasn't empty. Laying the suitcase on the floor, he kneeled and popped it open.

"Bingo," he muttered to himself.

The suitcase held three pairs of men's slacks, one pair of jeans, five shirts, briefs, several pairs of socks, a photo album and some papers in a plastic grocery bag. Cal pulled the bag back from the papers and thumbed through them. Looked like five or six short stories, Mabry's name on the title page of each of them. If he wasn't mistaken, they had been done on a typewriter, not a printer, and the pages were starting to yellow. Something Mabry had written way back when, he decided, probably while he was still in college in Eden. He slid the papers back into the bag and replaced it in the position he'd found it.

Turning to the photo album, he opened it and scanned each page quickly. Older pictures filled the first half of the book, some of them in black and white, some fading color shots done with a Polaroid camera. The toddler, child, and teen posed in many of them showed traces of the man Michael Mabry would grow into. Cal guessed the pretty woman in some of the pictures was Mabry's mother and the thin, tough-looking man was his father.

The last half of the book was a surprise. Page after page held pictures of Mabry and Rawlings. Cal recognized some as having been taken here in Eden on Raven's campus when they were young, happy, and obviously in love. Rawlings had been a pretty thing, Cal thought, with that honey-blond hair, great smile, and those innocent green eyes. The two of them made a handsome couple. They continued to make a handsome couple as they grew older, as testified to by the record Mabry had kept in pictures. Photo after photo showed the two of them posed in front of backgrounds not found in Eden, and as the photographic quality of the pictures improved, their faces took on the maturity of passing years.

The photo album and suitcase proved three things. One, Katherine Rawlings was important to Mabry. Other than his mother and a few females who were probably relatives in the older pictures, the only woman in the album was Rawlings. Two, they had kept in contact over the years. And, three, Mabry was in Eden, and he was still in contact with Rawlings. The stories could conceivably have been left behind when he skedaddled thirty-odd years ago, but the shirts and clothes were not thirty-year-old styles.

Cal had spent only one night in Holly House, but he'd seen Rawlings from his window when she came home last night and at breakfast this morning when she'd smiled and said hello. When she left this evening, he'd followed her to Price's where a backyard bash was going on. She'd been alone every time. The bag proved she'd had recent contact with Mabry, yet he was nowhere to be seen. If she was an innocent party, why would she keep his things for him while he stayed out of sight? Didn't make sense. Maybe the plan was for the two of them to leave town or even the country separately, and he'd left the bag for her to bring to him.

Cal carefully felt the surfaces of the suitcase inside and out but found nothing out of the ordinary. The Star wasn't hidden there. He got to his feet, groaning as his back and knees screamed a protest, and replaced the bag in the closet. He glanced at his watch. He'd seen Rawlings enter Price's backyard a half hour before. He figured he had at least another hour, probably more, before she'd leave Price's party. Plenty of time to go over the room with a fine-toothed comb, after which he had a call to make. It was time to report in to Chicago.

***

While Paul Holland and his groupies watched, Kate pulled away from the curb. She didn't want to stay at Jackson's party, but she didn't want to go back to Holly House just yet. She had too much on her mind to sleep. There was a time she would have called Lou, and the two of them would have found a cafe or a park bench and talked for hours. But those times were long gone. Lou had a family now, plus there was the little problem of explaining to Lou why she'd kept her in the dark about Michael. So she drove.

As she moved through the streets of Eden, past the groups of laughing students and the quiet houses and dark stores, she tried to remember exactly when she and Michael had gone from lovers to friends. It had been at least three years, maybe more, after that first time before Michael reappeared in her life. She was cold to him at first, but it was impossible to be angry with Michael for very long.

She was still in Toledo then. He stayed less than a week. At first she resisted his sexual overtures, but her won't power lasted less than a day. After all, he was still the good-looking sexy man he'd always been. She'd been afraid that sleeping with him would dredge up the old feelings, and to some extent it did. But it was different this time. She still cared for him and still enjoyed his body, but for the first time, she accepted him for what he was—a desirable, but damaged man. With that acceptance, her feelings for him morphed from romantic love into the more enduring love of long-time friends.

He recognized the change, and Kate suspected he was relieved. They could be what was now called "friends with benefits" but without the guilt and hurt. Over the following decades, he called her once or twice a year, occasionally sent her a postcard, and every few years showed up unexpectedly. He never said much about what he'd been doing between visits, and she never pried. She didn't want to know what she was pretty sure were sad details of a wasted life. Somewhere along the way, they stopped sleeping together. Michael still made half-hearted attempts, just as he had this evening, she turned him down, and that was that. They stayed friends, without the benefits, and it worked for them.

When Kate reached the city limits, she continued into the darkened countryside. Without being aware of it, she had aimed her car toward her hometown of Mayfield. Situated just under ten miles from Eden, it was a drive of less than ten minutes on the nearly empty roads.

Eden's population, including students, topped 10,000 most years. Mayfield's population was no more than a fourth of that. A bedroom community, its working residents found employment at the university or steel mill in Eden or made the longer commute to jobs in Lexington. It was a comfortable, quiet, middle-class town, with modest but nice homes, mom-and-pop stores, and unclogged streets.

The house she'd grown up in sat in an older section of Mayfield. A post-WWII ranch of dark red brick with a full basement, it shared the street with trees that were planted as saplings when the homes were built to house returning vets and their families. Harry and Bette Rawlings had bought the home in 1957, after Harry got out of the service. Soon after, Bette found out she was pregnant with twins. Because Kate commuted to Eden during her undergrad program at Raven, the house on Oak Street was the only home she'd known until she and Michael moved into their efficiency apartment during grad school.

Turning onto Oak Street, she remembered how relieved she had been to get away from the house that had become stifling in its silences. When exactly did that happen, she wondered. It hadn't been that way when she'd been small. She remembered smiles and laughter around the backyard grill and dinner table, and how it had felt when her father came through the door after his shift as a Raven groundskeeper ended, a big smile creasing his face as he picked her up and swung her into his arms. She had been his beloved Katydid, and Steven had been his "little man." By the time she entered high school, that man was beginning to disappear, and by the time she graduated, he was gone. She and Steven couldn't understand why.

Once, after an introductory psychology course her freshman year at Raven, she diagnosed her father as suffering from clinical depression. Sure that she had the answer, she approached him with her newfound knowledge and, know-it-all that she was back then, suggested he get counseling. He had simply looked at her while she babbled on, and when she finally ran out of steam, he'd gone back to his newspaper. She never had the courage to raise the issue again, even though to this day, she suspected she had been right. In the end, it made little difference. Legitimate illness or not, he had turned his back on his family.

Nearing the house, she saw her father's blue Toyota in the drive and a light through the picture window that opened onto the living room. Anger surged. It was just like him, she thought, abandoning his wife when she needed him most. Was Steven right, she wondered. Was another woman involved? Well, if there was some bitch in there trying to take her mother's place, she was in for the surprise of her life!

She parked at the curb, shut the driver's door quietly, and strode up the drive to the walk curving off it. Two steps led to a small concrete porch that stretched along the middle of the house. She reached for the storm door handle, prepared to barge in, verbal guns blazing, but hesitated. The drapes were open at the picture window, and she stepped quietly to it instead.

Her father was there, but he was alone. Stretched out in the worn leather recliner they'd had since she was a senior at Raven, he was asleep, his mouth hanging open, oblivious to the sitcom playing on the television. An empty glass and plate sat on the end table next to the chair, a bag of chips wedged between his right thigh and the arm of the chair.

Suddenly the anger was gone. In its place was a sadness so intense she felt as if she were drowning in it. Instead of the Lothario she'd been prepared to lambast, she'd found a sad old man, all alone in an empty house that had once been a happy home. She turned away and left as quietly as she had come, wondering as she drove away, if she had given up too easily back in her freshman year.

***

Just before midnight, Jo heard Nick come in. He banged around in the kitchen for a few minutes, and then came down the hall and paused outside her door. Don't even think about it, she thought to herself, but he continued past to the guest room. She fell back to sleep but woke again a little after five. Since then she'd lay staring at the ceiling.

They were at a crossroads. It was funny in a way. She hadn't wanted to come to Kentucky, and now she didn't want to leave. When Nick got the assistant chief of security position at Eden Steel, she had threatened to leave him rather than leave the City. That was fifteen years ago. Brianna had just started first grade. Nick used logic, arguing it was better to leave before Brianna had established friends, Jo arguing back that there was no reason to leave at any time. In the end, she followed him to Eden. She was surprised when, after a few months, she found she liked it.

Less than a year later she saw a notice in the paper that the Eden Police Department was hiring. She signed up for and took the civil service examination without telling Nick. She'd half expected not to do well and was surprised when she placed third. There were two openings. When the man who scored second highest withdrew thanks to another offer, she could no longer avoid telling him. He hadn't liked it, and she suspected it was because he was jealous. When they met, Nick had been in security for several years but hadn't given up his dream of being a "real" cop. After he worked his way up to supervisory positions, the money and hours had been too good to give up to start at the bottom in patrol somewhere.

They argued about her taking the job, but she refused to budge. Nick hadn't been the only one who had dreamed of being a cop. Jo had just turned thirty and could hear the clock ticking. If she was ever going to do what she had always wanted to do, it was now or never. The conflict continued for a while with him bitching about her shift work and making veiled accusations that she was a bad mother, but eventually things settled down.

She hadn't wanted to come, but now Eden was home. She knew she wasn't going anywhere, and she also knew he was. So now what? A long distance marriage with weekend visits every few weeks? As far as she could see, that was their only option short of separation and ultimately divorce. Even if they tried the long distance thing, how many couples with a good relationship could make that work for the long haul? Their relationship hadn't been good for a long time.

She was so deep in thought it took her a few seconds to realize the sound she was hearing was her cell phone. She swung her legs off the side of the bed, and grabbed it off the nightstand. The screen showed it was the department calling.

"Morning."

"Back at you," Vera said. "We got a body on campus. Hanover Hall parking lot. Ivan said it looks like he's been shot."

"Who's up with me?"

"Sticks. I called you first, though."

Eden detectives did not have permanent partners assigned like the big city departments. For the most part, they worked alone, only pairing when a case was large, involving multiple incidents as with the recent string of burglaries and car break-ins, or when a case was more serious. Murder qualified for the latter category. Cases were assigned on a rotating basis, depending on availability, and when a partner was required, the next free detective stepped up.

"Okay," Jo said. "Tell Sticks I'll meet him there."

Chapter 14

"Lou? Is everything okay?"

Kate rubbed her eyes, trying to clear the fog from her brain, as she stared at her friend standing in the hall outside her room. Edna, dressed in robe and slippers, stood behind Lou. She had an anxious look on her face. Outside the sun was still below the horizon, showing just a hint of the light that was to come.

"Is Roger okay?" Just as she said this, another thought struck Kate. "Is it my mom? Or Steven?"

"They're all fine, Kate." Lou came into the room.

"I'll make some coffee," Edna said, turning away.

"Thanks, Edna. We'll be down in a few minutes." Lou closed the door and turned to Kate. "It's Michael, Kate. He's dead."

Kate stared at her, the news slow to sink in.

"Dead?" she repeated. "Dead? We just saw him."

"I know, sweetie," Lou said. "But there's no question. It's him."

"Oh, God!" Her vision blurred as tears filled her eyes. She blinked several times to clear her vision and felt a few tears trickle down her cheeks. She wiped them away with her hand. "What happened? Was he in a car accident?"

"No. It wasn't an accident."

Kate stared at her, waiting.

"He was found beside his car in Hanover Hall's parking lot," Lou said. "It looks like he was shot to death."

Kate felt her legs give out, and she sat down hard on the edge of the bed.

"Hey." Lou sat beside her and took her hand. "Take a deep breath, girlfriend."

"Michael was murdered?" Kate said, not believing it even as she said it. It had to be a case of mistaken identity. "Are you sure it's him?"

"I saw him, Kate. One of our guys found him, and dispatch called me. I got there just after a city marked unit did. I ID'd him."

"Who would do that?" Kate felt as if she were in a fog. She couldn't wrap her mind around the concept of Michael being dead, much less murdered.

"Did he get into it with anyone at Jackson's party? Did he leave with anyone?"

"No," Kate said, shaking her head. "At least not while I was there. He was still there when I left."

"What time was that?"

"I don't know—it was early. Not long after you and Roger left. It was just starting to get dark, so I guess it was around nine."

"And you were here the rest of the night?"

"No," Kate said. "I wasn't sleepy, so I drove around for a couple of hours."

"Alone?"

Lou had a strange look on her face. A cop look, Kate suddenly realized. The look the cops on TV shows have when they're homing in on a suspect.

"Of course, alone," Kate said. "I didn't kill Michael, Lou. I went for a drive, that's all."

"I know you didn't kill Michael, Kate." Lou looked embarrassed, but she pressed on. "But you two have an unpleasant history, and the city cops don't know you like I do. They're going to want to know where you went after you left Jackson's."

"I went for a drive, like I said. First around Eden and then over to Mayfield."

"Did you see anyone?"

"Yes," Kate said. "I saw my dad. Sitting all by himself in our old house."

"But," she added, holding up her hand, as Lou started to speak. "He didn't see me. And neither did anyone else."

**

Mabry's body lay in a slumped position against the rear driver's side door, his chin resting on his chest, his dark hair still neatly combed, his left leg bent with the foot resting under the right leg. Except for the blood soaking the front of his blue shirt, he looked a lot like the many drunks Jo had found passed out during her years on patrol. The driver's door stood open, as did the glove box and the console storage box, the contents of both scattered across the bucket seats. Bob Smith, one of the two investigators sent over from the State Police forensic lab in Ashland, squatted by the open passenger door, carefully dusting for prints. Waste of time, Jo thought, especially on a rental.

Eden wasn't big enough to have their own forensic people. They had the option of collecting their own evidence and prints, but for more serious crimes, state investigators were called in. Bob and his partner, Lena Jackson, usually handled Eden calls. Jo had worked with them before and knew them to be thorough.

"No watch," Sticks Mullins confirmed from his squat beside the body. "Looks like he might have had a ring, too. There's lighter skin on his ring finger. "

Jo liked partnering with Sticks. Not only was he a good detective, he was easy to get along with, which translated meant he was able to put up with her New York attitude. He'd been on the department for ten years. His given name was Gerald, but he'd been called Sticks since high school. She'd asked him about it once. He told her he'd played basketball in high school and used to get ribbed about his skinny legs. He'd been pretty good at making free throws, he said, and once when he'd scored in a close game, his hometown radio announcer had broadcast, "That boy has sticks for legs, but he sure can shoot!" The name had stuck.

Jo dropped the wallet she was holding into an evidence bag. They had found the brown leather wallet lying on the pavement beside the body, empty of everything except a single picture and the Illinois driver license that confirmed the victim was Michael Mabry. She passed the evidence bag to Lena.

"So, whaddya think?" Sticks straightened his lanky six-feet-four-inch body into a standing position and stepped back. "Caught our car thieves going about their business, and they shot him?"

"They haven't shown any inclination to violence before now," Jo said.

"Everybody always says that the first time their dog bites."

"Mabry had some pretty bad characters out of Chicago looking for him. Be quite a coincidence if he got shot by petty thieves, now wouldn't it?"

"Coincidences do happen."

"Maybe. But I'd like to learn a little more about Mr. Mabry and what he was doing in Eden. Not to mention what he was doing in the Hanover Hall parking lot."

"Okay." Sticks nodded. "We gotta dot all the i's and cross all the t's. But our thieves may have helped themselves to his things even if they didn't kill him."

"And if they did, they might have seen something."

"I doubt they're going to come forward and volunteer the information," Sticks said. "Talked to Samuels last week. He and Lewis are coming up empty."

"Somebody somewhere knows who these guys are. People might not rat out a thief, but murder changes things."

"Samuels is probably in church today," Sticks said, "but Lewis is a heathen. I'll get him to come in and start putting pressure on his snitches."

"Good," Jo said. "Before you do that, though, we need to talk to our visiting mystery writer."

***

"I'm Detective Valentine, this is Detective Mullins." The two detectives proffered their IDs to Kate. "We'd like to talk to you about a Michael Mabry."

"She knows about the murder," Lou spoke up before Kate could reply. "We're old friends. I came by to tell her after I left the scene."

Valentine nodded, her jaw tightening for a moment. Kate could see the petite woman didn't like that Lou had usurped her right to make the death notification. Probably wanted to see my reaction, she thought.

"Is there somewhere we can talk in private?" Valentine looked at Ann.

Kate noted the woman's accent. Definitely not a Kentucky girl. It sounded like New York, probably the city.

"Certainly," Ann said. "We have a conference room that is removed from the main rooms."

Ann led the way down the hall leading to the rear of the first floor. The large conference room had been formed by removing a wall between two smaller rooms. A mahogany support beam crossed the ceiling where the dividing wall had once stood. An oval oak table surrounded by ten chairs dominated the center of the room. A matching buffet stood against one wall, while four additional chairs stood against another. The outside wall was dominated by French doors leading onto a flagstone patio enclosed by a low stone wall.

"Can I get you some coffee?" Ann said.

"That won't be necessary, thank you."

Ann nodded and left them alone, closing the door behind her.

Valentine turned to Lou. "We'd like to speak to Ms. Rawlings alone, Lou."

"Sorry." This time it was Lou's jaw that stiffened. "I'm not just here because I'm a friend. Michael was murdered on university property."

"Michael?" Jo Valentine's eyebrows rose a notch at the familiarity.

"You knew the victim?" Mullins interjected. The thin man was younger than Valentine—in his late thirties, Kate guessed—and his accent indicated he was a Kentucky native.

Lou nodded. "We all became friends back in our college days. Neither of us had seen him in years until he showed up here this week."

Valentine held up a hand. "Wait, please. This changes things a bit. Lou, you know how it works. We need to talk to you and Professor Rawlings separately now that we're aware you knew Mabry."

Lou opened her mouth to protest but shut it again. She looked at Kate.

"She's right."

Valentine turned to Mullins. "Take Lou out on the patio, Sticks," she said. "I'll talk to Ms. Rawlings in here."

"After you, Chief." Mullins gestured toward the French doors.

Lou hesitated, looking from Kate to Valentine. Kate guessed her friend wanted to ask the detective to take it easy on her, but her sense of professionalism stopped her.

"It's okay," she said. "I'll be fine."

Lou nodded. She opened the French doors and went out, followed by Detective Mullins, who closed the doors behind them. They moved to one end of the patio where they took seats on opposite sides of a wrought iron and glass table. Kate turned back to Detective Valentine and waited.

"You and Michael Mabry met in college?"

"That's right. We were both in the graduate writing program."

"Under Dr. Price?"

"Yes. He was advisor—and friend—to both of us."

"What was your relationship with Mabry?"

"We were a couple," Kate said. "We lived together for a short time."

"Why did the relationship end?"

"Michael found it difficult being faithful. He eventually left town with another woman."

"That must have made you angry."

"Of course, it did," Kate said. "I was hurt and angry and depressed and several other emotions. But that was over thirty years ago, Detective."

"True," Valentine nodded. "But then the man who broke your heart reappears in your life after his long absence. Old wounds can fester and reopen given the right trigger."

"No," Kate shook her head. "My old wounds, as you say, have not festered. I cried for a while, and then, as the kids say, I got a life."

"Yes, you did," Valentine agreed. "Not only are you a professor, you've written several successful mysteries. Which I thoroughly enjoy, by the way."

"Thank you."

Kate knew the compliment was meant as a distraction. She'd written the scene several times herself. In her books, she usually followed the distraction with the meaty questions, so if life was imitating her art, Detective Valentine would be getting down to business the next time she opened her mouth.

"When was the last time you saw Michael Mabry?"

And here we go, Kate thought.

"Yesterday evening," she said. "At Jackson Price's Summer Kickoff."

"What time was that?"

"I got there a little after six, I think. Michael arrived after I did—I'd guess around seven. I left just as it was getting dark so around nine or a little before."

"Was Mr. Mabry still at the party?"

"He stayed there, yes. Or at least I think he did."

Valentine tilted her head to one side, her eyebrows raised in a question.

"He followed me to my car," Kate said. There was little point in not mentioning it to the detective. She knew Paul Holland would be sure to call attention to their encounter. "We sat and talked for a while. Then I left. Michael walked back toward Jackson's, so I assumed he was returning to the party."

"You talked for a while. About what?"

"A lot of things," Kate said. "About getting old, our past together, my books, just the chit-chat of old friends who haven't seen one another in a while."

"Thirty years is more than a while."

Kate was silent. She could feel herself being herded into the trap like a steer being guided to the slaughterer's bolt gun. If she lied to this woman and was caught, she would look guilty, but how would she explain to Lou why she had remained silent for so long about her friendship with Michael? For that matter, admitting she had kept in contact with Michael might raise questions with the police. It was a lose-lose situation.

"Before last night, when had you last seen the victim?"

"He stopped by my office," Kate said, relieved, although she suspected the relief would be short-lived. "Earlier in the week."

"Can you be more specific?"

"Monday evening. He was waiting in my office after I finished my class."

"In your office? Don't you lock your office door?"

"Of course I lock my door," Kate said. "Michael had asked Hanover Hall's maintenance man, Robbie Applegate, to let him in."

"Is Mr. Applegate in the habit of letting people into locked offices?" Valentine made a note.

"I don't know," Kate said. "I wouldn't think so."

"But he let a stranger into yours?"

"Michael wasn't a stranger. Robbie had just started working at Raven when we were in graduate school, so they knew one another."

"They were friends?" Valentine looked skeptical.

"I don't know if I would call them that," Kate said. "But they were friendly. Michael was that way with everyone who crossed his path."

"Help me understand this," Valentine said. "A janitor lets a man he hasn't seen in over thirty years—and was never close friends with, according to what you say—into a locked university office. I wouldn't think that's accepted university practice, particularly considering the break-ins lately."

"I'm sure it's not university practice," Kate said. "I spoke to Robbie about it the following day, and he promised not to do it again. You'd have to know Michael to understand. Michael is a born charmer. He can talk anyone into just about anything. It's just the way he is."

She stopped for a second, surprised to find tears stinging her eyes. "Was," she corrected. "It's just the way he was."

"So," Valentine said, letting Robbie's transgression go for the moment, "were you surprised to find Mabry in your locked office?"

"Of course," Kate said.

"What did he want?"

Kate shrugged. "He was back in town and wanted to say hello, I guess."

"You guess?"

"He said he was in town for a few days and wanted to see Jackson and me, to congratulate us on our books."

Valentine waited.

"He also asked if he could leave his bag with me. He had a room at the Shady Nook and didn't trust their security."

"That was wise of him. Where is the bag now?"

"Upstairs. In my room."

"We'll need to take possession of that," Valentine said.

"I understand."

"We didn't find a watch on the victim. Did you happen to notice if he was wearing one last night?"

Kate thought for a moment. "Yes, I'm pretty sure he was."

"Can you describe it?"

"Not really. It was a gold color, and I think it had a stretch band, but I couldn't tell you the brand or anything else about it."

Valentine made a note of the information. "What about any other jewelry?"

"Just his class ring," Kate said. "From Western. Michael was proud of that ring. He was the first person from his family to go to college, much less graduate."

"Can you describe it?"

Kate did her best to describe the ring while Valentine made notes.

"Since you're asking me this," Kate said. "I can only assume Michael's watch and ring were taken. Do you think he was killed in a robbery?"

"Too soon to say." Valentine finished writing and then looked up, switching tack. "Were you upset to see Mabry after all these years?"

"Not really," Kate said. "It surprised me, of course."

"And that's all?" Valentine leaned back in her chair. "Even after thirty years, if I suddenly came face-to-face with a man who had broken my heart, I think I might be a little upset."

"I'm not you."

Valentine stared at her for several seconds, without speaking, a little smile on her lips that did not reach her eyes.

"No, you're not," she said. "Were you aware that your old boyfriend was being sought for questioning in the Drayer Museum theft and murders?"

Kate stared at her, unable to believe she had heard correctly. "What?" she managed.

"Michael Mabry was working under an alias as a security guard at the Drayer," Valentine said. "He disappeared from Chicago right after the heist. Word is his partners are organized crime figures. Apparently not only were the authorities looking for him, but his partners were as well. Which leads one to believe that he double-crossed them and took off with the Star."

She leaned forward, and Kate involuntarily pulled back. "My question to you, Ms. Rawlings, is why would a man in possession of a stolen item worth at least fifteen million dollars who is being pursued by both the police and his partners drop by Eden to congratulate you on your books?"

Kate's mouth opened, but nothing came out. She was still trying to process what the detective had told her. She swallowed hard and tried again.

"Are you sure about all this? There couldn't be some kind of mistake? Couldn't he have just run when the theft happened? Because he was afraid?"

"Was he working under an alias because he was afraid?"

"Maybe there was some other reason for that..." She stopped, her voice trailing off. What reason could there be?

"Well, I'll give you that," Valentine said. "He may have used an alias so his employer wouldn't learn of his criminal record."

"Criminal record?"

"He'd been in prison twice, once for grand theft and once for felony fraud. He'd also served three stints in county jails for the same types of crimes—at least under his own name. It wouldn't surprise me to learn he'd been in jail under an assumed name or two as well."

Kate felt sick. All those times Michael disappeared from her life in between his visits—had he been in jail or prison? He'd never said anything, but then he never said much at all about his life away from her. She hadn't pushed when he sidestepped her questions because she'd been afraid of what she would hear.

"I didn't know," she mumbled.

"Sorry, I didn't catch that."

"I said I didn't know," Kate spoke louder.

"You're saying you weren't aware of Michael Mabry's criminal activities, past or present?"

Kate nodded.

"Are you also saying you hadn't seen or talked to Michael Mabry at any time in the past thirty-odd years before he showed up in your office last Monday night?"

Kate hesitated. She knew she should admit she and Michael had seen each other over the years, but how could she make this woman understand that, in spite of how Michael had treated her, they had become friends? And Detective Valentine would never believe that Michael had kept his criminal activities from her.

Kate made her decision. "Yes, that's what I'm saying."

"Interesting." Valentine reached into her jacket pocket. When she removed her hand, she was holding a 4x6 photograph, the edges of which had been folded. "Then how do you explain this picture we found in the victim's wallet?"

She held it out to Kate. It was of Michael and her, arms around one another, smiling, the sun on their faces, posed for the tourist Michael had asked to take the picture. It had been taken seven years before, the last time she'd seen him before this week. She'd been at Nebraska then, and the brilliant flowers and verdant shrubs of Lincoln's Sunken Garden were visible behind them.

"Correct me if I'm wrong," Detective Valentine said. "But you and our victim don't look like you were in graduate school when this picture was taken."

Chapter 15

"Looks like we're late to the party," said Sticks Mullins.

"Shit!" said the manager of the Shady Nook.

Jo and Sticks surveyed the wreck that was Michael Mabry's room. Dresser drawers had been pulled out and left lying on the floor, and the dresser itself pulled out from the wall. The bed was a ruined mess, bedclothes in a heap on top of the room's table, the mattress and box springs slit in several places and upended against the headboard. The cheap pictures had been torn loose from the walls, and the vinyl of the one upholstered chair slit open. As Jo stepped in and turned from side to side surveying the mess, she saw that even the dirty, frayed carpet had been torn loose and pulled back along the edges.

"I don't think this was the work of our burglars," she said.

After interviewing Rawlings and Lou, Jo and Sticks had headed for the Shady Nook for a quick look. Jo hadn't expected to find much. If Mabry had been in possession of the Star, he'd have to be more of a fool than he seemed to be to leave it in his room. Apparently someone else hadn't been so sure.

"Think the killer found what he was looking for?"

"No way of knowing for sure, but I'd guess no. If Mabry had the Star, he probably hid it some place safer than here. And we can't be sure whoever tore this room apart is the same person who killed Mabry."

"Pretty likely, though."

Sticks was right. It was likely. Still, the search might have occurred whether Mabry had been killed or not. It might be that whoever searched the room simply took advantage of the fact that Mabry wasn't in it. She pulled out her cell.

"It's me," she said, when Lena answered. "When you and Bob finish up over there, head over to the Shady Nook, room 18. Somebody tossed Mabry's room. If we're lucky, maybe they left something behind."

"Even if they did," Sticks said, when she disconnected, "it'll be hard to link it to the doers. I hate to think how many fingerprints, hairs, and stuff I don't wanna know about has been left behind in this place."

She called dispatch for a patrol officer to secure the room until Lena and Bob arrived. While they waited, she thought over what the next move should be.

"Call Lewis," she told Sticks. "I want him to collect whatever he has on any burglary suspects. Tell him we'll be in before noon to go over it with him."

"Where are we going first?"

"Not 'we.' I want you to talk to Price. Verify the times Rawlings and Mabry showed up at the party and when each of them left. Find out if Mabry got into it with anyone, and get the names of all the people who were there."

"What are you going to do?"

"I'm going to run by the Holiday Inn and talk to Mr. Becker."

"The insurance investigator?"

Jo nodded. "It's been a few days since he stopped by. I want to know if he located Mabry. And while I'm at it, I intend to find out where he was last night."

***

"Look at him! It's been at least forty-five minutes and he hasn't moved!" Gabby was whispering. She shivered and moved closer to Wendell. "It's not normal!"

They were stretched across the king-size bed, watching Leonard through the open bedroom door. He was seated in one of the six chairs that flanked the dining table in the living room of their suite at the Lexington Hilton. They had gotten rooms in Lexington after deciding it was safer to stay out of Eden in case the Professor was there. Wendell didn't want to think about what Baby would do if the Professor spotted them before they spotted him.

So far they'd had no luck. They had tried the Shady Nook Friday after leaving the Main Street Diner, but that had been a dead end. The desk clerk, a bald fat fuck with white hair sprouting out of his ears and nose, had been no help.

"Where's your badge?" he'd said when Wendell asked if a man fitting the Professor's description had checked in.

"Badge? Not a cop, man." Wendell had been surprised. He'd never been mistaken for a cop before.

"Then I'm afraid I can't help you," the old man replied. "Guests expect privacy here, and that's what they get."

"What is this, the fucking Hilton?" Wendell pulled a twenty from his wallet and slid it over to the old man.

The man slid it back and turned back to the game show playing on the battered analog TV sitting on the counter. Wendell sighed and upped the ante to a fifty with the same result.

"Look, son," the old man said. "I don't need your money. I got a good pension from the service, and I got my paycheck. I don't give out no guests information, and that's the end of it."

Wendell had wanted to grab the old fucker by his nose hairs and choke the information out of him. The man must have seen it in his eyes. Instead of backing off, he straightened and stared back at Wendell, one hand resting on something under the counter. Wendell had to give him credit for having balls, but he was pretty sure his balls weren't what the old dude had his hand on.

He and Gabby sat on the motel for several hours before deciding to give it up. Saturday they made the rounds of the chain motels, asking desk clerks and maids if anyone fitting the Professor's description had checked in. The only thing they learned was that they were not the only ones inquiring about him.

So they were surprised when Gabby reported that news to Baby Saturday evening and learned Leonard was on his way to Kentucky. Baby had ears in a lot of places, and those ears had heard that the Professor was definitely in Eden. Gabby's end of the conversation was limited to "We've been looking, Dom" and "I'm sorry, Dom, we tried, we really did" and "Yes, Dom, I understand."

"Are we in deep shit?" Wendell asked her when she hung up.

"I'm sure it will be okay," she said, but the look on her face told Wendell she wasn't sure at all.

Leonard had woken them shortly after seven Sunday, strolled in without a word, and flipped on the TV, tuning it to a Lexington news channel. The three of them watched a blonde with tired eyes reporting the murder of an unnamed suspect in the Drayer heist. The creepy fuck watched it standing, a muscle twitching in his left cheek, and then he sat down at the table. Since then only his eyelids had moved.

"Did he do it?" Gabby kept her voice low.

"What do you think?"

"Does he always act like this after one of his"—Gabby hesitated for a second—"jobs?"

"The only time I been around him was at the museum, and we were busy gettin' the hell out of there. So I dunno. I've heard stories about what he did on regular jobs, not how he acted."

"Do you think he found the Star?"

Wendell didn't answer. That was the fifteen-million-dollar question, wasn't it? If Leonard had popped the Professor, he must have found the Star. Otherwise, he'd have kept the Professor alive long enough to tell him where it was. But if he had it, why wasn't he on his way back to Chicago with it?

"Wendell?"

"I don't know," he finally said. "But I'm starting to get a bad feeling."

Chapter 16

"Have a seat, Mr. Becker." Jo Valentine wadded her Egg McMuffin wrapper into a ball, tossed it into the wastebasket and dusted off her hands while she finished chewing and swallowing. She nodded toward the coffee machine to the left of the door. "Coffee?"

"Sure, why not?"

She poured his into a Styrofoam cup from the stack used for visitors and topped off her mug. Cal took a sip.

"Not bad," he said. "Better than the cop coffee I remember."

"So, Mr. Becker." Valentine reclaimed her seat behind the desk. "I admit I'm a bit surprised that you're still in town. When I stopped by the Holiday Inn, they told me you'd checked out two days ago."

"After I found out Katherine Rawlings was staying at the Holly House, I decided it might be a better place to lay my head."

"How did you know where she was staying?"

"Called around when I first got to town and asked for her. Desk clerks and B&B owners aren't as suspicious down here as they are up north. Not a one refused to confirm or deny they had someone by that name checked in."

"How did you know she wasn't staying with family or friends?"

"I didn't. Figured it was worth a few phone calls to be sure."

"What have you found out since we last talked?"

"Not much. I showed Mabry's picture around at all the motels and hotels in the area, but nobody admitted seeing him. I thought I'd make the rounds again today to talk to the weekend staff and then start checking in other towns near here."

He tried to decide if he should admit knowing Mabry had been in contact with Rawlings. He knew how he would have felt as a cop if someone withheld information, but he couldn't think of a good way to explain how he'd come by that information without admitting he'd entered Rawlings room illegally.

"I did find a reason to think I was on the right track by coming here," he said instead.

"What was that?"

"I went by Holly House Friday morning to see Rawlings. She was just pulling out of the driveway, so I followed her. She drove to the Main Street Diner and met some lady friends. Turned out I wasn't the only one watching her. Dominick Duda's brother-in-law, Wendell Halsey, was there, and I doubt it was for the food."

"Mabry's former cellmate?" Valentine sat up straighter.

"One and the same," Cal said. "He was with his wife, Gabby, Duda's sister."

"Interesting," she murmured.

"Got even more interesting when Rawlings left," Cal said. "The Halseys left right after she did. By the time I got outside, the three of them were a couple doors down, talking. They all looked pretty friendly, if you ask me."

"What was your take on it?"

"Made me wonder if Rawlings is involved. I had figured I'd talk to her, see if she'd heard from Mabry, and warn her against helping him. After seeing their sidewalk confab, I got to wondering if maybe the two couples were in it together."

"The Halseys, Mabry, and Rawlings?"

"Everybody in Chicago knows Halsey is a screw-up. If he wasn't married to his sister, Baby would've dumped him in Lake Michigan years ago."

"Baby?"

"Duda's nickname. He's a fat guy with a baby face."

"I see," Valentine said. "So you think Duda's sister and her husband might want to get out from under?"

"It's a theory." Cal shrugged. "Gabby is a lot younger than her brother. Word is, he's always run her life and she doesn't like it. She eloped with Halsey, probably just to spite Baby. Halsey and Mabry were close, according to prison reports, so it's not too farfetched to think they might have decided to keep the Star for themselves and take off for parts unknown with their ladies."

"Katherine Rawlings has a lot to lose."

"Love makes women do strange things," Cal said. "No sexism intended. I did some checking on Dr. Rawlings. She's never been married, and as far as I could find out, she's never been seriously involved with anyone. Maybe she and Mabry had a thing back in the day, maybe not. But we know she knew him, and women like her are just the type he likes. Easy targets."

"Are you aware that Michael Mabry was found shot this morning?"

"What?" Cal sat up straighter, and set his coffee cup on the desk. "No shit? He's dead?"

"I'm afraid so."

"Do you have the shooter?"

"Unfortunately, no."

"What about the Star? Did you find it?"

"Again, unfortunately, no."

"So what do you know?"

"Before we talk about what I know," Valentine said. "I need to know where you were last night."

"Sure," Cal said. "Been there and understand how it works. I was at the Holly House most of the evening and all night. Got in around four yesterday afternoon, followed Rawlings to Price's party. That was around six. The party was at the back of the house, so I couldn't keep an eye on her without crashing it. Figured that'd be a bad idea, so I went back to the Holly. Didn't go out again until I came here. "

"Can anyone confirm that?"

"Edna and Ann were nice enough to invite me to share their dinner with them," Cal said. "We ate right after I got back from tailing Rawlings to Price's and then talked for an hour or so. I made some calls after that and watched TV until around eleven when I went to bed. Ann stuck her head in the TV room around ten and told me good night. She was on her way to her place, I guess.

"So, no," he concluded. "I don't have anyone who can swear I was there all night. Didn't kill Mabry, though, but I realize you can't take my word for it."

Valentine looked at him without speaking for a few moments. Becker could guess what she was thinking. With something as valuable as the Star in play, it wouldn't be unheard of for a cop to turn crook, much less an insurance investigator. What she couldn't know was that his main reason for being in Eden was to find Sam's killers. Finding the Star would simply be a bonus.

"I'm glad you're so understanding, Mr. Becker." She leaned back in her desk chair and took a sip of her coffee before continuing. "You're right about Rawlings and Mabry having a thing, as you say. She says it ended badly, but she has no hard feelings. Not sure I buy that. Regardless, we know he's in town, and we know she's seen him."

"You do?"

"According to her, he showed up at her office Monday night and left a bag with her. She says he told her he was staying at the Shady Nook and didn't trust their security."

Cal tried not to let his face show his relief.

"We took possession of the bag, of course."

"Anything interesting in it?"

"No Star, if that's what you're asking," Valentine said. "Just clothes."

"Just clothes?"

"That's all we found. Why? Should there have been something else?"

She was looking at him funny. Back to the big question, Cal thought. She hadn't mentioned finding Mabry's short stories or the picture album. That meant Rawlings or somebody had taken them out before handing it over to Valentine, probably to hide the fact that Rawlings and Mabry had spent a lot of time together in the years since they were in graduate school. But if he told Valentine about the stories and album, he'd have to tell her how he knew.

"Not that I know of," he said. "Just a letdown, that's all. Finding the Star hidden under some socks is too much to ask for, but I was hoping for two plane tickets out of the country at least. That would give my theory some credence."

"Sorry to disappoint." She pushed back from the desk and stood. "Thank you for coming in, Mr. Becker. I assume you'll be staying in town?"

"Definitely," he said. "My job is to find the Star. Mabry's death doesn't change that. Unless I see the Halseys heading out or one of my contacts in Chicago tells me they're home, I have to assume the Star is still here."

***

"What?" Foreman said when Cal told him the news. "Hold on."

He'd phoned Foreman from the car as soon as he left Valentine's office. Based on the background noise when the phone was answered, he'd interrupted Sunday dinner. Foreman's wife hadn't sounded happy when she answered the phone, but she sounded a lot happier than Foreman did when he learned Mabry was dead.

Cal heard a door shut and the background noise disappeared. "You found him and now he's dead?"

"I'm afraid so," Cal said.

"The Star wasn't found with his body?"

"Afraid not."

"So his killers have it." Cal hated to think what Foreman's blood pressure must be about now. He sounded like he was about to stroke out.

"Not necessarily," Cal said. "According to the locals, Mabry's room had been taken apart. Sounds to me like someone was searching for the Star. If they got it from Mabry before they killed him, they wouldn't still be looking."

"Do you think Halsey killed him?"

"Maybe. Halsey doesn't have a history of violence, but you can never tell with these guys."

"Maybe he searched the room, didn't find the Star, and then got it from Mabry before he killed him."

"It's possible," Cal said. "But until we know for sure, I think we should operate under the assumption that the Star is still out there. If Baby's got it, we'll know soon enough."

"How? He's certainly not going to tell us."

"No." Cal took a deep breath and rubbed the spot between his eyebrows. Seemed like every time he talked to Foreman, he got a headache. "We'll know if and when Baby calls Halsey off and he goes home."

"Oh." Foreman was silent for a moment, and when he spoke again, he sounded calmer. "That makes sense."

"If Halsey shows up back in Chicago in the next day or so, I'd say they got the Star," Cal said. "Otherwise, I think he'll stay in the area and keep looking. If I know about Katherine Rawlings, you can bet Duda does, too. If she and Mabry were involved, she might have the Star or know where it is."

"Can't you question her?"

"Well, sure, I could, but I doubt she's going to admit to being involved in theft and murder." Cal knew he was doing a poor job of hiding his sarcasm. He tried to soften his tone. "I think it would be better to continue watching her."

"I'll get Watson and Miles down there to help."

"No need," Cal said. "I think for now it's better to keep a low profile. I've got a room down the hall from Rawlings, so I'm in a good position to keep an eye on her. Besides, if Halsey or some other Duda goon did get the Star, Andy and Mike need to be up there to find that out."

"All right." Foreman didn't sound convinced. "I want a report every day."

"No problem," Cal said. "Tell your missus I apologize for disturbing her dinner."

Chapter 17

"Katherine. I'm so sorry." Jackson hugged Kate close, his eyes red and moist. He kissed the top of her head, and she felt her own eyes fill up.

They were in Jackson's office. It was a little after seven. She had come in early in the hopes of catching him before the usual hustle-bustle was underway and had been surprised to see that he was already in his office.

"I was in Lexington most of the day yesterday." He held her back at arm's length, his hands on her shoulders. "I didn't know about Michael's death until I got back last night and found a note on my door asking me to call a Detective Mullins. By the time he left, it was late and I didn't want to wake you."

"I was probably awake anyway," she said. "Not that I was in the mood to talk to anyone. Jackson, they're acting like they think I killed Michael!"

"What? Why, that's ridiculous!"

"Detective Valentine doesn't think so." Kate took a deep breath. It was time to be honest with all her friends. "And I understand why she might feel that way."

"What are you talking about?"

Kate hesitated. "Can I have some coffee? I didn't sleep much last night."

"Certainly." Jackson crossed to a door in the side wall of his office that led to a short hall and a break room used by the English faculty and staff. He came back a few minutes later with two cups of coffee and stir sticks. Placing one in front of her, he dug packets of sugar and creamer out of his jacket pocket.

"Now, my dear, explain why you think this detective considers you a suspect." He placed a disdainful emphasis on "detective." He moved behind his desk, but remained standing while he opened a sugar packet and added it to his coffee.

Kate stirred creamer into her coffee and took a sip before speaking. She knew she was delaying the inevitable, but she dreaded the look she knew she would see on Jackson's face when she told him what she had to tell him. It would be the same look she had seen on Lou's face the day before.

"I haven't been honest with you, Jackson. I haven't been honest with anyone, not you, not Lou, not my brother."

"What is it you haven't been honest about?"

"Michael," she said. "I let everyone think that, until last week, I hadn't seen him since grad school."

Jackson stared at her, the hand holding the stir stick poised motionless over his coffee. She looked down at the cup in her hands, unable to meet his gaze.

"He showed up in Toledo in '86—five years after I'd last seen him. He stayed a week then disappeared again." She paused for a breath and another sip of coffee. "He showed up again a few years later and then a few years after that. It didn't matter where I was. He always knew. Sometimes he phoned in between visits or sent a card on the holidays. He sent me roses when my first book was published."

"Isn't that just precious!" Jackson sat down hard in his chair, his coffee forgotten. "Katherine, I cannot believe you continued a relationship all these years with Michael! Not after what he did to you!"

"It wasn't a relationship, Jackson. At least not the kind you mean. I guess that first time in Toledo, it was, but after that...I don't know how to explain it, but we became friends. Nothing more. Michael and I were both satisfied with that. I loved him, but I was no longer *in* love with him, if you know what I mean."

She leaned forward. "Haven't you noticed, Jackson, that as you get older the things that bothered you so when you were young cease to have any importance?"

He looked at her for a moment before replying. "Actually, no," he said. "I haven't noticed that."

"Well, that's how it was with Michael and me," she said. "I remembered he hurt me terribly, but it was only a memory. There was no longer any pain associated with it. So I could accept him for who he was and love him as a friend."

"And how did he feel?"

"Relieved, I think. He had someone in his life who knew him for the damaged man he was but still cared for him. He had a friend. In fact, I wouldn't be surprised if I was the only real friend he ever had."

"Why didn't you say anything?"

"I should have," she said. "I wish I had. Lou's pretty disappointed in me."

"She didn't know?"

"No one did. I wasn't living here anymore. When I came home to visit, there were several times I almost told Lou, but you know how she felt about Michael. I knew what she would say, and I guess I didn't want to hear it. I thought things would continue the way they were, that I'd never return to Eden, and no one would ever have to know that I still saw Michael from time to time."

Jackson leaned back in his chair, looking up at the ceiling. After a few moments, he lowered his head and looked at her. "Maybe you didn't tell anyone because you were ashamed to admit you were still being a doormat for Michael."

Katherine stared at him, shocked. "I was *not* being a doormat," she said between clenched teeth, her anger growing. "As for not telling you, it was, in fact, none of your damned business!"

She stood up, slamming the half-empty coffee cup down on his desk. A few drops splashed out onto his blotter. She started toward the door.

"Katherine, wait, I'm sorry!" Jackson stood and came out from behind the desk. "That was unnecessarily harsh."

He took her by the shoulders, turning her to face him. He had tears in his eyes, and her anger dissipated as quickly as it had come. "Forgive me. Please. That was unfair of me. You're right. I have no reason to be upset with you for not telling me something I had no right to know."

She stared at him for a moment before smiling slightly. "You're forgiven. You know I can't stay mad at you, Jackson." She shook her head. "Obviously I can't stay mad at anyone for very long."

"It's one of your many good qualities, Katherine, only one of which I intend to make Detective Valentine aware." He led Kate back to her chair and resumed his seat behind the desk. "But I ask that you think long and hard about why you so easily forgave Michael. I remember the sweet girl who used to cry on my shoulder over the cold father who rejected her every attempt at love. The same girl who subsequently fell in love with a man who was as emotionally crippled as her father."

"What are you saying? That I settled for whatever Michael could give me because that's what I'm used to?" Katherine was starting to feel angry again.

"You're a beautiful and intelligent woman, Katherine." Jackson leaned forward, his eyes earnest. "I'm sure you've had many men interested in you since you left Eden. Yet you've never married and never been seriously involved with anyone since Michael. At least, not that you've told me about on your visits home."

"Maybe I just never met the right man."

"And Michael was? Or did you keep seeing him because you knew how to play the role in that relationship? The same role you'd played with your father most of your life?"

Kate tried to laugh, but the sound that emerged from her lips was harsh and ugly. "So your diagnosis is that I'm emotionally crippled? You didn't tell me you'd become a licensed psychotherapist."

"Don't trivialize what I've said by making jokes. I've said all I'm going to say on the subject. Consider it closed." He leaned back in his chair. "You're a good person, Katherine. I intend to tell Detective Valentine that as well."

"What did the detective who came to see you want?" Katherine said, reminded by the mention of Valentine that Jackson had had a visit from her partner. She was relieved at the chance to change the subject.

"He questioned me about when Michael arrived at the Kickoff and when he left, whether he got into any disagreements with anyone there and the names of the guests. Recalling who all was there took a while, believe me.

"And," he added, "he also wanted to know what time you arrived and left. He was clever about it. He saw your name among the others I'd given him and asked if you were the Katherine Rawlings who wrote mysteries before asking about your attendance. I simply thought he was a fan at the time, but what you told me certainly puts his questions in a different light."

"There's more, Jackson." Kate picked up her coffee. She took a sip, not relishing the idea of having to tell him about Michael's criminal activities.

"Yes?"

"I assume you've seen the news about the theft and murders at the Drayer Museum in Chicago?"

Jackson nodded.

"Detective Valentine told me that Michael is a suspect."

"What?"

Kate nodded. "He was working as a security guard at the Drayer under an assumed name. He disappeared after the Star was stolen and those people killed. The police think he was involved with some organized crime figures in Chicago."

"Michael? Involved with organized crime? How can that be?" Shock was evident on Jackson's face. "It was obvious he'd not done much with his life but organized crime?"

"Detective Valentine also told me that Michael had been in jail and prison. More than once. For theft and fraud. Maybe that's how he met those people."

Jackson stared at her, his mouth hanging open. He closed his eyes for a moment. When he opened them, he'd regained his usual composure.

"Well, well, well," he said. "It seems we didn't know Michael as well as we thought we did."

***

"Just because she's your friend, Chief Pelfrey, doesn't mean she's not a suspect until I have reason to think otherwise."

"Knock off the 'Chief Pelfrey' crap, Jo!"

"Figured you need to be reminded of where your loyalties should lie."

Jo had been reading the preliminary coroner's report when Lou came storming into her office early Monday morning. The report was discouraging. The cause of death was given as gunshot wound—a .38 hollow-point—to the chest. No surprise there. The discouraging part was the fact that no trace evidence had been found on the body. Because too many people had spent time in the motel room and the rental car, the body had been their best chance for evidence. Jo had hoped for a stray hair or piece of skin—something, anything. But there was nothing. If only life could do a better job of imitating an episode of CSI....

"I know damn well where my loyalties lie—with the truth!" Lou had sent a steady barrage of voice and text messages all day Sunday, each one protesting the accusations directed at her friend. Jo had ignored them all. "Damn it, Jo, do you honestly think someone like Kate could be a murderer?"

"I believe anyone could commit murder given the right circumstances."

"Well, whoever it was, it wasn't Kate. And if you'd passed on the info you got from Chicago, we wouldn't be having this conversation. I'd have slapped Michael in cuffs at Jackson's party, and that would have been that."

Jo had given the information called in from Chicago to the department secretary with instructions to pass it on to the university police. The woman claimed she had done so, but Lou's people claimed they never got the call. Lack of communication, Jo had observed over the years, caused most of the world's problems. In this case, it may have cost Michael Mabry his life.

"Kate wouldn't hurt anyone," Lou continued. "I've known her since we were kids, and I'm telling you, you're barking up the wrong tree!"

"Are you sure of that?" Jo said. "You knew her when you were both young, but she's been gone for a lot of years. Are you sure you know her now?"

"Of course, I'm sure!"

Lou looked at the ceiling, partly in frustration and partly because she didn't want to look Jo in the eyes. Ever since Kate had admitted to keeping in contact with Michael all these years, the nagging suspicion that maybe she really didn't know her friend as well as she'd thought had been setting up shop at the back of her mind. But one thing she was sure of—Kate was not a killer except between the pages of her novels.

"Okay, okay." She took a deep breath. "Look, I know you can't rule anyone out this early in the investigation. But surely

Kate isn't at the top of your list. Michael's partners should be who you're looking for."

"And I am, along with anyone else who might have a motive."

"Actually," Lou said. "That's the main reason I stopped by. I do know someone else you need to check on."

"You just got sidetracked giving me hell, right?" Jo spread her hands. "Okay, who? And why?"

"Johnny Crouch," Lou said. "Used to be a pipe fitter at Eden Steel. Has a house and a few acres out on Elk Lick Road. He's from Perry County, where Michael grew up."

"Why would he want Mabry dead?"

"Because of his daughter," Lou said. "Michael was a senior in high school, Lucy a sophomore—just fifteen—when Michael got her pregnant. I've got family down there that told me the story back when Michael was shitting on Kate. According to my cousin, Michael had just gotten his college acceptance letter when Lucy told him she was pregnant. He promptly ditched her and spread it around town that the baby wasn't his, that she'd been screwing around."

"Nice guy."

"Yeah, a real prince. He was already at college when Lucy committed suicide. My cousin told me back then Johnny had just gotten hired at Eden Steel and Michael had better steer clear of him because Johnny swore he'd kill him if he ever saw him. Michael left town before Johnny got here, so the two of them never ran into one another then. Maybe Michael wasn't so lucky this time."

Jo had been making notes while Lou talked. "This guy would be what, in his seventies by now?"

"In his sixties, anyway. A lotta guys become daddies early in southeastern Kentucky. He's not an old feeble guy, if that's what you're getting at. I saw him at the VFW fish fry Memorial Day. He's got more muscles on him than Roger does."

"Besides," she continued. "Since when did age matter when it comes to pulling a trigger?"

Chapter 18

Kate had been dreading the Monday night class, fearing the looks, whispers, and maybe outright questions of the students. She was surprised when the only questions were related to their writing, not Michael's murder. She reminded herself that these were adult students with jobs and families. They may or may not have heard the news, but they were apparently unaware it involved their teacher.

She soon found herself relaxing. While she didn't forget, she was able to push Michael's death and Detective Valentine's suspicions to the back of her mind, and focus instead on the budding authors in the room. The interlude was welcome, and she was sorry when the clock told her it was time to end it.

She gathered her papers together and left the classroom. She was tired, not having slept more than a couple of hours the night before. She had lain awake, going over the day's events, first the news and then the police interview—interrogation would be a better word, she thought—and, finally, the scene with Lou.

Detective Valentine had motioned to Detective Mullins that she was finished, and he and Lou had come back into the conference room. Immediately Lou had come to Kate's defense.

"Look, Jo, I know you have a job to do," Lou had said. "But Kate isn't your killer."

"You know how it works," Valentine replied.

"Yeah, yeah," Lou didn't bother to hide her irritation. "Look, what happened between Kate and Michael was a long time ago. Hell, it's been thirty years since she's even seen him. Surely you don't think she's been nursing a broken heart just waiting for revenge for *that* long?"

"I wouldn't think so if it had been that long," Valentine replied, and Kate knew what was coming next.

"Lou," she started.

"I think you and your friend need to talk." Valentine motioned to Detective Mullins, and the two of them left.

After they were gone, Kate told Lou. As she tried to explain how it had been between Michael and her, she watched her friend's face register surprise and then harden, and she knew the trust that had always existed between them had taken a blow that might never be overcome. Lou asked a few questions in a monotone voice, told her goodnight, and went home.

Kate had cried more than once during that long night, both for Michael and for Lou's friendship. Then she'd had to come clean with Jackson that morning and her brother that afternoon. Steven had been the easiest of all. He'd been surprised but said he understood how she felt.

"It says something good about you, sis," he said. "You don't hold grudges, and when you love, you keep on loving. That's nothing to apologize for."

They'd hugged, and she'd cried some more.

Now as she trudged the hall to her office to pick up her purse, she tried to think what, if anything, she could do. Maybe I should try to look at this as a story, she thought. I'm my own main character, falsely suspected of the murder of a friend. Maybe I should do what one of my characters would do and solve the case. The trouble is, she thought, inserting the key into her office door, that's easier to do on paper than in real life.

That was the last thought she had before everything went black.

***

Edna took the proffered credit card and ran it through the swipe terminal. All registrations were processed at the walnut secretary located in the large Holly House foyer. She sat at the secretary, while the man stood to one side and slightly behind her. She had offered him a seat in the upholstered armchair that sat next to the secretary specifically for incoming guests, but he had refused. It wasn't the first time a guest had declined to be seated nor was it the first time one had stood as he did now, but for some reason, he gave her the willies as he loomed over her. That's exactly what it feels like, she thought. It feels like he's looming.

The card was approved as valid. Edna released the breath she hadn't been aware of holding, hit the Reset button, and handed the card back to the man.

"Do you know how many nights you'll be staying, sir?"

"No."

Edna hesitated for a second. In her experience, guests typically followed their "Yes" or "No" with further details, such as "Yes, two nights" or "No, not sure what my plans are." The man who had registered as William Jones stayed silent. Suddenly Edna realized what it was about him that gave her the willies. He didn't move. Well, he did move but only when necessary and only as much as necessary.

"Oh," she said. "Well, we'll finish processing the card when you check out."

She took the key to the Rose Room from the pegboard on the wall to the right of the secretary and handed it to him. "I've put you in the Rose Room. It's the second door to the right at the top of the stairs. We're not very full so if you aren't pleased with it, we can certainly move you."

He took the key, nodded slightly, picked up the small suitcase by his feet and went to the stairs. Edna watched him as he climbed the stairs and turned right. She heard the door to the Rose Room open and close.

"Well, he's certainly an odd duck," she said to herself, and went to find Ann to tell her about their strange new guest.

***

The bed was harder than Kate remembered, so hard that lying on it made her head hurt. Where was the pillow? There should be a pillow. Somewhere close by she heard a siren blaring, but then it stopped. It sounded like it had come right into the Holly House's parking lot. She started to open her eyes and raise her head to see what was going on, but the sharp pain that shot from her head into her neck made her lie back down, groaning.

"Lie still, Dr. Rawlings," an unfamiliar male voice said. Kate felt hands on her shoulders. "You've had a head injury. It's best not to move until the paramedics have checked you out."

Kate opened her eyes and focused on the face of the young man kneeling over her. He wore a campus police uniform. Behind him, she could see Robbie Applegate, a worried look on his wrinkled face.

"What happened?" she said. "Did I faint?"

"What's the last thing you remember?" the young officer said.

"I don't know." She tried to think. "Class. I was going to my office—is that where I am now?"

She tried to rise up, but his hands held her steady. "Not yet, Dr. Rawlings. Wait for the paramedics, remember?"

"Wait for the paramedics," she repeated.

"Do you remember what happened after you got to your office?"

"I unlocked the door. I think." She tried to remember more, but it hurt too much. "I must have fainted then."

She heard a door opening in the direction of the stairwell and the sound of hurrying feet coming along the hall toward them. The officer stood up and stepped away, and a man wearing an Eden Fire Department EMT uniform took his place. Another man knelt on the other side of her and slipped a blood pressure cuff around her arm.

Their examination was quick but thorough. They slipped a neck brace around her neck, checked her vitals and her pupils, and asked her where it hurt while probing along her spine and limbs. The one who had taken her blood pressure disappeared and came back pushing a stretcher.

"I'm fine," she protested as they moved her onto the stretcher. "I just fainted, that's all."

"We need to get you checked out by a doctor, Dr. Rawlings." The name tag on his uniform read Bill Maggard. He had nice eyes, so Kate smiled at him.

"Bill," she said. "You have nice eyes."

He smiled at her and winked. She giggled. The two men raised the stretcher, and the ceiling swooped down at her. Suddenly she felt nauseated and closed her eyes, willing herself not to throw up, and everything went away.

She woke up as they loaded her into the ambulance. She smiled at Bill and closed her eyes again. The vibration of the ambulance's motor and the streets they passed over was pleasant, and she dozed until they stopped. The night air felt good after the closeness of the ambulance, but the lights were too bright. She scrunched her eyelids into slits and watched the ceiling tiles go by as they wheeled her into the emergency room.

After that there was more prodding and poking, more questions about where it hurt, lights shining in her eyes, and medicinal smells. By the time they took her for x-rays and a CAT scan, she had become more alert and the pain in her head had subsided a bit. She tried to remember what had happened, but between unlocking her office door and waking up lying on what she now knew was the floor of the hall outside her office, everything was a blank.

When she came back from the CAT scan, Lou was pacing back and forth in front of the nurses' station, her brown eyes broadcasting her anxiety. When she saw Kate, she rushed over. "Kate, sweetie! I got here as fast as I could. How do you feel?"

"Like I have one of those hangovers we used to get back in college."

Lou laughed, obviously relieved that Kate could joke. Was all forgiven, Kate wondered. Lou didn't seem to be angry or disappointed with her now.

"Do you remember what happened?"

"Not really. I remember going back to my office after class and unlocking the door, but then I guess I fainted because I don't remember anything else."

"You didn't faint," Lou said. "Somebody clobbered you."

"What?"

"Somebody was apparently in your office. Your desk lamp was on the floor just inside the door. We think that's what he hit you with."

"Why would somebody hit me with my lamp?" Kate was starting to feel confused again.

"Looks like he was looking for something," Lou said. "Your office was a mess—drawers dumped, books pulled off the shelves. Your purse was on the floor by the door. A Visa and American Express were still in it, along with your ID and some money. Did you have your purse with you?"

"It was in my office," Kate said. "That's why I was going back there after class."

"How much cash was in it? Any other cards besides the ones I found?"

"No other cards. I had forty, maybe fifty dollars. Not sure of the exact amount." She was silent for a few seconds, processing what Lou had said. "Was it the burglars? Did I surprise someone breaking into my office?"

"Maybe, but I doubt it," Lou said. "Our resident burglars have been grabbing anything of value and getting the hell out, not trashing offices the way yours was trashed. I think whoever was in your office was looking for the Star."

Chapter 19

Deputy Sam Gentry had a natural talent for lip reading. As he pulled his cruiser onto the graveled parking area in front of the dilapidated trailer, he saw the scrawny man behind the yard sale table say, "Aw, shit!" and chuckled. Day is getting off to a good start, he thought to himself. Looks like Lenville's got some merchandise he doesn't want me to find.

Sam had a theory that most criminals were criminals because they were too damn dumb to be employable. Lenville Sorrell was a poster boy for that theory. Sam had busted him six times in the last four years for possession of stolen property, all confiscated from Lenville's yard sale table. Yet the boy persisted in setting up his table any day there was good weather, knowing that Sam and a couple of the other deputies made it a practice to stop by and check out the wares. Most days there was nothing to find, but sooner or later Lenville would slip a stolen item in amongst the junk, and the revolving door of arrest, plea bargain, thirty-to-sixty days county time, and back at it would begin again.

Sam notified dispatch where he would be and then took his time putting on his sunglasses and hat, all the while watching Lenville twitch and sweat, thrusting his hands into his pockets in an effort to keep them from grabbing whatever it was he wanted to hide. Getting out of the cruiser, Sam straightened slowly and stretched.

"Mornin', Lenville," he said, drawing out the name. Lenville Sorrell hated his given name, preferring to be called Lenny. "Saw you out here and thought I'd stop and say hello."

"Aw, man—why you keep hasslin' me? I ain't doin' nuthin' wrong."

"Why, Lenville!" Sam feigned shock. "I'm just trying to be friendly, that's all. And do my job. You're out here all by your lonesome on a country road. Figure you could use some police protection."

The ripped screen door on the trailer opened, and a skinny blonde with sores on her face and a fussy baby on her hip stepped out.

"Mornin', Christie." Sam touched the brim of his hat.

Christie scowled and jiggled the baby.

"Cute baby," Sam said. "I heard a few months back that Lenville was a new daddy. Boy, right?"

"Caleb," Christie said, standing straighter. "Named him after my granddad."

"Well, Christie," Sam said. "If you know what's best for little Caleb there, you'll get away from Lenville and off the meth."

"I don't do no meth!" Christie protested, jutting her chin out.

"Tell that to the child welfare people when they ask you about those sores on your face." Sam turned back toward Lenville. "But that's not why I'm here today. I just thought I'd stop and see if Lenville's got anything good for sale today."

"Aw, man—why you keep callin' me that shitty name? I'm Lenny."

"Lenville! Shame on you! Your momma and daddy gave you that name, and you should wear it with pride."

Lenville mumbled something and kicked at the dirt.

Sam began walking slowly down the length of the table, picking up an item here and an item there, inspecting them and putting them back down. Most of the items were junk, likely purchased in bulk from other yard sales that hadn't been able to sell them. As he moved down the table, he kept Lenville in his peripheral vision and saw him nervously glance toward the far end of the table several times while slowly inching in that direction. Christie sat down on the steps of the plywood stoop in front of the trailer and watched as the scene unfolded. She had a resigned look on her face.

Lenville began rearranging the items on the table, trying to give the appearance of tidying up. Sam saw him pick up a stuffed bear three feet from the end of the table, brush an imagined speck of dust off it before putting it down in a different spot from where it had been. Bingo, Sam thought.

When Sam reached the bear, he idly ran his index finger over it and poked its belly. Lenville stopped fidgeting and froze, still as a statue. The boy's like a damn Geiger counter, Sam thought. Instead of picking up the bear, Sam picked up a toy car next to it, inspected it carefully, put it back down and moved on to a scratched and dented Magic Eight Ball. Out of the corner of his eye, he saw Lenville let out the breath he was holding and glance at Christie.

Sam moved on to the end of the table, turned and started back, walking slowly. Lenville went still again as he approached the bear and relaxed as Sam moved past it. About three feet past the bear, Sam suddenly stopped.

"You know," he said, turning back toward the bear. "I got a little niece that'd probably like that stuffed bear there."

"Aw, man." Lenville swallowed rapidly, his Adam's apple bobbing up and down. "You don't want that piece-a-shit. It's old and dirty. Git her a new one."

"You think I'm made of money, Lenville? You know how kids are. You buy 'em something new, they just tear it up in a week anyway. I'd rather get her this one that's already broke in."

Sam picked up the bear. Under it was a gold watch and a ring.

"Aw, shit!" Lenville said.

Chapter 20

Nan Davis was the first in a parade of visitors to Kate's room the following morning. She poked her head in the door at six-thirty and came the rest of the way in when she saw Kate was eating breakfast.

"Hey, there." She gave Kate a quick peck on the cheek. "How are you?"

"I'll have to wait for the doctor to be sure." Kate grimaced. "My neck hurts, and I've got a sore spot on my head. No headache, though, so that's good."

The emergency room diagnosis was a mild to moderate concussion caused by the blow to the head. X-rays had ruled out a neck fracture, but as the doctor explained, the blow to the head or her hitting the floor likely traumatized a ligament in her neck, resulting in a sprain and the pain she was experiencing. Because of the concussion, she had been admitted overnight for observation. The night nurse had applied a cold pack periodically to her neck during the night, and although it still hurt, it was better.

"I got the news last night," Nan said. "I thought about coming by, but I doubted I would get to see you."

"I doubt you would have wanted to," Kate said. "I wasn't at my best."

"Do you know who attacked you?"

"No. I didn't even know I'd been hit until they told me. I thought I'd fainted." She pushed the half-eaten tray away. "Are you here professionally?"

"Of course," Nan said. "It's definitely news. But that doesn't mean I'm not visiting you as a friend as well."

Kate smiled. "Thanks."

"The incident report says your office was searched. Do you have any idea what the intruder was looking for?"

"No, although Lou does."

"Lou Pelfrey?"

Kate nodded and then winced. She made a mental note to avoid nodding until her neck healed. "Lou and I are old friends. She thinks my attacker was looking for the Shooting Star."

Nan looked surprised. "The Shooting Star? The item that was stolen from the Drayer in Chicago?"

"That's the one." Kate could see Nan was having a difficult time making sense of what she was hearing. "Another thing you probably don't know is that the man who was murdered over the weekend, Michael Mabry, was also a friend. We were romantically involved in graduate school here at Raven."

"Ah!" Kate could almost see the light bulb going off above Nan's head. "And he's a suspect in the Drayer theft and murders."

"That's what they tell me. Apparently Michael kept a lot about his past from me, but the fact that he came to Eden and was murdered drags me into it. I seem to officially be a suspect."

"For murder?" Nan looked shocked. "That's ridiculous!"

"Thank you," Kate said. "I think I'm just one among many on their list, but I'm still on the list. And now that I've been attacked and my office searched, I doubt Lou will be the only one who thinks the Star is involved."

"Michael Mabry's partners must have killed him but didn't find the Star. Obviously this puts you in danger." Nan thought for a moment, tapping her pen against her lips. "Maybe I can help. It's not much, but I can do my usual snooping and find out what I can about the investigation both here and in Chicago. I have a couple of friends from my freelance days who ended up on newspapers there. I'm sure they'd be glad to have an insider on the story here, so we should be able to scratch one another's backs."

"Oh, Nan, thank you!" Kate sat up straighter in the bed, feeling her spirits lift. "I was wondering if I could ask you to find out what's going on here, but it didn't occur to me you would have contacts in Chicago."

"My tentacles reach pretty far." Nan smiled. "I'll find out what I can about your friend's role in the theft and who he might have been partnered with. I'll get pictures if I can, so you'll know who warrants a 9-1-1 call."

Jackson arrived then with a huge vase of yellow roses. Nan exchanged a few words with him before excusing herself. Jackson had no more than found a place for the roses on her windowsill when Ann and Steven showed up. They informed her that Edna was sitting with Bette. The doctor arrived in the midst of the socializing and, after a cursory examination, declared her fit to be discharged. After some discussion, it was decided that Ann would take Steven home, and she and Edna would come back for Kate.

"It always takes a while for the paperwork to be finished," Ann said. "The timing should be about right."

The three of them left. Over the next hour, Kate listened to instructions, promised to make a follow-up appointment with a family doctor, and signed several forms. A nursing assistant stayed with her while she dressed in case she felt unsteady and then left to go about her other duties. Kate sat in the reclining chair by the bed, waiting for Ann to return. The television was tuned to a morning talk show, but she heard little of it, preoccupied with thoughts about how fast and unpleasantly her life had changed over the last few days. She didn't see her father enter the room until he was right in front of her.

"Hello, Katydid." He had his hands shoved into his pants pockets and looked nervous. "I heard you had a little trouble."

"Hi, Daddy."

"I see you're dressed and out of bed," he said. "Are they about to kick you out of here?"

She nodded, wincing again as she did so. "Just waiting for my ride."

"Steven only said you'd been hurt and were in the hospital. He didn't say what happened?" He looked at her expectantly.

"I'm told someone hit me."

"Hit you?" His face registered surprise, followed by what looked like anger. "Why would anyone hurt you?"

"Lou says my office was torn apart. I guess I surprised someone in there."

"Did you see who it was?"

"No. I didn't even know I'd been assaulted until they told me."

He looked frustrated at the lack of information.

"That's all I know, Daddy." She decided not to get into the lengthy story of the Star, Michael, and the fact that she was a suspect in his murder. Her father had taken an immediate dislike to Michael when she'd introduced them. He'd warned her Michael would hurt her, and she hadn't listened. When Michael had abandoned her, her father hadn't rubbed it in with an "I told you so," but his silence and glowering looks made it clear he was angry with her for not listening to him.

Or maybe he was angry with Michael, she thought suddenly. Why had that not occurred to her before?

They were silent for a moment. He stared at the floor, she stared at the television, neither of them sure what to say. "So, you're okay?" he said finally.

"My neck hurts a little, but the doctor says that will go away."

"Well, then, I guess I'll be on my way." He turned to leave but stopped at the door and looked back at her. "I'm glad you're okay, Katydid."

"Thanks, Daddy." She hesitated. "I'm glad you came by."

He nodded, smiled slightly, and left. When Ann and Edna arrived ten minutes later, Kate was still replaying the conversation in her mind. It hadn't been much, but it was the most they had talked at one time since she'd left home. Maybe, she thought, I should get clobbered more often.

***

The suite was large, but Wendell felt it closing in on him as he paced from the bedroom through the living room and back again, his attention focused on Gabby. She was sitting in a chair at the end of the dining table, her cell phone pressed against her ear, talking to her brother in Chicago. For the most part, it had been a one-sided conversation.

Baby had called Gabby's phone, not his, and that fact alone made Wendell sweat. Try as he might, he couldn't glean much from Gabby's responses. He had heard her explain that they weren't absolutely sure what had happened to their "old friend"—Baby was careful what he said on any phone—but that their "coworker" had been acting stranger than usual lately. No, she said, they hadn't found any good "souvenirs" yet, and, no, they didn't know if their co-worker had either. After that, Gabby had mostly listened, responding with the occasional "umm-hmmm" or "yes, I understand."

It was not going well. The Professor had got himself shot by somebody—the creepy fuck was still at the top of Wendell's list of suspects—on Saturday night. It was already Wednesday and still no Star. Things were more complicated now because of the murder investigation. He didn't have to be in Chicago to know Baby wasn't happy. The only good news was that so far Baby didn't know that Wendell had almost been caught searching Rawlings's office. The Star wasn't there, he'd made sure of that, but it had been a close call.

"We're working on that," Gabby said. "Our co-worker is on site. We've started scouting around ourselves, but so far no luck."

Wendell stopped pacing, feeling his stomach drop. She waved her free hand at him in an "it's okay" gesture. He sat down and waited.

"Yes, yes, we will. I'll call you later. Love you, too." She disconnected the call and leaned back in the chair, letting go a big sigh of relief.

"Dom is pretty pissed off," she said. She never called her brother by his nickname. "He says Leonard claims he didn't do Mick, but I get the impression he's not sure he believes him."

"He doesn't think we had anything to do with it, does he?"

"I don't think so. You heard me tell him we didn't know what happened. He wants us to pick up a burner phone and call him later." She leaned forward, a worried look on her face. "Do you think Leonard could have lost it and did Mick before he got what he wanted?"

"I dunno." Wendell stood and began pacing again. "It doesn't seem like him, though. He's as cool as a damn snake, you know that."

"Maybe it was an accident? Maybe Mick went after Leonard's gun?"

"I guess that's possible," Wendell admitted. "But why wouldn't he just say so?"

"Maybe he's afraid of Dom?"

"I don't think that creepy fuck is afraid of anybody."

"You don't think he could have the Star, do you? If he's not afraid of anyone, like you say, maybe he figures he'll just keep it for himself."

"I dunno." Wendell's head was beginning to hurt. "I sure as hell hope not. Because if Baby starts thinking that, he might want us to do something about it."

Chapter 21

The pain in her neck had improved from the day before, but looking up to pick a pair of shoes from the shelf in her closet was not the most pleasant experience. The hell with it, Kate thought, grabbing a pair of athletic shoes. I'm going for comfort, not style today. Dropping the shoes by the desk chair, she retrieved the pair of slacks from the bed and hung them back in the closet. Going to the dresser, she opened the bottom drawer and selected a pair of green jeans that went with the top she'd chosen. Even if she decided to run by her office, they'd look fine.

She stood for a moment looking into the drawer. Tucked away in the back of the drawer, partially covered by her other jeans, was the plastic grocery bag containing Michael's stories and the photo album he had so treasured. When Lou broke the news of Michael's murder to her, she'd realized the police would want the bag he'd left with her. She hadn't been able to bear the idea of Michael's stories and pictures, things he'd valued enough to carry with him all these years, ending up in a police evidence room, or even worse, the trash bin. She'd also had the selfish motive of not wanting the pictures of Michael and her brought to light, although after Valentine's interrogation, that no longer mattered. When Lou left the room while she showered and dressed, she'd hidden them under her jeans. She'd counted on the detectives not opening the bag in front of Lou, and they hadn't.

She'd just finished dressing when her cell phone rang.

"Hey, Kate," Nan said. "How are you feeling this morning?"

"Much better. Thanks for asking."

"I wanted to touch base with you," Nan said. "I talked to my Chicago friends yesterday morning after I left the hospital, and they both got back to me last night. They emailed some information and a couple of photos. I'm close to Holly House if it's okay to come by."

"Of course," Kate said. "I was just heading down to breakfast."

"See you in a few."

Only three tables were occupied when Kate entered the dining room. Two older couples sat together at a window table, poring over tourist brochures and discussing what to see. The rumpled man Kate had first seen at the Main Street Diner sat at the corner table nearest the door reading the Lexington paper. He looked up when she came in and smiled.

"Good morning," he said.

"Morning." She smiled back. She didn't know the man's name, but she'd noticed Ann and Edna chatting with him, and they seemed to like him.

A table at the far side of the room was taken by a man Kate hadn't seen before. Slender almost to the point of emaciation with thinning brown hair, she guessed him to be in his forties. He was dressed in brown slacks, a white pullover shirt and a tan sports coat. He also had the Lexington paper next to his plate.

"There you are," Nan said, coming up behind her. "Think Ann and Edna will feed me this morning?"

"If they won't, I'll share my breakfast with you."

Kate led Nan to a table in the far corner, two tables down from the new guest. Kate wasn't sure how full Holly House was this morning but guessed any late breakfast arrivals would choose tables closer to the door and windows. She preferred discussing what Nan had found in private.

"Freeloading again, I see," Ann joked when she brought their coffee.

"With Edna's cooking? Definitely! Why else do you think I stay friends with you?" Nan joked back.

Ann took their orders and left to make a coffee round of the rest of the tables. Nan had laid an accordion file folder with a tie on the table when they'd first sat down. Opening it now, she pulled out some papers.

"I didn't have any photo paper at home," she said. "So I had to print these out on a piece of regular printer paper. Still, they're pretty good."

She slid one of the papers over to Kate. On it were what appeared to be two booking photos, one a frontal view, the other a profile.

"This man is Wendell Halsey," she said. "He's the brother-in-law of a major Chicago bad guy. The cops up there believe he was in on the Drayer heist with your old friend. Apparently they used to be cellmates in prison."

Kate closed her eyes for a moment and shook her head. Opening them again, she found Nan looking at her with a concerned look on her face.

"Sorry," she said. "It's just that I'm still having trouble reconciling the Michael I knew with the Michael he'd apparently become. It's like I'm watching one of those science fiction movies where there are alternate universes with people who look the same and sound the same but are very different people. You know what I mean?"

"I think so," Nan said. "I think we freeze people in time in our minds based on when we know them."

"I guess you're right." Kate picked up the paper, looked at it, and her eyes widened. "Oh, my God! I've seen this man. Here in Eden."

"What?" Nan automatically pulled a pen from her pocket, preparing to jot down the details. "Where?"

"Friday—when we all met at the diner. He was there with a woman."

"Are you sure?"

"Yes. I noticed him while we were eating. I suppose I might have forgotten about it except for the fact that he stopped me outside and asked me to autograph one of my books. He introduced the woman with him as his wife and said she was a fan. They said they were just passing through but thought they'd stay a couple of days. They wanted to know a good place to stay."

Nan was taking notes as Kate talked. "Did they indicate where they might get a room?"

"They said they'd probably try one of the chains out by the interstate." She rubbed her sore neck. "Is he dangerous? I mean, could he have been the man in my office?"

"According to my friends, he's not usually violent. In fact, he has a reputation for being a bit of a screw-up. The word is his brother-in-law only tolerates him because he's married to his sister. The brother-in-law is very dangerous, though. I would imagine that anything he tells Mr. Halsey to do, he'd do." Nan took a sip of her coffee before continuing. "His wife is Gabriella—goes by Gabby. Her brother is Dominick Duda—nickname Baby. The authorities have been after him for a long time, but witnesses have a way of clamming up or disappearing. Your friend, Michael, and Halsey were cellmates at Big Muddy—that's a prison in Illinois. The thinking is that Halsey put Michael in touch with Duda."

Kate was silent for a few moments, leafing slowly through the two pages of printed information and the sheet with the pictures. "Can I keep these?"

"Sure. I've got the email so I don't need them."

"Are you going to put this in the paper?"

"Not until I talk to Jo Valentine. I've got a good relationship with the local police, and I don't want to ruin that. She'll likely want to talk to you after I tell her you've seen Halsey."

Ann brought their breakfasts then. Even though the omelet was perfect, Kate found her appetite had fled. As she forced herself to eat and make small talk with Nan, she didn't notice the man two tables down get up and leave.

Chapter 22

The house on Elk Lick Road was a small, one-story, white frame building with a front porch wrapping around three sides. A barn and two smaller outbuildings—one of them a chicken house— stood behind and to the right of the house. A battered red F-150 pickup was parked near the barn. A scattering of Rhode Island reds scratched and pecked the barnyard dirt in their search for insects. As Sticks pulled the unmarked to a stop, four mixed breed dogs tore around the side of the house, barking at the intruders, and the chickens scattered.

"Damn it!" Jo said. "Doesn't anyone keep their dogs tied?"

"No leash laws in the county." Sticks opened the driver's door. "Dogs just doing what they're meant to do—serve and protect, just like us."

He grinned at Jo. He knew she wasn't comfortable around dogs and never missed a chance to needle the city girl about her fear of being bitten.

Jo stayed where she was in the passenger seat until she saw the dogs welcome the ear rubs and "good dog" praises that Sticks heaped on them. Then she tentatively opened her door and stepped out, raising her hands away from the dogs when they came around the car to sniff her.

She turned as she heard the front door of the house open and saw what Lou meant when she said that Johnny Crouch wasn't a feeble old guy. He was gray-haired and his tanned face was wrinkled, but his body was more muscular and firm than most of the twenty-year olds she saw in Walmart these days.

"Help you?" He didn't move from the porch or call off the dogs.

"Morning," Sticks said. "You John Crouch?"

"I am. Who's asking?"

"Detective Mullins, Eden P.D.." Sticks held up his identification. "This is Detective Valentine."

Sticks moved toward the porch. Jo slowly moved around the car, keeping one eye on Johnny Crouch and the other on the dogs that shoved and chewed on one another as they jockeyed to keep their position close to her. She had to admit there was nothing threatening in their body language. That was one thing she'd noticed about dogs. She didn't like them or trust them, but the ones she'd met didn't seem to know or care. They wanted a human's attention, and it didn't matter to them whether or not the human was interested in giving it to them.

"We'd like to ask you a few questions, Mr. Crouch." Sticks stepped onto the porch and offered his right hand. Crouch hesitated for a second before accepting Sticks's hand and shaking. "We understand you're familiar with a man named Michael Mabry."

Jo had pulled her attention away from the dogs and was looking at Johnny Crouch when Sticks said the name. She saw Crouch's eyes go blank, hiding whatever emotion was elicited by the mention of Michael Mabry's name.

"Why you askin' about that son-of-a-bitch?"

"Do you know him, Mr. Crouch?" Jo said.

"I know he's a no-good bastard, that's what I know."

"When did you last see him?"

"Hell, I dunno—thirty, thirty-five years ago? Right before he skipped out on my little girl and his baby she was carryin'."

"Are you aware he was found shot to death here in Eden Sunday morning?"

Crouch's eyebrows rose a notch, and a big smile creased his face. "Well, now," he said. "I sure appreciate you folks driving all the way out here to bring me good news. I wish I'd pulled the trigger, but I'm still glad to hear somebody did."

He stopped for a second and then laughed.

"Oh, I get it," he said. "You think maybe I did pull the trigger."

"Where were you between eleven Saturday night and two Sunday morning?" Sticks said.

"In my bed. Right here. Alone, unfortunately, just like I been since my wife, Martha, died twenty years ago."

"So there's no one who can verify you were here?" Jo said.

"Them dogs there, but I don't guess you'll take their word for it." Crouch couldn't keep the smile off his face. "You know, I never woulda thought I'd be happy to be suspected of anything by the police, but this tickles me no end. I'm sorry I wasn't the one to do it, but I'm kinda proud to be suspected of it."

"Do you own any weapons, Mr. Crouch?"

"Little lady, this is Kentucky. Of course, I own weapons. Got two rifles, a shotgun, and two pistols. I'm guessing you'll be wanting to take a look at them?"

"We'd appreciate it," she said.

"Well, in that case, get yourself a warrant."

"It would be easier if you'd just let us check them now," Sticks said.

"I'm sure it would be, but I got no reason to make your life easier. I watch enough cop shows on TV to know I don't have to turn them over to you."

"The faster we can eliminate you as a suspect, the faster we can find who really committed the crime," Jo said.

"You don't get it, do you, little lady?" Crouch said, his face turning red. "That no-good son-of-a-bitch destroyed my family. Thanks to him, my little girl killed herself. My wife got depressed—no big surprise there. Damn doctors threw pills at her, and those pills took out her kidneys. My boy'd always been a good boy, but he blamed himself for not protectin' his little sister. Started drinkin' and druggin' and gittin' into trouble and never stopped. So if I can slow you down a little by making you get a warrant, then that gives the man—or woman—who did kill that son-of-a-bitch more time to get away. Hell, if I knew who it was, I'd give them a ride out of town myself!"

"I have to warn you against helping the person who committed this crime," Jo said. "Knowingly doing so would make you an accessory."

"Warn all you want, little lady," he said. "I'm sixty-eight years old, my wife is dead, my daughter is dead, and my son might as well be for all the good Adam's doin' with his life. I can die a happy man now that I know the son-of-a-bitch that killed my little girl is dead, and if I can help the person who pulled the trigger, I damn sure will. You catch me, you can put me in prison as an *accessory,* and the state can take care of me in my old age. Now git off my porch."

"So…what do you think, little lady?" Sticks said as they pulled out of Johnny Crouch's driveway and started down Elk Lick Road.

"Fuck you, Mullins," Jo said. Sticks chuckled.

She took a deep breath. It wasn't the first time a citizen had made a less than respectful comment about her height and gender, but it still pissed her off and made her want to hit something or someone. Guess men aren't the only ones who can get a "little man complex," she thought.

"I think," she said, "that we can't rule Crouch out yet. He didn't look all that surprised to hear that Mabry was dead. You'd think if he hadn't seen or heard of the guy in thirty years like he said, he'd have been surprised just to hear his name."

"I noticed that," Sticks said. "I noticed something else, too. He said his son is basically a no-good who ruined his life thanks to what Mabry did to his sister. Maybe he ran into Mabry and decided to get payback."

"Could be." Jo took out her cell phone and hit speed dial for the station. "Hey, Vera, it's Jo. I need you to run a name for me. Adam Crouch. I don't have a DOB or SSN, but his father is John Crouch, lives in the county on Elk Lick Road. Arrests, outstanding warrants, and a recent address, if you can find one. Run him through NCIC as well."

She listened for a moment.

"Tell them to wait for us. We're only about fifteen minutes out." She disconnected and turned to Sticks, smiling. "Lewis got a call this morning from Powell County. A deputy over there found what looks like Mabry's watch and class ring at a yard sale. The guy that was running it is in custody. Donnie and Rick are heading over there now, and so are we."

***

"I swear that guy gives me the willies!" Ginger shuddered.

"Did he try something with you?" Cal tried to look concerned. Which he was. He liked Ginger. But he also wanted to know more about the Holly's new guest for his own reasons.

"No, no, it's not that. I can handle that." Ginger waved a hand at him, dismissing the suggestion as ridiculous. "He's just—I don't know—creepy."

When Ginger had stopped by his room to drop off fresh towels, Cal had casually brought up the topic of the newest Holly House guest. Breakfast this morning was the first time he'd seen the man. He was nondescript, dressing and looking like a salesman or a mid-level executive, but something about the way he held himself caught Cal's eye. Ginger was right. He *was* creepy, although it was hard to say why.

Even more interesting than his unexplained creepiness, however, was the fact that he had obviously been interested in Katherine Rawlings and her conversation with Nan Davis, a woman Cal had learned was a local reporter.

"What's this creepy fellow's name?"

"Supposedly William Jones." Ginger smacked her own forehead. "Oh, Lordy, don't tell Ann I told you that. I'm not supposed to discuss one guest with another." She thought for a moment. "And I never have until now. What is it about you, Mr. Becker, that makes me go running off at the mouth?"

"My good looks and charm?" Cal winked at her.

"Oh, you!" Ginger slapped him on the shoulder.

"Seriously, if he scares you, I'd like to know who he is. What's he driving?"

"A blue Focus," Ginger said. "Newer model. He gave his address as St. Louis. The car's got Kentucky tags, so it's probably a rental."

"You'd make a good detective," Cal said.

"You mean, I'm nosy?" Ginger raised her eyebrows and gave him a look.

"I didn't say that." He held his hands up in a defensive pose.

"Well, I am, but I find out a lot of interesting things that way." She laughed but then turned serious. "Take you, for instance. Unless I'm very much mistaken, I'd say you're the insurance investigator who's in town looking for the person who killed those people at that museum up in Chicago."

Cal's mouth dropped open. He'd been joking with her when he said she'd make a good detective. Apparently it wasn't a joke after all.

"What makes you think that?"

"I've watched you, Mr. Becker," she started.

"Cal," he said, interrupting her. "I told you to call me Cal."

"Okay, *Cal*," she said. "I see you watching everyone and everything. Nothing gets by you. And you make sure to buddy-up with everybody so they won't think anything when you start asking questions. Like you've done with me. 'Call me Cal.' I mean, could you be more obvious?"

Lordy, Cal thought. This woman is a finely tuned bullshit detector, if there ever was one. "So I'm friendly, and that makes you think I'm a detective?"

"Well, that and the fact that the folks who have seen the insurance investigator describe him as a chubby teddy bear of a man wearing clothes that look like they've never seen an iron."

Ginger grinned.

"Ouch! That hurts!"

"If you want to be incognito, you're going to have to learn to blend in better. That includes learning to use an iron. So am I right? Are you the insurance investigator?"

Cal reluctantly nodded. "You got me."

"Well, your secret's safe with us," Ginger said.

"Us?"

"Ann, Edna, and me. When I told them who I thought you were, they saw it, too." She shrugged. "Me and my big mouth."

"I'd rather you didn't talk about it with anyone else. Especially here."

"I promise." Ginger raised her right hand, as if swearing an oath. "Anyway, since you are the investigator, are you going to see if you can find out who the creepy Mr. Jones really is?"

"That might not be a bad idea." He thought for a second. "Maybe you can help."

"Really? How?" She was obviously thrilled with the idea.

"Do you think you can get hold of something he's touched?"

"Oh, you mean for fingerprints? Sure, no problem."

"I need it to be something clean, something no one else has touched. Otherwise, there'll be too many other prints on it. Maybe a glass from his room?"

"That won't work," she said. "He doesn't let me in. Says he doesn't need maid service while he's here. But he's been here since Monday night and he's eaten breakfast both mornings. I'll make sure all the water glasses and coffee cups are polished clean before I leave tonight. Ann and Edna put those on the tables early, before I get here, so I'll tell them to wear plastic gloves when they do it. That way, no matter which table he sits at, you'll get your prints."

Cal stared at her. Maybe I should get this woman an application for Gallagher, he thought. Then again, maybe not. She'd probably put me out of a job.

"Do you think he's got something to do with the Chicago thing?" Ginger was excited.

"No reason to think that," he said. "I'd just like to know who he is."

It was true. There was no reason to think that except for the fact that he couldn't see Baby Duda sending only his sister and a screw-up like Halsey after Mabry. He also couldn't see Halsey and Gabriella as killers. Something about Mr. Jones, though…call it cop instinct, but he didn't think Mr. Jones was a salesman.

***

It was nearly noon before Kate mustered up the courage to face her office. She'd been told it was a mess and dreaded what she would find. The hall was empty as she unlocked the door. The isolation made her nervous, but she shook it off. Whoever had assaulted her wasn't likely to try it again in daylight when anyone could come walking down the hall. For that matter, he wasn't likely to try it again at night either, although she thought she'd take her purse to class with her from now on and leave the building when her students did.

She'd been prepared for a mess but not for the tidy office that greeted her. Her books were on their shelves, although closer inspection showed them to be in a different order than she liked them, papers were stacked in tidy heaps on her desk and the carpet appeared freshly vacuumed. Other than the missing lamp, there was no evidence of the ransacking her office had undergone.

She found Mary in the break room enjoying a lunch of salad and a Diet Coke. Mary dropped her fork and jumped to her feet when she saw Kate.

"Kate, honey! How are you?" She gave Kate a hug but jumped back when Kate winced. "Oh, honey, I'm sorry! Did I hurt you?"

"It's okay," Kate said. "My neck is still a little sore is all. I try to avoid sudden movements. The doctor promised it would go away."

"I could not believe it when I heard what happened! Worrying about the offices being broken into was bad enough, but now this…I swear, I don't know what's happening to the world today! Do the police have any idea who did this?"

Kate didn't want to get into a discussion that would ultimately lead to Michael, the Star, and her suspected involvement. If she knew Eden and Raven, Mary would hear the rumors sooner rather than later, but she didn't want to talk about it now.

"Not that they've told me," she said and changed the subject. "I just left my office, and it looks a lot neater than I was told it did. Did you clean up the mess?"

"Not me," Mary said. "I would have, but I never got the chance. After the police gave the okay Tuesday morning, Dr. Irons and his teaching assistant—Jerry something, I never can pronounce his name—cleaned it up."

"Chris?" Kate was surprised. "That was nice of him."

"He was really angry when he heard what happened." Mary sat back down. "He wanted to come see you at the hospital, but Jackson had just come from there and said you were being discharged. So he cleaned up your office instead."

"Is he in today?" Kate said. "I'd like to thank him."

"He was this morning."

Kate excused herself, retrieved her mail, and headed for Chris's office. His door was closed and locked. She returned to her office and spent the next hour rearranging the books on her shelves and the papers on her desk. She was relieved to find the assignments her students had turned in Monday were intact. She had just settled back in her chair and started reading the first one when her phone rang.

"Hello," she said. No one answered. "Hello?"

She waited a few moments and hung up. Probably just a misdial, she thought, feeling uneasy. She got up and closed and locked her office door.

Chapter 23

"Any luck?" Wendell said, closing the door behind Leonard.

It was early evening. He and Gabby had been about to head out for dinner when Leonard showed up. For a second, Wendell thought Leonard's appearance in Lexington was good news that meant the Star had been found and they could head home. One look at his face dashed those hopes.

"It's not in her room," Leonard said.

Wendell glanced at Gabby. She looked as nervous as he felt. The creepy fuck was unpleasant to be around under the best of circumstances, but they'd spent enough time with him the last few days to know he was beyond unpleasant when things weren't going his way.

"So what's next?" Wendell wasn't sure he wanted to know.

"You come back with me," Leonard said. "We have a house to search."

"What house?"

"The one belonging to Jackson Price—the man who wrote the other book that was in the Professor's room. I went by his place. It's large. Even with both of us, it's going to take a long time to search."

"You think Price is in on it?" Wendell had forgotten about Price.

"I think we need to search the house."

"And you want me to go with you?" Wendell didn't like the idea of returning to Eden now that the Professor's murder had the cops on high alert. He'd already drawn too much attention asking questions around town. He'd been pushing his luck searching the broad's office.

Leonard didn't reply. He stood motionless, waiting, for what Wendell didn't know. Probably for me to piss my pants, he thought. The creepy fuck made him nervous enough to do just that.

"So when do we go?"

"Tomorrow," Leonard said. "While he's at the university."

"You said it's gonna take a long time to search the place." Wendell thought he detected the hint of a whine in his own voice and tried to make himself sound normal. "What if he comes home?"

"Let's hope for his sake that doesn't happen."

"I could go and keep watch outside," Gabby spoke up.

"No, babe, I don't want you there," Wendell said, but Leonard raised a hand.

"That's a good idea. We'll have our cells," he said. "You can ring us if he comes home early."

"Baby won't like it if something happens to Gabby," Wendell protested.

"Nothing will happen, honey," Gabby said. "I'll be outside. It'll be safer for everybody if I keep a watch."

Wendell started to argue but stopped. The look on the creepy fuck's face made it clear he wanted Gabby as a lookout. And Gabby was right. It would be safer for all of them, including the dude who lived in the house, if they had a lookout.

"Okay. Just don't get out of the car. No matter what. Promise me?"

"I promise." Gabby made a cross-my-heart gesture.

"What if we don't find it at this dude's place?" Wendell said.

"We'll try another method."

Wendell waited for him to elaborate, but the creepy fuck just stood there staring at him. Could he have the damn thing, Wendell wondered. He couldn't see the creepy fuck doing the Professor before he got the Star, not even accidentally. But if he had it, what was he waiting for? Why not get the hell out of the country now while he had some distance between himself and Chicago? He was a scary dude, but Wendell didn't think he was stupid enough to take on Baby. Unless—Wendell wondered why this hadn't occurred to him before—the creepy fuck had the backing of someone who wanted Baby out of the picture.

They spent the next half hour going over details and agreeing on where and when to meet the following morning. After Leonard left, Wendell and Gabby decided they weren't really hungry after all.

Chapter 24

The gloomy gray morning did nothing to improve the curb appeal of the rusted, single wide mobile home occupying number thirty-six, a corner lot at the rear of the Morningside Trailer Park. Number thirty-six's location limited the trailers they had to evacuate to one on the left and a couple across the street. Four Powell County deputies set up at locations giving them a view of all sides of the trailer so they could watch for movement at the doors and windows, while the park's manager went door to door with Jo and Lewis. The trailer directly across from number thirty-six housed an older lady having her breakfast, but they had to rouse the occupants of the other trailers from their sleep. Jo guessed that would be the case with the occupants of number thirty-six as well.

Lenville Sorrell's story was that he had "found" the watch and ring. According to Jo's watch, he stuck to that story for exactly ninety minutes, but the threat of being charged as an accessory to murder finally loosened his tongue around six the previous evening. That's when he told them Tommy Applegate had asked him to sell them for him.

Tommy and his father, Ivan, shared the trailer at number thirty-six. The pattern of burglaries at the university made sense now. Hanover Hall's offices had remained untouched while every other building on campus had been hit at least once. Robbie Applegate was Ivan's father. Leaving the building he worked in untouched was apparently their way of showing familial respect.

By ten after six the surrounding trailers were empty, the occupants grouped in the manager's office at the park's entrance, disgruntled, but out of the line of any gunfire that might occur. Samuels and Sticks positioned themselves to each side of the trailer's rear door, weapons drawn. Jo stood to the left of the front door, while Lewis on the right reached up and knocked heavily. Here goes, she thought. While the Applegates had never been known to use weapons, murder changed everything.

There was no response to Lewis's knock, so he banged again. Jo heard a sound inside the trailer toward the rear and glanced that way just in time to see a curtain flutter.

"I think you woke somebody up," she said.

"About time." Lewis knocked again.

Jo heard heavy footsteps moving from the rear of the trailer to the front door, and a moment later, the door opened a crack.

"Yeah?" said a voice hoarse with sleep. "Whaddya want?"

Lewis pushed open the door, Jo on his heels. Ivan Applegate stumbled backward, nearly falling over a dirty ottoman. Lewis grabbed him and spread-eagled him against the living room wall, while Jo moved toward the rear of the trailer, weapon drawn. Behind her she heard Lewis say, "You missed me, Ivan?"

"Ah, man, I ain't done nuthin'," she heard Ivan protest, as she moved through the filthy kitchen and into a short hall.

The trailer's layout had the living room at the front. The kitchen was to Jo's left as she stepped through the front door, and a hall led from it to the bath and bedrooms. The first hall door opened into a small room intended as a second bedroom. It was filled with cardboard boxes, several computers, and tangled copper wiring. Fruits of their labors, Jo thought. The next door revealed a bathroom. The toilet and sink looked like they hadn't been cleaned in months, and the shower curtain was dingy and barely attached to the rod. The buildup of dirt on the floor made it impossible to tell the color of the linoleum, and a small hole in the flooring under the toilet tank indicated a past leak that had been allowed to rot out the floor. At the end of the hall was a closed door. Jo turned the knob and kicked it open.

"Police!" she said, moving quickly into the bedroom, her heart pounding.

The curtains were pulled, making it difficult to see, not that there was much to see anyway. The room contained bunk beds, a dresser, and a kitchen chair. Considering the condition of the rest of the trailer, it was surprisingly neat, the floor clear of discarded clothing and two pairs of shoes arranged side by side under the dresser. The bottom bunk was unmade and empty, but a leg poked out of the bedding on the top bunk. She found a switch on the wall and flicked on the overhead light. Down the hall she heard the heavy footsteps of Sticks, Samuels, and the uniforms as everyone piled into the trailer. "Police!" she said again, louder this time. The bunk's occupant stirred slightly.

"Outa there, Tommy!"

Jo winced as Samuels's voice boomed in her ear. Rick Samuels was a big man, well over six feet and bulky, with a voice to match. He was a good guy, an easygoing man with a sense of humor who seldom had to use force to effect an arrest. Jo liked him, but he made her nervous. Whenever he stood near her, she felt like a mouse about to get trampled by an elephant. That feeling was heightened in the confines of the small trailer bedroom, and she fought the impulse to back away.

"Huh?" Tommy Applegate rose up on his elbows. He'd been sleeping on his stomach, and his face was reddened on the left side.

"Mornin', Sunshine," Rick boomed jovially. "Climb on down from there."

"Detective Samuels?" Tommy sat up. His head grazed the ceiling, and he scrunched down a little. Jo watched his eyes dart back and forth, the way an animal does when cornered and looking for an escape route. As he came further awake, she saw the realization hit him that there was no escape.

"Aw, hell," he said and dropped down from the bunk.

***

"Have a seat." Jo motioned to the chair at the side of her desk.

Kate sat, feeling a little like a child who has been called to the principal's office. She looked around the room, measuring how it looked against the descriptions she'd written. It was considerably smaller than the detective sections she had described in her books, but the overall atmosphere was the same. Utilitarian, she thought. If I had to describe it with one word, utilitarian would be it.

She'd spent most of the day with her mother. After breakfast, she'd taken Bette to her hairdresser for a haircut, shampoo, and style. Bette seemed to enjoy it and chatted with Mary much as she would have before the Alzheimer's. Afterward, they'd strolled along the main street downtown, checking out the antique shops that had sprung up like mushrooms after a rain to replace the mom-and-pop stores of Kate's childhood.

It was during lunch at the Main Street Diner that she noticed Bette growing vague and forgetting to take bites of her food. They had returned to Steven's, and after Bette had lain down for a nap, she and Steven visited for a while. She was still there at three when Jo Valentine called and asked her to stop by the station. Although she didn't say why, Kate guessed it was to discuss the man from the diner.

"Nan Davis tells me you've seen this man in Eden." The detective slid two photos across the desk. They were the same two booking photos that Nan had shown her, but these had been printed on photo paper.

"Yes," Kate said. "I saw him in the Main Street Diner last Friday. Nan and I had brunch there with friends. He was with a woman."

"I understand he spoke to you?"

"Yes. After I left. He and his wife—at least, that's who he said she was—stopped me on the street and asked me to autograph a copy of *Flee.*" She hesitated a moment. "That's my latest book."

"I'm familiar with it."

"He apologized for having stared in the diner. I had noticed him looking at me. He said his wife was reading *Flee,* and he'd recognized me from the book jacket."

"So you autographed the book for him?"

"Yes. They also asked me where were good places to stay in Eden. They said they were on a road trip but thought they might stay in town for a couple of days. I told them about the Holly House and the chains by the interstate."

"Anything else?"

"No. They left and so did I."

"Did you see what they were driving?"

"I'm sorry, no." Kate cleared her throat. "Could he...do you think he's the man who attacked me?"

"No way of knowing."

"I guess it could have been the infamous Eden burglars," Kate said. "Maybe it's just a coincidence that this man was in town a few days before."

"I doubt that."

Kate started to ask why she thought that, but the phone on the desk rang before she could. The detective answered with a curt, "Valentine."

After listening for a few moments and jotting what looked like an address on a slip of paper, she said, "I'm on my way. Tell Sticks I'll meet him there."

She hung up and looked at Kate. "It seems that when your friend, Dr. Price, arrived home a little while ago, he found his house had been broken into."

"What? Is he okay?"

"He's fine. He didn't surprise the doers, just found the results." She stood up. "Thank you for coming in, Dr. Rawlings. I expect you to call me immediately if you see this man again."

"Can I go with you? To Jackson's?"

The detective looked surprised. She shook her head. "I'm afraid it's a crime scene, Dr. Rawlings."

"I understand that, and I wouldn't get in the way or contaminate anything. I just want to make sure Jackson is all right. I mean, I know he didn't get hurt, but this has got to be upsetting for him."

"Well, I don't suppose I can stop you from driving over there," the detective said. "But stay out of the way."

"I will," Kate said. "Thank you."

As Kate hurried to her car, she wondered if the man in the booking photos had been at Jackson's home. Michael's former cellmate was interested in one thing—the Star. For the first time, it occurred to her that Michael could have hidden the Star in Jackson's home the night of the Summer Kickoff. If he had, he had put their friend in danger. For that matter, even if he hadn't, he had still put both Jackson and her in danger simply by leading his criminal friends to Eden.

"Damn you, Michael," she muttered, pulling out of the lot behind Detective Valentine's unmarked car. "Why couldn't you have just stayed gone?"

***

A marked unit and Sticks's unmarked were parked side-by-side in front of the open garage doors. A white Lexus Jo assumed belonged to Price occupied the center bay of the three-car garage. The other two bays were empty.

Jo had seen the opulent Tudor from the street but never close up. With two full stories and an attic, she guessed the house boasted at least 6,000 square feet of living space. Behind it she could see a spacious backyard with a large slate patio leading to what looked to be a fancy backyard grilling area. Beyond that was a garden with benches, tables, and a fountain. So this is how the one percent lives, she thought. Not too shabby.

Jackson Price was standing at the front of the cruiser. He looked stunned. He didn't move as she stepped from her car, but as Katherine Rawlings pulled in behind her, he came alive. He met Rawlings halfway to the house, and they hugged.

"Jackson, are you okay?"

"I'm fine, Katherine. When I saw my kitchen, I didn't go any farther. I was afraid they might still be in there." He shuddered and looked at Jo. "I've never had any trouble here. This has always been a safe neighborhood."

"I'm not sure there is such a thing in this day and age," Jo said. "Unfortunately. Would you excuse me a moment? I want to look around inside, but I'll want to talk with you after."

"Of course," Price said.

Jo noticed he was holding onto Rawlings arm as if he needed it to keep himself upright. She hoped the old man didn't have a heart condition and was suddenly glad Rawlings was there. He seemed to take comfort from her.

"We'll be in the garden." Rawlings nodded toward the back yard.

Inside Jo found a uniformed officer stationed at the door leading from the garage to the house. "Hey, Jeff," she said to the man.

"Back at you." He stood aside to let her enter the house. As she did, she noticed a security system keypad just inside the door.

The door led into a mud room and from there into a kitchen that Jo estimated was at least a third the size of her entire house. The shining granite countertops and gleaming stainless steel appliances looked out-of-place amid the clutter left by the burglars. The contents of the drawers, pantry, and refrigerator were strewn across the counters, much of it spilling onto the tiled floor.

She went through another door into a butler's pantry that connected the kitchen to the dining room, and from there into the living room. The butler's pantry had been searched but was less of a mess in that contents of cabinets remained on the countertops. The dining room was more or less in order, probably because the china cabinet and buffet had been the only two pieces of furniture to search. At a quick glance, it appeared that Price's china had not been damaged. Jo doubted it was out of respect but more because there had been no need to move it to verify that nothing was hidden under it.

The living room was a disaster. Sticks stood in the middle of the mess. When he saw her, he waved his hand at the overturned furniture with its stuffing oozing out of the slashes in the upholstery. "Deja vu all over again, huh?" he said. "Only with nicer stuff than the Nook."

"What's the rest of the house like?" Jo said.

"More of the same. Lena and Bob are on their way. I told them they might bring along a couple of their buddies since this is a big house."

"It *is* a big house," Jo said. "This would have taken some time."

"Dr. Price says he left for the university around seven-thirty this morning," Sticks said. "He got home just before four. So the jackasses that did this had plenty of time. Found an empty bread wrapper in the sink. Price said he had a half full loaf when he left this morning, so it looks like they even had time for lunch."

"I wonder how they knew he wouldn't come home for lunch."

"Maybe they didn't know. Maybe Price was just lucky."

Jo looked around at the trashed house. Price had been lucky, she thought. If he had come home and surprised this, she had little doubt they would be investigating another murder instead of a burglary. She walked over to the fireplace wall and picked up a painting of a western scene. In the lower right corner, she saw the name "Remington." If this was an original Remington—and she suspected it was—the burglars had seen fit not to take it. Glancing around she saw other paintings, prints, and sculptures lying amid the destroyed furniture.

"Our burglars appear to have left an awful lot of valuable items."

"It's the same in the rest of the house," Sticks said. "Price'll have to be the one to say for certain if anything is missing, but I've seen a bunch of what looks like valuable art, a pretty nice stereo, a couple computers, and even some jewelry in his bedroom. No TVs, though, but I also didn't see any TV stands so maybe he doesn't own one. Didn't see any medications in the bathroom or bedroom, so they might have been taken."

"I think we know what they were looking for. Question is, did they find it?"

She did a quick walk-through of the house. Every room, including the attic rooms, had been turned upside down, but in every room she saw objects of value. Even small objects, such as several pieces of diamond and gold jewelry, had been left. Apparently not only were the intruders uninterested in Price's valuables, they were uninterested in making it appear they were. Leaving the way she'd entered, she walked to the back of the lot. Price and Rawlings were huddled on a concrete bench in front of the small fountain. Rawlings was holding Price's hand, but neither was talking. They looked up as Jo approached.

"Detective?" Price's voice trembled.

"What you saw in the kitchen...," Jo hesitated, hating to tell the old man that his house was a shambles. "Well, the rest is pretty bad, too. They searched every room."

Price groaned and leaned against Rawlings.

"You say 'searched'," Rawlings said. "You think they were looking for the Star, don't you?"

Cuts right to the point, doesn't she, Jo thought. Not that it took a genius to come to that conclusion. "It's too early to say. But at first glance it doesn't look like anything has been stolen."

Price looked surprised. "Nothing?"

"Not that we can tell, but of course, you'll have to verify that. I can tell you that your computers, sound components, and a lot of artwork and jewelry are still in there. Did you keep any cash or guns in your home?"

"A little cash," Jackson said. "In my nightstand drawer. No more than a couple of hundred. No guns."

"What about televisions?" Jo said. "We didn't see any."

"I've never owned one, Detective." He drew himself up straight. "They are junk food for the mind."

Well, excuse me, Jo thought.

"What about medications?"

"I'm fortunate enough not to be on any," Price said. "Although I could certainly use a Valium now."

"I noticed you have a security system. Was it set?"

"No." He looked sheepish. "I'm afraid I only set it when I go on trips. I used it religiously when I first installed it, but like I said, this has always been a safe neighborhood. I got out of the habit of setting it years ago. I'm so sorry."

"Damn it!" Rawlings said. "This is all Michael's fault!"

"Katherine," Price began, but she stopped him.

"Jackson, what if you had come home while these people were still here? They knocked me out Monday night. Don't you think they'd have done that to you—or maybe worse?"

Jo hadn't thought Price could get any paler, but he did.

"You really think they were looking for the object that was stolen from the museum?" He looked from Rawlings to Jo and back again. "Why would they think it's here?"

"Because Michael was here Saturday night," Rawlings said. "They killed him, but they didn't find the Star."

"Do you think...," Price began but didn't finish.

"Do I think they found it here?" Rawlings finished for him. "I don't know. I hope so. Because if they didn't, what's next?"

After more conversation it was decided that Price would go with Rawlings to Holly House. The state forensic people would need a lot of time to process the scene. Jo informed Price not to expect the house to be cleared until the next morning at the earliest. She would call him when it was okay for him to return and would go through the house with him to determine if anything was missing.

"I think you should plan on staying at Holly House for the weekend," she said. "The house will need a lot of straightening up."

"You'll have help, Jackson," Rawlings said. "You won't have to deal with this on your own."

They left soon after for Holly House, leaving Price's car since he was in no condition to drive. Jo watched them pull out. Rawlings was right. Mabry had brought a lot of trouble with him when he ran to Eden. His partners weren't going to quit until they found the Star. If simple searches didn't yield results, it was easy enough to figure out what the next step was likely to be.

Chapter 25

Kate's Thursday evening class wasn't as much of a distraction from all that was going on as her Monday night class had been. News of her attack had spread among her students. Each expressed concern for her well-being and agreed they would all leave for their cars as a group. They seemed to think the attack was random or connected to the recent burglaries and that they might be at risk. Kate didn't disabuse them of that conclusion. She didn't want to get into the whole sordid Michael and Star story and couldn't think of any way to tell them what was really going on without getting into that. Still, she felt a little guilty for not relieving their anxiety.

She tried to concentrate on her students and their creative writing attempts, but her attention kept wandering back to Jackson and the break-in at his home. He had looked so frail when she'd left Holly House that she'd been tempted to cancel class, but she knew he was in good hands with Ann and Edna. If anyone could distract him from what had happened, they could. Jackson had a lot of people who cared about him—herself included—and he would get through this. What worried her was what might still be to come.

Kate had given Lou a quick call on the way to class. Lou had just gotten off the phone with Eden P.D. a few minutes before Kate called and was as upset as Kate was. Lou promised either she or one of her officers would be there to escort Kate to her car that evening, so she wasn't surprised to see Lou waiting in the hall as she and the others filed through the door at the end of class. However, she was surprised to see Chris Irons.

"Hey, girlfriend." Lou gave her a quick hug. "I stopped by to escort you to your car and found out you already have a guard."

Chris looked embarrassed. "I heard about what happened Monday night. I had some work I needed to do anyway, so I just hung around. Lou was just telling me about the break-in at Jackson's. Is he okay?"

"Physically, he's fine." Kate felt a little awkward and noticed Lou watching her, a smile on her face. "He's obviously upset. They left his house in shambles."

"Surely he's not staying there?"

"No, he's at Holly House, at least for the weekend. The police are going over the house now. The detective said it would probably be okay for him to go back tomorrow, but it's going to take a lot of work before he can move back in. I told him I would get some people together to help him. Would you be able to help?"

"Glad to," Chris said. "I'm sure I can count on Jerry—my TA—as well."

"Which reminds me," Kate said. "I never got a chance to thank you and Jerry for straightening my office. I really appreciate it."

Kate noticed Lou's eyebrows go up a notch.

Chris waved it off. "The least we could do."

The three of them began walking down the hall. Kate's students had left in a group after seeing she had people waiting for her. As they reached the stairs, Kate heard them leaving the building two floors below. As they descended, they talked about what had happened and decided that Kate would give Chris and Lou a call once Jackson had been given the all-clear to return to his house. Separating in the parking lot, she thanked Chris again and watched him drive off.

"Well, well, well," Lou said. "I think you have an admirer, girlfriend."

"He's just a nice person," Kate said. "I'm sure he's worried about Jackson."

"I think he's more worried about you."

Kate ignored that. "Have the police told you anything they haven't told us?"

"Nope," Lou said. "Jo thinks the doers were looking for the Star, but you already know that. She's concerned if they didn't find it, they may escalate their efforts to something a little more direct. Unfortunately Eden doesn't have the manpower to give either you or Jackson any protection other than increased patrols around Holly House. That's why I'm here tonight and why I'm following you home and making sure you get inside."

"Thank you." Kate felt tears sting her eyes. "This has been a truly shitty week. I don't know what I would have done without you."

"That's what friends are for."

"I feel so bad for Jackson. Everything was going great for him—a successful book, a movie, even retirement. He was on top of the world and now this." She shook her head. "Remember how worried we were that Michael had come back to hit Jackson up for more money? I wish that's all it had been."

"No kidding! I knew Michael was bad news the minute I saw he was back, but I had no idea how bad. But we'll get through this, Kate, and we'll make sure Jackson does, too." She opened Kate's door. "Now get in your car and let's get you home. I've got a horny husband waiting for me."

Chapter 26

Chief Brody Daniels looked tanned and rested after his Hawaiian vacation. One of those jiggly Hawaiian hula dolls meant for car dashboards sat on one corner of his desk, along with a new picture frame containing a 5" x 7" photograph of Daniels and his wife, Gloria, posed smiling in brightly printed Hawaiian shirts, leis draped around their necks, the brilliant blue Pacific in the background.

"Looks like you had a good time." Jo nodded at the picture as she sat down in the chair across from Daniels. "Welcome back."

"We had a great time," Daniels said. "Gotta say, though, I'm glad to be home. The older I get, the more I hate being away from my own bed. Never can get a decent night's sleep when I travel. Although considering all that's going on, maybe I should have extended my trip."

Brody Daniels was a big man, both in height and girth, with thinning gray hair and a quick smile. He'd played center for the Eden High football team but surprised everyone when he turned down a football scholarship offered by the University of Louisville. Instead, he enrolled at Eastern, majoring in criminal justice. After all these years, it was still talked about around town. Nick had asked him about it once at a department barbecue. Daniels told him that all he'd ever wanted to be was a cop. He had made it through high school football with no injuries, but as the time for college neared, he decided he was pushing his luck. He didn't want an injury from a sport that was just a game to him to derail his chances to do what he really wanted to do.

"Before you fill me in on your murder investigation, though, I gotta ask you about a rumor I heard this morning."

"You mean that we might have some Chicago thugs in town looking for the artifact stolen from the Drayer Museum?"

"Heard about that, too, but that's not what I meant. I heard you're leaving us."

"What?" Jo was surprised. She hadn't told anyone at the department, not even Sticks, about Nick's new job. The news must have originated at Eden Steel before traveling the Eden grapevine to the department.

"I understand Nick's leaving Eden Steel for a high-paying job in D.C.," Daniels said.

"He's going to D.C. I'm not."

"Uh-oh." Daniels leaned back in his chair. "Guess I just stuck my nose in something that was none of my business."

"No problem," Jo said. "You have a right to know if one of your people's quitting on you."

"You okay with this?"

"I'm okay," Jo said. "We're going to try the long distance marriage thing. D.C. isn't all that far away. But I'm not kidding myself about how it's probably going to end up. Things haven't been great between us for a long time."

Daniels looked sad. "I'm sorry to hear that. I'm glad I'm not losing one of my people, but I hate to hear about anyone's marriage coming apart."

"Yeah, well, who knows? Maybe a little distance between us will reignite the spark." She knew she sounded flippant, but she really didn't want to dwell on her home life right now.

The evening before she and Nick had finally sat down for a long and reasonably civilized discussion. He wanted his new job as much as she wanted to keep her old one, which didn't leave many options. They finally decided to give a long distance marriage a try. With his new salary, it wouldn't be a financial hardship for him to fly home frequently or for her to fly to D.C. Nonstop flights from either Lexington or Charleston, West Virginia, only took about an hour, so travel time wasn't a big issue either.

That decided, the only thing left was telling Brianna. They ate a pleasant dinner together and then FaceTimed her in her dorm room at Ohio State. She took it well, congratulating her dad and telling Jo she was glad they weren't selling their home and moving. The relief that Jo felt was reflected on Nick's face when they hung up. They celebrated with a glass of wine, followed by another, and Nick returned to the master bedroom that night.

"When's Nick starting in D.C.?" Daniels said.

"Monday. He's driving up tomorrow. He's going to stay in one of those hotels that have efficiency apartments until he finds a place to rent or buy."

"I hope it works out, Jo. I really do."

"Guess we'll find out," Jo said. "Now about the murder and the Chicago thugs...."

For the next hour Jo filled Daniels in, starting with the phone call from the Chicago detective and ending with the break-in at Price's. "Sticks and I met Dr. Price at his home this morning. As far as he could tell, nothing is missing. He had cash in a nightstand, and even it was left."

"You think they were looking for the Star?"

"That's my take on it. Mabry was at Price's just hours before he was killed. He would have had the opportunity to hide the Star on Price's property. Whether he did and, if he did, whether it's been found is anybody's guess."

"What about the Applegates? Are they talking yet about the watch and ring?"

"Roy Prescott left a message this morning," Jo said. Prescott was the Applegates' attorney. Since he wasn't a public defender, Jo figured Robbie Applegate was paying the toll for his useless progeny. "Said his clients are ready to deal."

"Are we?"

Jo shrugged. "Depends on what they have to say. I don't see them for the murder, but I'm sure Prescott's made it clear we've got enough to charge them with it. We linked the biggest share of the items found in their trailer to the most recent burglaries, so we've got them on possession of stolen goods. And there's the pills and meth they had stashed in their dresser drawer, so they're not going anywhere. The best they can hope for is no murder charge and a good word to the D.A. on sentencing for the other charges, and Prescott knows it."

"Are Dr. Price and Dr. Rawlings in danger?"

"If the Star wasn't found at Price's, yes," Jo said. "Lou Pelfrey is a old friend of both of them. She's putting her officers on overtime to provide extra protection in Hanover Hall while they're at the university. Rawlings has two evening classes a week, and campus police will escort her home. Our guys know to make extra patrols by the Holly House where both Rawlings and Price are staying."

"All right." Daniels nodded his approval. "When are you talking to the Applegates?"

Jo looked at her watch. "In an hour."

"Catch me when you're done. I want to know what they said. Besides, by then I'll need a break from the paperwork that piled up while I was gone."

***

"Sorry, Cal," Mike said when Cal answered his cell. "Nothing on the prints. Good clean sets on both items, too, but the guy's not in the system."

"Damn it!"

Ginger had made good on her promise to get the mysterious Mr. Jones's fingerprints. She had brought him both the water glass and the coffee cup used by Jones at breakfast the day before, and he had overnighted them to Chicago. The more he'd thought about the new guest, the more he'd convinced himself that the man had some connection to Mabry and the Star. Was that just wishful thinking, he wondered now? While his wild goose chase had proven correct in so far as Mabry running to Eden, the Star was still in play. He was no closer to finding it now than he'd been when he boarded the plane in Chicago. Maybe he had latched onto the idea of the odd man down the hall being involved just to make himself feel better.

"What about the description I gave you?"

"Andy and I have asked around, but nobody seems to recognize the man. Or so they claim. The description you sent sounds like an average Joe, and that by itself should make him stand out in Duda's crowd. Everybody we talk to claims to know nothing about the Drayer, Mabry, Halsey, or this dude, and that makes me think they know a lot but are too afraid to talk."

"Yeah, well, no big surprise there. Duda scares the shit out of everybody."

"If you could get a picture, maybe that would help."

Cal had hoped to snap a picture of Jones with his cell, but so far he'd had no chance to do so without being spotted. When Jones was at Holly House, he kept to his room except for breakfast where he sat with his back to a wall and faced the rest of the room. Cal tried to follow him once when he'd left Holly House but lost him within a few blocks. Cal didn't think it was simply luck that Jones had evaded him. The man had been watching for a tail and only someone with something to hide did that.

"I'm working on it," he said. "I don't suppose the Halseys have turned up back home?"

"Haven't seen them. Anything new down there besides this guy?"

"Oh, yeah," Cal said and proceeded to bring Mike up-to-date on the break-in at Price's.

Cal had been enjoying the Holly House's spacious front porch when Rawlings had shown up with Price. The old man had looked pretty shaky. Rawlings had her arm around him, supporting him, and Cal jumped up to get the door for them before taking Price's other arm and helping Rawlings get him into the parlor. After they told Ann and Edna what had happened, he helped Rawlings get Price to his room.

"It looks like Kentucky is where the action is," Mike said after he finished. "Which leads me to ask, you need some help?"

Cal thought for a moment. "Not yet," he said. "You and Andy need to be there in case the Halseys show up. But if they don't return to the roost this weekend, I can use all the help I can get."

"If you do, it'll have to be somebody other than Andy or me. You talked to Foreman lately?"

"Been sending him email updates every day but haven't talked to him since Sunday. Why?"

"Andy's off the case for now. Called the office Monday. His sister in Phoenix was in a bad accident and is in the hospital. Sounded like she's in pretty bad shape. We don't know how long he'll be off. Foreman about had a litter of kittens. You know how freaked he is over the Star, and now he's losing one of the people familiar with the case."

"So who's helping you out up there?"

"Foreman assigned Jack Lennox and Helen White. If you decide you need help, we'll send one of them down. Foreman figures it's best to have someone who's been in on this from the beginning in each place, and he's probably right."

Cal thought for a moment. Now that Foreman had assigned two people to take Andy's place, there wasn't a good reason not to have somebody working with him in Kentucky except for the fact that he didn't want anybody looking over his shoulder. He preferred to work alone on this case for as long as he could.

"Let's play it this way," he said. "Keep Jack and Helen up there for the weekend. Gives them some time to get up to speed and gives you two extra pairs of eyes to keep a watch for the Halseys. If they don't show up by Monday, send Jack down to me. Helen's got a husband who might not like her being out of town with a good-looking guy like me."

Mike laughed. "You keep thinkin' that, Casanova."

They talked for a few minutes more and hung up. One more weekend, Cal thought. Two more days to take care of business.

***

Ivan Applegate looked bad. Not that he looked good on the best of days, Jo thought, what with the rotten teeth and sores on his face compliments of his meth use. But now, at least twenty-four hours after his last meth hit, he really looked like shit. He looked like he was ready to fall asleep on the interrogation room table, while at the same time he couldn't seem to sit still.

"Hey, can I get some coffee and something to eat?" he said as soon as Jo, Lewis, and Roy Prescott stepped through the door.

"Good morning to you, too, Ivan," Donnie said. "Yes, I'm doing well. Thanks for asking."

"Aw, come on, Detective Lewis," Ivan whined. "I got a headache and I'm hungry and you wanna yank my chain."

Jo set the coffee she was carrying on the table. "This is the best we can do for now, Ivan."

"Thank you, Detective Valentine." Ivan drank a third of the cup before setting it down, seemingly oblivious to the hot liquid. He leaned back in the chair and sighed. "Man, I needed that."

Two chairs were arranged on each side of the interrogation table, Ivan occupying one. Roy Prescott took the chair next to Ivan, while Jo and Lewis took the other two. Jo knew Tommy Applegate and Linda Carter, Prescott's associate, were similarly arranged in the station's only other interrogation room with Sticks and Rick Samuels.

"Mr. Prescott tells us you're ready to have a meaningful conversation, Ivan," Donnie said.

"As long as we have some assurances that Mr. Applegate's cooperation will be rewarded," Prescott said.

"We don't reward murderers," Jo said.

"Murderer!" Ivan sat up straight. "I didn't kill nobody!"

Prescott put a hand on Ivan's arm and shook his head at him. "My client had nothing to do with Michael Mabry's death. All you have on him and his son is possession of stolen property and drug possession."

"We have them dead to rights on those charges," Donnie said. "But I think a jury can put two and two together and get murder when they hear your clients sold a ring and watch that the victim was wearing when he was killed."

"What if my client has information about Mabry's murder?" Prescott said. "Can we be assured that you will not press charges for murder?"

"You can't be assured of anything," Jo said. "Just because Ivan tells us he's innocent and claims to have information isn't proof to us he didn't do the deed."

"But," Donnie picked it up, "if what he tells us checks out, then we won't hit him with a murder charge. And we might consider putting in a good word for him regarding sentencing on the other charges."

Prescott went through the motions. He frowned, tapping his pen on his legal pad and sighing a few times before nodding at Ivan. It was all an act, Jo knew. Prescott had to make it look like he was earning his fee. "Go ahead, Mr. Applegate. Tell them what you told me."

"Sure, sure." Ivan bobbed his head, passing his coffee cup back and forth in his hands. "Yeah, me and Tommy stole some money and a watch and ring from that dead guy. We went through his car first, but there wasn't nothin' worth takin' so that's why we took the watch and ring. We didn't want to touch him, you know, but we had to get something."

He looked at them as if waiting for them to agree with him. When no one said anything, he took a quick gulp of coffee and continued. "Anyways, we took that stuff. But we didn't kill him. He was already dead."

"You ever heard that story before, Jo?" Donnie turned to her. "Dude cops to a lesser crime, hoping it will make us believe him when he says he didn't do the more serious one?"

"All the time. You'd think the dudes would learn a new story."

"I'm tellin' you the truth!" Ivan protested. "We wasn't even gonna do anything around Hanover. My dad works there. I don't like to cause him no trouble."

"Now that's really sweet," Donnie said. "Don't you think so, Jo?"

"I do," Jo said. "So if you weren't going to do anything around Hanover, what were you doing there?"

"We was on our way to Fenton Hall. We figured we'd hit an office or two in there, maybe some cars if there was any around."

Fenton Hall, which housed offices and classrooms for the Botany department, was located on the right of Hanover Hall. It had been one of the first to experience office burglaries, but that had been several months ago.

"So what changed your mind, Ivan?" she said.

"We was already at Fenton, workin' on the door lock," Ivan said. "We heard some dudes arguing, kind of yellin', you know? Then we heard a gunshot. We got curious."

"You got curious?" Donnie said. "Now I've heard it all. Two meth heads breaking into a building hear a gunshot and go toward it because they got curious? Either the meth has burned out your brain, or you're lying through your teeth!"

"We just wanted to see what was goin' on." Ivan looked petulant. "Ain't no law against looking, is there?"

"Lordy!" Donnie rolled his eyes and looked at the ceiling.

"What did you do?" Jo said.

"We sneaked over there." Ivan shot Donnie a dirty look and directed his comments to Jo. "We was workin' on the back door at Fenton's so when we heard the shot we ran to the other side and then came around the front. Then we sneaked along the front of Fenton and over to Hanover. We was just about to come around the other side where the parking lot is when we saw the truck."

Jo and Donnie looked at one another. "What truck?" Jo said.

"The one that was haulin' ass out of the parking lot," Ivan said. "It come around the corner of the building, goin' real fast. Me and my boy could have been hit if we'd stepped out about then."

Hanover Hall's parking lot was located at the rear of the building. The original entrance to it was a drive that passed along the opposite side of Hanover from Fenton. Around the time Jo had come to town, the city and university had created a new street running behind both buildings' lots, each of which now had an entrance from that street, as well as the original drives.

"You're saying the truck was on the drive that runs along the side of the building?"

"Yeah, that's right." Ivan bobbed his head. "It was goin' real fast. When it got to the end of the driveway, it turned right and really hauled ass."

"Could you see who was in it?"

"Are you kiddin'? It was goin' too fast, and we was hidin' up against the building."

"What did you do then?"

"We thought maybe we ought to get out of there, too, but we still wanted to see what happened, so we went on back to the lot. That's when we saw the dead guy. Wasn't nobody around and the lights aren't real bright right there, so we tossed his car. Didn't find a damn thing."

Ivan seemed to resent the fact that the murder victim hadn't been considerate enough to leave valuables in his car.

"We knew we wasn't gonna have time to do Fenton what with the dead guy and all, so we checked him out real quick. What else could we do? Anyways, we got a couple hundred out of his wallet and the watch and ring. Then we hauled ass."

"Did you see anyone else around?" Jo said.

"Hell, no! You think we'd stuck around if we had?" Ivan looked at her as if he found it hard to believe she was that dense.

"Let's go back to the truck," Jo said. "Can you describe it?"

"Sure. It weren't real new. An F-150. And red. It was red. Hey, can I get somethin' to eat now?"

Chapter 27

The light was just beginning to fade from the sky as Kate climbed the stairs to her room, feeling the ache in muscles she didn't know she had. She had spent the day at Jackson's with Lou, Roger, Ann, Ginger, Chris, and Jerry. Linza and Mary had helped out in the morning, while Georgia, Mark, and Bill had put in a couple of hours in the afternoon between other commitments.

The only member of the summer staff who hadn't shown up to help was Paul Holland. Not that his absence surprised anyone. Jackson informed her that Paul had stormed into his office the day before, demanding that Jackson retract his nomination of her for chair, his reason being that she was "involved in a sordid murder." He made a point of telling Jackson he had personally witnessed her being "intimate with the victim in a car on a public street."

Paul had picked a bad day to demand anything of Jackson, who wasn't in the best of moods after the trouble at his home. Jackson told him that the search committee members were perfectly capable of making their own decisions about the unsuitability of a candidate, be it for undesirable personal relationships outside the university or for gossipmongering within it. That hadn't gone over well with Paul, according to Jackson, who chuckled as he told the story.

Several grad students popped in and out during the day as well. Many of the men owned pickup trucks, and several loads of items that couldn't be salvaged were taken to the county landfill. Jackson held up well, but several times Kate saw his eyes mist up as he watched his trashed possessions being hauled away.

She and Lou spent most of the day getting the kitchen in order. It was one of the worst rooms in the house, thanks to food items from cabinets, fridge, and freezer having been opened and dumped.

Only items too small to contain the Star had been left intact. Ann had left an hour or so before Kate, and Jackson had ridden back to Holly House with her. He was probably asleep by now or close to it. The whole experience had been hard on him.

She showered, dressed in her most comfortable pajamas, and had just settled in bed with a paperback that she didn't expect to read much of before nodding off, when her cell rang. The display showed the caller was Steven.

"Hi, Stevie," she said.

"Kate." The tone of his voice caused her to sit up straight in the bed. She could hear noises in the background. "It's Mom. She collapsed. The EMTs are here and getting ready to take her to the hospital."

"Oh, my God!" Kate threw the paperback aside and swung her legs out of bed. "What happened? Did she fall?"

"They think she's had a stroke." Steven's voice broke on the last word.

"I'll be right there," Kate said.

"No, no, the ambulance is getting ready to leave. Meet us at the hospital."

"Okay." Kate held the phone in one hand while pulling jeans and a T-shirt from the dresser. "Have you called Dad?"

"Believe it or not, he was here when it happened. He's riding to the hospital with me," Steven said. "Listen, I gotta go, sis. They're wheeling her to the ambulance now."

She hung up, dressed quickly in the jeans and T-shirt, and at the last minute threw on a light jacket. She knew she'd probably be at the hospital for hours, and the A/C could be chilly. Dropping her phone in her jacket pocket, she grabbed her keys and purse and hurried out the door. As she descended the stairs, Ann came from the direction of the kitchen. Kate quickly filled her in on the news.

"Edna and I will meet you there," Ann said.

"Thank you," Kate said, blinking back tears. "Don't bother Jackson, though. If he finds out what's going on, I know he'll want to come, and he needs his rest after all he's been through."

Ann was heading toward Edna's rooms at the rear of the house as Kate hurried out the front door. Neither of them noticed the Holly's latest guest standing quietly in the shadows at the top of the stairs. As the door closed behind Kate, he descended quickly and followed her outside.

***

Jo and Sticks had picked Johnny up at his house Saturday morning and interrogated him off and on during the day for all the good it did. He continued to deny he'd killed Mabry, but he was unconcerned that he might be charged with the murder. Jo thought she saw a fleeting look of surprise in his eyes when she told him they had a witness who had seen his pickup leaving the Hanover lot, but he'd remained unruffled. He had also remained unruffled when they told him they were having trouble locating his son, Adam.

Vera's record check on the younger Crouch—now forty-five years old—had turned up a juvenile record in Eden, but nothing since. Lexington was a different story. He was a frequent flier in their jail, having been picked up several times for drunk and disorderly, twice for DUI, once for petty theft, and twice for assault. Booze was his drug of choice, according to the Lexington officer Vera spoke with, and bar fights his favorite form of recreation.

At his last arrest, six months earlier, he'd been living in a weather-beaten frame house in Lexington that had been divided into sleeping rooms with a shared bath. A Lexington patrol unit checked but reported back the landlord told them he'd kicked Adam out four months earlier for nonpayment of rent, and, no, he didn't know where he'd gone.

Jo wasn't sure she believed Johnny when he said he didn't know the whereabouts of his son, any more than she believed him when he said it wasn't his truck the witness saw leaving Hanover Hall's lot, but they didn't have enough to charge him. They'd had to release him just after dark.

"I don't know about you, but I'm ready for some shuteye," Sticks said now, stretching, his back making popping noises that could be heard from across the room.

"Head on out," she said. She was as tired as Sticks, but he had a wife waiting for him at home. Her house was empty. "I've got the paperwork."

"I won't fight you for it." Just as he stood, his desk phone rang.

"Probably Lois wanting me to pick something up on the way home," he said as he picked up the receiver. He listened for a minute, his posture straightening.

"We got it." He hung up. "That was dispatch. Katherine Rawlings's mama had a stroke and was taken to the hospital. Rawlings left Holly House half an hour ago, but never made it there. She's missing."

Chapter 28

Well, this is certainly a cliche, Kate thought. Being forced into the trunk of a car, then tied to a chair in what appears to be a cheap motel room—you would think the Halseys and Mr. Jones could come up with something more original. Michael had certainly been associating with people who did not share his own creative abilities.

On the other hand, she *was* tied to the chair, no one knew where she was, and they did have guns. Their methods might be cliche, but she couldn't deny their effectiveness.

She had just unlocked her car in the Holly House lot when someone had grabbed her, holding his hand over her nose and mouth until she passed out. When she came to, she was bouncing around in the dark, a strange humming noise all around her. Confused at first, she nearly panicked when she tried to sit up and her head hit something above her. For a few terrifying seconds, she thought she had been buried alive—such thoughts likely the result of seeing too many B-movies over the years—but then memory came flooding back and with it common sense. She realized she was in the trunk of a car, likely put there by Michael's partners. When the car stopped moving a few minutes later and the trunk opened, she had expected to see Wendell Halsey peering down at her. Instead, she was surprised to see the man who had checked into Holly House a few days before—Jones, she thought his name was. Edna had remarked he was a "strange one," and Ginger said he gave her the creeps.

Now, tied to a chair, her fingertips starting to go numb, she watched Mr. Jones flick open a switchblade knife. Except for the movement of his hand on the knife, he was motionless, the expression on his face blank. Ginger's assessment of his creepiness was dead on. Kate shivered, unable to pull her eyes from the gleaming blade.

Wendell Halsey sat on the side of the bed, a semi-automatic handgun in his lap, his eyes locked on Jones. Kate had the impression he was as frightened of Jones as she was. The woman Halsey had introduced as his wife outside the diner—Gabriella, Nan had said her name was—was standing by the bed, going through the contents of Kate's purse that were dumped on the bed. When Jones had pulled her out of the trunk, he'd searched her, running his hands in her pockets and her bra and crotch. If she hadn't been so repulsed by his touch, she might have found it amusing that he thought she would hide a $15 million dollar jewel in her underwear.

"What do you want?" Kate was surprised her voice wasn't shaking. "Where are we?"

Jones didn't answer. He was taller than Kate had realized from only seeing him seated in the dining room, but he stood with his shoulders hunched and his head pushed forward, like a vulture with its eye on dead meat. He began to stroke the blade of the knife, his fingers moving up and down its length.

"Anything?" he said, without looking away from Kate.

"Nothing," Gabriella said. "No phone in her purse either."

It wasn't the Star Jones had been looking for when he searched her. It was her cell phone. But then why hadn't he found it? Kate tried to remember what she had done with it. Surely she must have picked it up before rushing out to go to the hospital. She always kept it with her. Had she been so upset over the news of her mother's stroke that she left it on her dresser?

"Where are we?" she said again. "What do you want with me?"

"Where is your phone?" Jones asked, ignoring her questions.

"I don't know where my phone is! I don't know where I am!" Kate's vision blurred as her eyes filled with tears. She blinked them back, furious with herself for showing weakness to this monster.

"You are in a cabin in the woods," Jones said. "No one can hear you if you scream, but if you do, I will use this knife to cut out your tongue. I won't kill you because I have a question I need you to answer, but I will cut out your tongue. Then you'll have to write the answer to my question. Do you understand?"

Kate nodded, her mouth going dry. A cabin in the woods, he'd said. On the inside of the door, she could see a piece of paper framed in plastic like that found on motel room doors. So this isn't a private cabin, she thought, but a rental. When she'd been growing up here, there had been several motels with freestanding cabins instead of connected rooms. She guessed she was in one of them now, but she was not encouraged by the realization. If they were like she remembered, most were isolated in wooded areas with each cabin well removed from the others.

"What do you want?" she said again, even though she knew exactly what they wanted.

"I want what was stolen from us," Jones said. "I want the Star."

"I don't know what you mean," she tried.

"Oh, I think you do, Professor Rawlings."

Jones leaned over her suddenly, one hand resting on the chair seat, the other pressing the flat part of the knife blade against her neck, his face inches from her own, his lips slightly parted. He rubbed the knife slowly across her skin and exhaled slowly. She felt his breath fan her cheeks and smelled a hint of garlic mixed with what smelled like rotting vegetation. She turned her head in revulsion, trying hard to ignore the cold of the metal against her skin.

"I didn't know Michael was involved in the theft." She averted her eyes from his. "Not until after you murdered him, and the police told me."

Jones chuckled, moved the hand holding the knife and poked the tip of it under the point of her chin. She yelped at the sudden sharp pain.

"I'll cut out your tongue if you scream," he said. "I'll do more if you lie."

From the time Kate woke up in the trunk of her car until now, she had felt as if she were in a movie or a novel. On some level she recognized she was in denial, that she should be afraid, but with the mind of an author, she had edited the experience—too cliche, too B-movie, over-the-top threats, an overdrawn villain. Now, as she felt a trickle of blood dribble down her throat, reality snapped into focus. This wasn't a novel or a movie. The man standing before her was very real. She could no longer deny the danger she was in.

Behind him she saw Gabriella staring at her, face pale, eyes wide. Her right hand gripped Wendell's arm hard, the nails pressing into his skin. He didn't seem to notice. He wasn't looking at her but at Jones, his fear evident. They were criminals, Kate thought, but they weren't like Jones. They would be no help because they were afraid of him.

She looked back into Jones's blank dead eyes and felt her bladder threaten to loosen. He was going to hurt her and then he was going to kill her. And there was nothing she could do about it.

***

While Sticks went to Eden General to get statements from the Hills, Jo headed for Holly House, followed by a uniformed officer. According to the Hills, only thirty minutes had elapsed between the time Rawlings had left the house and the time they'd arrived at the hospital and found she wasn't there. Dispatch confirmed there were no reports of accidents or stalled vehicles, so the best place to start was the last place Rawlings had been seen.

As she pulled into the Holly House lot, she saw Rawlings's car. A quick check showed it was empty. She instructed the uniformed officer to make sure no one entered the lot and went to the door. She'd check first to verify that Rawlings hadn't returned to Holly House for some reason, and then she'd examine the lot for any indication she'd been taken.

As Jo stepped onto the front porch, Cal Becker opened the door. He was holding his cell, a worried look on his face. "Ann just called. She says Rawlings is missing."

"We don't know that for sure yet." Jo stepped into the foyer. "But it doesn't look good. Her car's in the lot. I don't suppose she came back for some reason."

"I've been downstairs ever since Ann and Edna left," Cal said. "I heard the women talking and came down. Ann told me what happened. I told her I'd stay down here in case anyone showed up wanting a room, but no one's come in and that includes Rawlings. We can knock on her door to be sure."

They did, but just as expected, there was no answer. Jo tried to decide if the circumstances justified entering the room without a warrant. She could claim she needed to make sure Rawlings wasn't lying inside in need of help, but considering Becker had been in a position to see whether Rawlings had returned, she doubted it would fly. So if she did find something linking Rawlings to the Star and the murder, it would likely be thrown out in court. Disappointed, she turned back to the stairs. Probably for the best anyway, she thought. The main thing now was that the woman was missing.

"Stick around," she said to Becker. "I want to look around the lot."

"Need help?"

"No. I've got a uniform for that."

It didn't take long to find the keys at the rear of an empty parking space. Two Ford keys and a small plastic drugstore discount card were attached to a key chain holding a small pewter novel with the name Agatha Christie and the outline of a train—the Orient Express, Jo guessed—on one side and a quote from the famous lady of mystery on the other. It was a good bet they belonged to Rawlings. It was also a good bet she hadn't dropped them voluntarily.

Back inside, she told Becker what she had found. He stood silent for few seconds before heading for the stairs.

"Where are you going?"

"You might not want to know," he said.

"I do want to know. Right now."

At the top of the stairs, he turned right and stopped two doors down. He knocked hard, waited, and pounded again. When there was no answer, he pulled a set of lock picks from his pants pocket and went to work on the door's lock.

"What the hell...what's going on, Becker?"

He stopped and looked at her. "Why don't you just go back downstairs, Detective Valentine."

"I'm not going anywhere. What do you know that I don't?"

"A new guest checked in this past Monday night. Goes by the name of William Jones. This is his room. Something about him isn't right. I think he's one of Duda's guys."

"You have any proof of that?"

"Not a bit," Cal said. "But he's had my antennae quivering ever since I saw him in the dining room Tuesday morning. When I was on the department, I learned to pay attention to that quiver. Rawlings is missing, but her car's in the lot. I saw him come in earlier this evening, but now he's not in his room. He drives a rental, a blue Focus with Kentucky tags. Did you see it in the lot?"

"No," Jo said. "Only cars in the lot are the ones belonging to you and Rawlings."

"I'm going in this room and having a look around, Detective," Cal said. "Unless you arrest me. Are you going to do that?"

Jo looked at him for several seconds before reaching into her jacket pocket. She pulled out two pairs of latex gloves and handed him one. "Don't forget your gloves."

He smiled, slipped them on and had the door open within fifteen seconds.

The room was a disappointment. William Jones traveled light—one suitcase, still holding his underwear and socks—and two pairs of pants and three shirts in the closet. No discarded papers in the wastebasket, no used boarding passes to indicate where Jones had come from, not even any empty food containers. It wasn't normal for someone to be this careful about what he left laying around his room. Jo felt her own antennae begin to quiver.

"Maybe we can get some prints." She spread gloved fingers on the inside of the used bathroom glass and pulled an evidence bag from her pocket. "Find out who this guy is."

"Don't bother," Cal said. "Been there, done that, got nothing."

"You ran prints?"

"Yep. Got his coffee cup and water glass from breakfast one day—had a little help, of course," he said. "Overnighted them to Chicago. Got good prints, but he's not in the system."

"Not doubting your methods…," Jo said, bagging the glass.

"Suit yourself."

"I'll get the description of his car on the air," she said, "Patrol might spot him. You said it has Kentucky tags. You wouldn't happen to have the number, would you?"

"So glad you asked," Cal said.

Chapter 29

Kate felt the chair scoot sideways as she was knocked back and to the right with the force of the slap Jones had delivered. Tears welled up in her eyes, both from the pain and from fear.

"Did you like that?" he said. "We can do this all night. I don't mind at all."

"I don't *know* where the Star is!" Her voice broke. "I swear Michael never told me anything about it."

Halsey and his wife had jumped from the bed when Leonard slapped her. They were fidgeting, looking at one another as if they thought they ought to be doing something.

"Hey, Leonard," Halsey said in a high shaky voice. He sounded like a scared little boy about to ask a bully to take it easy. "Maybe we should call Baby. Whaddya' think?"

So his name isn't William, Kate thought, but Leonard. Interesting to know but hardly helpful at the moment. William or Leonard, he is still going to kill me. I'm going to die in a cheap room at the hands of a psycho, and there's nothing I can do about it. She tried to hold back the tears, but in spite of not wanting to let the man see her cry, she began to sob quietly.

"I think," Leonard said, without looking at Halsey, "that all Mr. Duda wants to hear is that we have located the Star."

"But what if she's telling the truth?" Halsey persisted. "Maybe the Professor really didn't tell her anything. Maybe he hid it somewhere before he even got to Eden."

"If that's the case," Leonard said. "This lovely woman will have suffered and died for nothing. As will Dr. Price."

Kate stopped crying at the mention of Jackson.

"Ah, I think I hit a sore spot. You care for the old man, don't you?"

Kate glared at him, fear for herself forgotten for the moment. He would kill her and then he would go after Jackson. The way Jackson looked when he found his home had been violated flashed into her mind—how frail he had looked, how old and vulnerable. This monster had done that to Jackson.

"If you don't tell me what I want to know," he said, "when I'm done with you, I will visit the esteemed Dr. Price. I might keep you alive so you can watch. Would you enjoy that?"

"You sick bastard!" She looked at Halsey, blinking back tears. "You don't seem like a bad person. Are you going to let him do this?"

Halsey stared at her, his Adam's apple bobbing in his throat. Kate could see the torture sickened him, but his fear of Leonard was greater than his desire to see it stopped.

"I know who you are," she said. "Your name is Wendell Halsey. You and Michael were in prison together. You were his friend. So was I. Would he want you to let this happen to me?"

"How do you know my name? Did the Professor tell you about me?"

"If by 'the Professor,' you mean Michael, no, he didn't. He never talked about any of you. Or the Star." She glared at Leonard. "Like I keep telling you."

"Then how do you know my name?"

"A reporter showed me your picture. She got it from Chicago. The police have it, too, and they've been looking for you in Eden. She told me about your wife, too, how she's the sister of some gangster." She nodded at Gabriella. The woman stepped behind her husband, as if to shield herself from Kate.

"Shit!" Halsey ran a hand through his hair, leaving the top sticking up in spikes. "Shit, shit, shit!"

"Calm down," Leonard said.

"Calm down? Calm *down?* The cops aren't looking for you! You're a damn ghost! They know my name and they got my picture and they know about Gabby."

"All the more reason for us to complete our task quickly." Leonard turned back to Kate. "One more time—where is the Star?"

"I don't know." She began to cry, hating herself for it, but unable to stop. "Please...I really don't know."

This time the front chair legs came off the floor.

***

Jackson Price reached for the whiskey with a trembling hand, gave it up and picked the glass up with both hands. He took a long drink before setting it back down. Tears trickled down his face, and he drew his arm across his cheeks, wiping them with the sleeve of his robe.

Jo had asked Cal Becker to wake Price. He and Rawlings were close friends. If she had gone somewhere on her own, Jo thought he might know about it, but he hadn't seen Rawlings since they'd returned from his house. He hadn't even been aware of her mother's stroke. When she told him Rawlings was missing, the blood drained from his face, and he would have collapsed if not for Becker grabbing hold and keeping him upright.

She watched as the man tried to compose himself. The picture on the jacket of Price's book, lying on the table beside him, showed a robust and distinguished older gentleman. The person in front of her was a shriveled and pale old man. He sat huddled in the wingback chair in the Holly House parlor, wearing blue plaid pajamas, a blue flannel robe and slippers, his face pale and his hands shaking. She wondered what shape his heart was in.

"I never thought it would come to this," he muttered now.

"I'm sorry?" Jo only caught part of his words.

"I never thought..." he started but stopped and waved his hand at her.

"Dr. Price, are you all right?"

"No, I'm not all right," he said. "My friend is missing and in danger. How could I be all right?"

"Maybe we should go to the hospital." She glanced at Becker. "Get you checked out."

"I don't need medical care." Price's voice gained strength, and he pulled himself up straight. "Don't concern yourself, Detective. I'm not going to collapse on you."

"I am concerned," she said "about your health and about your safety. You have already been a target of these people once."

"You think they might come after me?" He sounded shocked. Apparently his concern for Rawlings had kept him from realizing he might also be in danger.

"I don't want to take that chance. If you insist on staying here rather than going to the hospital, I'm leaving a uniformed officer with you and another outside."

"I'll stay, too," Becker spoke up.

Price glanced at him, a grateful look on his face. He seemed to trust Becker and find comfort in knowing he would be there.

"Thanks." Jo meant it. The last thing she needed right now was for Eden's most famous citizen to have a heart attack because she had scared him to death. Becker seemed to have a calming effect on Price, an effect for which she was grateful.

"How will you find her?" The tone of Price's voice was pleading like that of a small child. "How will you find Katherine?"

"I can't go into it," she said, "but we have some leads."

Standing behind Price, Becker arched an eyebrow at her. You should be ashamed of yourself, his gaze seemed to say, for lying to an old man.

***

"Please…please stop." Kate felt a bubble of blood and saliva burst on her lip as she whispered the words. She had meant to say them louder, but they came out barely loud enough for Leonard to hear. "Please…."

He slapped her again, harder than before. She groaned. She had lost count of how many times he had slapped her, sometimes openhanded, sometimes backhanded. The backhands were the worst. He wore a large ring on his right ring finger, and every time he backhanded her, the ring cut. He had started out hitting her once for each time she denied knowing anything about the Star but had graduated to hitting her two or three times for every denial. Once the chair started to go over with her. He had grabbed her shoulder hard and slammed the chair back upright, jarring her still sore neck in the process. Through it all, he remained expressionless, his eyes blank. He could have been a robot, programmed only to hit and hit again.

She had to tell him something, anything, just to get him to stop. She couldn't take any more. How, she wondered, do abused women stay with their abusers? How do they survive this kind of treatment day in and day out?

"Where is the Star?"

She blinked at him, trying to focus through eyes that were swelling shut, as the glimmer of an idea began to form. Noodle it, she thought, referring to the mystery writer George Chesbro's term for mentally working an idea until it became a complete story. She used that technique herself, "noodling" an idea in the recesses of her mind as she went about her teaching and student consultations and the other tasks that made up her life. Now she didn't have the luxury of time. She would have to make the story believable enough to get Jones to leave the cabin, and she would have to do it quickly.

Behind him, she saw Wendell Halsey sitting on the edge of the bed, his head in his hands. His wife had gone into the bathroom a while back and hadn't come out. The Halseys knew the police were looking for them. If she could make up a convincing story about the location of the Star, they might be afraid to go look for it, leaving only Leonard. They seemed to be sickened by what he was doing to her. If he was out of the picture, even for just an hour or so, she might be able to convince them to let her go.

"I…" she tried, her voice failing. She wanted to tell him, but she couldn't form the words.

"What's that?" Leonard leaned closer. "You need a little encouragement to speak up?"

He stepped behind her and grasped the little finger of her left hand. He leaned over her shoulder, his mouth next to her ear, and began to twist the finger. She cried out at the sharp stabbing pain.

"I'm going to break this one," he whispered, his warm breath tickling her ear. "And each time I ask you where the Star is and you don't tell me, I'm going to break another one. When we run out of fingers, I'll think of something else."

"No, no!" Kate cried, as he twisted harder. "I'll tell you! Please, stop! I'll tell you!"

Leonard released her finger and straightened. On the bed, Wendell Halsey lowered his hands, a look of surprise on his face.

"What did I tell you, Wendell?" Leonard said. "A little persuasion was all it took."

He came around in front of her and stood looking down at her, like a stern parent with a wayward child. His crotch was level with her eyes, and she felt her stomach turn as she saw the bulge. He had more than enjoyed the pain he had inflicted on her.

She raised her head. His eyes were as blank as ever. It was as if his lower half wasn't connected to his top half, as if his brain wasn't able to process the arousal signals from below. Somehow this frightened her more than all the slaps and threats had done. She prayed he would believe what she had decided to tell him. If he didn't, she would not survive the night. And then he would go after Jackson.

She also prayed that her father had stayed at the hospital.

"It's at my parents' house." She strained to get the words out through her swollen lips. "In Mayfield."

"Your parents' house?" Leonard didn't look convinced. "Why would the Professor hide it there?"

"Michael didn't," she whispered. She cleared her throat and tried to speak louder. "I did."

"Where are your parents?"

"They're not involved," she said. "You have to leave them alone. Please! They don't know anything about it. They don't even live there anymore."

"I don't have to do anything." She flinched as Leonard started to draw his arm back. "Except get the truth."

"It *is* the truth! I swear it!" She cringed and closed her eyes, waiting for the blow, but it didn't come. When she opened her eyes, she saw Leonard had dropped his hand to his side.

"Explain."

"My mother has Alzheimer's. She and my dad moved in with my brother. The house is for sale. It seemed like a good place to hide the Star. No one would think of looking there."

She talked fast, hoping she'd noodled the idea enough. The first draft of this story would have to work. If it didn't, she wouldn't live long enough for revisions. And neither would Jackson.

"Address?"

She told him.

"Where in the house?"

She thought fast. "In the basement. Behind the furnace. There's an old cabinet, a built-in one. My dad keeps nails and drill bits—things like that—in buckets there. I hid it at the bottom of a bucket of nails."

There had been an old cabinet behind the furnace when she still lived at home, and it had contained nails, drill bits, nuts and bolts, even a few tools. Her dad had kept it stocked for household repairs. Whether the cabinet was still there or whether it was still full of her dad's things was anybody's guess. She hadn't been in the basement of the house in Mayfield in years.

Leonard turned and walked the length of the room and back again, thinking. He turned to Wendell.

"Go," he said. "See if she's telling the truth."

"Me?" Wendell stood, his hands out, palms up. "You heard her before. The cops have my picture. I can't go. If I get spotted, we're all screwed."

"Then Gabriella," Leonard said.

"No! You can't send Gabby either. You wanna face Baby if Gabby gets arrested?"

For the first time Kate saw Leonard look human. It was only for a second, but a flicker of indecision crossed his features. A cold chill ran through her as she realized Leonard was afraid of crossing Baby Duda. Any man who could frighten a man like Leonard was a man she never wanted to meet.

She waited, holding her breath.

"All right," Leonard said. "I'll go."

Kate tried to hide her relief. One good thing about having your eyes swelling shut, she thought, was that it made it difficult for other people to see what you were thinking.

Chapter 30

"Why do you insist on asking me these inane questions, Detective? I don't know anything. I've told you. You should be out finding Katherine."

Jo felt like she was in a bad dream, one of those where you're trying to run from or to something, but you can't move. Katherine Rawlings was out there somewhere, maybe already dead, maybe just wishing she was, and Jo had no clue what to do or where to go. She was helpless, and she didn't like the feeling.

She and Sticks had met up back at the station. He quickly filled her in on what he had learned from the Hills, which wasn't much. Rawlings had left for the hospital after receiving word that her mother had been taken there by ambulance, but she never arrived. After receiving a call from Jo, Sticks had questioned the Hill women about their guest, Mr. Jones, but they had no information other than the name he used when he checked in and their observations that he seemed strange. Jo filled him in on the keys. His eyes widened when she told him she and Becker had searched Jones's room, but he made no comment.

She'd also phoned Lou and filled her in. As Lou's phone rang, Jo had a fleeting hope that maybe—just maybe—Lou might know where her friend was, but she knew even as she thought it that she was grasping at straws because she didn't have anything else to grasp. Lou had listened to Jo, asked a couple of questions, given her the information on Rawlings's cell carrier, and hung up to make calls to her people at Raven.

She'd left Sticks at the station rousting someone out of bed at Verizon to get a trace started on Rawlings's cell, while she returned to Holly House to harass an old man with questions because she couldn't think of anything else to do.

Jackson Price had regained some of his color, along with his outrage at the ineptitude of the Eden Police, but he still looked bad. Jo wondered when he had last eaten. He seemed to have lost weight since she met him at his house after the break-in only two days ago. Maybe it's his posture, she thought. He was stooped, his shoulders hunched, his midsection sunken in.

"This is part of finding Katherine." Cal Becker patted the old man's shoulder. "I've learned over the years people often have information that will help without even knowing they have it. Just talk to the detective, Jackson. Tell her any and every bit of information you can remember about Mabry since he showed up in Eden. You never know when something that doesn't seem like much to you could be just what's needed."

"Michael should never have come back!" Price clenched his fists. "He had no right! He didn't deserve it!"

"Deserve what, Dr. Price?"

Price looked puzzled for a moment, as if he'd forgotten Jo was there. "What?"

"You said Michael didn't deserve it. Deserve what?"

Price's mouth worked, but no sound came out. His hands relaxed and his shoulders sunk even more. Jo saw a glimmer in his eyes, the beginning of tears.

"I should have given the money to him," he said. "I should have given it to him to make him go away. If I had, none of this would have happened."

"He asked you for money?"

Price nodded. A tear trickled from his right eye and ran down his cheek. So, Jo thought, Becker had been right. Mabry had come back to Eden to hit his old friend up for money. The old friend had said no, and now he was blaming himself for what had happened to Rawlings.

"This isn't your fault, Jackson," Cal said, squeezing the old man's shoulder. "Don't blame yourself."

Jo started to ask him for more details but stopped as Lou Pelfrey entered the room carrying a laptop case.

"Any luck on the cell trace?"

"Not yet," Jo said. "Sticks is working on it. The night supervisor wouldn't give the okay. Said Rawlings might not even be missing. He pointed out we make people wait twenty-four hours to file a missing persons report. The guy finally agreed to get *his* boss out of bed."

"We might not need them. I remembered something on my way here."

As Lou talked, she unzipped the case and removed the computer. Flipping it open, she powered it up.

"A couple years ago, Kate went to Europe—some trip offered by the University of Nebraska for their faculty and staff. Lasted a month and they went all over." She glanced at Cal. "What's the password for the Wi-Fi here?"

Cal told her. She typed it in and continued.

"I always wanted to go to Europe, so I made her get an app called EagleEye on her phone that would show me her location. That way I could live vicariously by following her everywhere she went."

"An app?" Cal said. "You mean, an application? Like a software program?"

"Basically, yeah," Lou said. "If someone has it installed and has designated you as a friend, you can see where that person is at any time if the phone is turned on."

"That's a big if," Cal said.

"It's worth trying," Jo said. "If this doesn't work, there's still the phone company. Even if the phone is off, they can track it via GPS."

"Not Kate's phone," Lou said. "She's still using a first generation iPhone. No GPS. EagleEye can track using just cell towers, although it won't pin the location down as accurately as it would with GPS."

"Let's hope it works," Jo said. "Although the Halseys—and Jones, if he's involved—probably got rid of the phone on their way to wherever they took her."

Jo and Cal held their breath as they watched Lou sign in to EagleEye. A list of her friends displayed on the left side of the screen. She selected Kate, and a map appeared with a blue square containing a picture of Rawlings displayed in the center. Lou clicked on it, and a text box popped up displaying Rawlings name. Under her name was a road name—Morgan Glen—followed by Eden, Kentucky, the zip code and USA. In lighter text under that, it said "2 hours ago."

"That's where she was two hours ago," Lou said, stabbing her finger at the screen.

"What's that mean?" Cal asked. "That she's somewhere else or that her phone's been disabled?"

"I don't know," Lou admitted. "Cell service is hit and miss in that part of the county, so it could be she's moved out of range of a tower. Or she's still there. If a phone hasn't moved, EagleEye doesn't update the time."

"No street number," Jo said. "Can you get a cross road to narrow it down a bit?"

Lou clicked on the zoom bar, and the orientation moved out enough for them to read the name of a road that crossed Morgan Glen to the south. Jo punched a speed dial number on her cell.

"Sticks," she said when the call was answered. "We got a location where Rawlings's phone was two hours ago. How's not important—I'll tell you later. What do you know about the area around Morgan Glen Road? Maybe a few miles north of Polksville Road? Any cell service?"

She listened for a few moments.

"Okay. Get a couple deputies headed our way. I'm on my way to the station." She disconnected. "Sticks says cell service drops right where EagleEye last picked her up. Just houses and farms in that area—Sticks says they all belong to local people as far as he knows."

"Maybe Kate isn't the only person we should be worried about," Cal said. "Maybe the Halseys and Jones have taken over someone's house and are holding her there."

"Let's not imagine trouble we don't need," Jo said. "Becker, come with me. Lou, you follow us."

She turned to Jackson. She had almost forgotten he was there. He shouldn't be left here alone and not just because he looked like he might collapse at any moment. As long as Mabry's friends were still at large, he was in danger.

"Lock the door when we leave," she instructed him. "I'll get a uniformed officer heading this way. Do *not* open the door for anyone but him. You understand?"

Jackson nodded. "I won't. I promise."

"Will you be okay until he gets here?" Cal looked worried. "I don't like to leave you."

"I'll be fine." Jackson took a deep breath and struggled to his feet. He patted Cal's shoulder. "Go. Find Katherine. Please."

Cal looked at him for a moment and nodded. They went out, pausing for a second on the porch until they heard the lock engage behind them.

Chapter 31

"You don't want to do this. I know you don't. You're not killers."

Kate strained against the ropes holding her to the chair, pleading with her body language as well as her voice. Wendell Halsey was pacing back and forth, his wife watching him, both looking as if they wished they were anywhere but where they were.

Kate's torturer had left only a few minutes before, taking the key to the house that she'd carried in her purse all these years and leaving the Halseys with strict instructions to watch her. She had no idea how far the cabin was from Mayfield, but she knew she had to act fast if she had any hope of getting away. It wouldn't take Leonard long to search her parents' basement and realize she'd lied to him. Then she would be dead, and he would go after Jackson.

"Please…" she started.

"Shut up! Just shut up a goddamn minute, will you!" Wendell shouted.

His wife put a hand on his arm, murmuring something Kate couldn't hear. He took a deep breath and put his arm around her shoulders. The two of them turned away and began talking low, but the cabin was small enough that Kate caught most of it.

"I don't like this," she heard Wendell say, "…no murder rap."

"What can we do?" Gabriella said. "He'll kill us if we let her go."

"The cops know who we are, Gabby. We need to get out of here."

"And leave her?"

Kate's stomach did a flip. She had wanted to get Leonard out of the way so she could try to convince the Halseys to let her go. She hadn't considered the possibility they might run and leave her for Leonard to deal with.

"Please, no," Kate pleaded. "You can't leave me here with him. He'll kill me."

Wendell turned and stared at her. He started to speak, but she continued, talking fast, trying to make her case while she had the chance.

"If he kills me, you both will be guilty of murder. The courts don't distinguish between who pulls the trigger and who lets it happen. You'll still be charged with murder." They looked at one another. Maybe she was getting through to them. "The police only know about the two of you. Do you think Leonard is going to stick around? He'd be afraid you'd turn him in. He'll disappear, and you two will be the ones sitting on death row."

She had another thought. Noodling still in progress, she thought.

"Or he might not come back at all. Maybe he'll just take the Star and go. Why should he share all that money with you?" She looked at Gabriella. "Or with your brother?"

"Shit, shit, shit!" Wendell flopped down on the side of the bed, burying his face in his hands. "What do we do, Gabby?"

Gabriella straightened, a determined look on her face. She was the stronger of the two, Kate thought, and probably smarter than her husband as well. She would be the one to decide what they would do. Kate didn't know if that was good or bad for her. Gabriella might be more sympathetic to another woman's plight, but what was it Kipling said? The female of the species is more deadly than the male? That might go double for the sister of a gangster.

"I'm calling Dom," Gabriella said. "We'll do whatever he says to do."

Wendell raised his head and looked at her, relief in his eyes. "That's good, babe. That's a good idea. He ought to know what's going on here, especially since you're here."

"I'll have to go out," Gabriella said. "I checked while I was in the bathroom, and there's no service here. Will you be okay if I leave you here with her?"

"Sure, sure, I can handle her." Wendell nodded his head. "Just get back before the creepy fuck does."

Kate realized she was going to have to revise her plan. Having watched Wendell's interaction with his wife, Kate knew she would never be able to convince him to let her go on his own, just as she knew there was no chance Gabriella's brother was going to tell them to set her free. The police might be looking for the Halseys, but without her as a witness, it would be difficult to charge them with anything. No, Gabriella's gangster brother was more likely to tell them to let Leonard do his job and dump her body where it wouldn't be found.

***

"You gotta be kidding me!"

Kate had waited for what she estimated was ten minutes after Gabriella left before informing Wendell that she really had to use the bathroom. It had not gone over well.

"Please! I really have to go." Kate squirmed in her chair, trying to use body language to convince him that she was close to peeing her pants—which, in fact, was not all that far from the truth. Getting smacked around by a sociopath tended to do that to a person.

"Gabby can take you when she gets back."

"I'll wet myself by then." She began to cry, surprising herself. The tears weren't an act. "I can't deal with that, too."

"Goddamnit!" Halsey stepped behind her chair. Kate felt the ropes loosen and slip off her wrists. "You try anything, I'll give you a worse beating than Leonard did."

"I won't. I promise. Thank you so much." Kate rubbed her wrists, feeling her fingers start to tingle as circulation was restored.

Halsey grabbed her right arm, yanked her out of the chair, and shoved her into the bathroom. As she turned to shut the bathroom door behind her, he pushed it back open.

"Leave the damn door open."

"I can't do that." She tried to look embarrassed. "I can't go with you watching. Besides," she looked around the small bathroom, "what can I do in here?"

Halsey pushed past her and checked the window. It was painted shut. Kate's hopes for an escape through that route vanished, and she wondered what, indeed, *could* she do in there?

"Leave it cracked," Halsey said, exiting the bathroom and leaving the door open a few inches. "You'll have your goddamn privacy."

Kate pulled the toilet lid up, making sure it clanked against the toilet tank, and turned on the faucet in the basin. Halsey would think she needed it to help her urinate, and its sound would cover the fact that she wasn't. She turned slowly, examining the bathroom for anything she could use to fight her way out. This is the only chance I've got to stay alive, she thought. And the only chance I'll have to save Jackson.

***

"This is it," Lou radioed over the secure channel they had established on the police radio. "This is the general area. I just checked EagleEye on my phone, and it's still showing Kate's phone as having last been here. No updated location."

A county car containing two deputies who knew the area was in the lead, followed by Jo and Cal. Lou was behind them in her personal vehicle, and Sticks brought up the rear. The night sky was overcast, with only a crescent moon occasionally peeking out from behind the clouds, and it was late enough that the windows of most of the houses were dark. The only light they had to work with was limited to their headlights and the security lights in the barnyards of the farms they passed.

"What now?" Cal said.

What now indeed, Jo thought, her frustration growing. Odds were that Rawlings wasn't even here. Her phone was probably in one of the ditches they were passing, tossed there by her kidnappers. They were engaged in an exercise in futility, but it was the only choice they had.

"We know what Jones's car looks like," she said, trying to sound upbeat. "We'll look for it."

She radioed the instructions to the others, along with the vehicle description for the benefit of the deputies, and passed a handheld searchlight to Becker. He plugged it into the dash's power outlet.

"You check that side, I'll check this one," she said. For all the good it will do, she thought, but didn't say. She knew Becker and the others were thinking the same.

She flipped on the searchlight mounted on the driver's side of the cruiser she had traded her unmarked for when they stopped at the station. Ahead of her the county cruiser's searchlights came on.

Twenty minutes later, after three passes up and down Morgan Glen Road in the area where EagleEye showed Kate's phone had last been, Jo was ready to admit defeat. They had had a clear view of all the vehicles parked outside the houses, barns, and trailers they passed. There was the chance that Jones's car was inside a garage or a barn they were passing, but Jo didn't really believe that. Either the kidnappers had moved out of the range of the cell towers or they had discarded the phone.

She radioed to the others to convene at a barn that sat by itself between two pastures, a half-mile away from the nearest house. The barn was apparently still used and the graveled pull-off in front of it well maintained. The six of them got out of their vehicles and gathered around Jo's cruiser as she spread a map over the hood.

"What about these side roads?" she asked, tapping the map at the location of two narrow county roads that cut off Morgan Glen. "Where do these go?"

"This one dead ends a couple miles down," one of the deputies said, pointing to the road that led off the west side of Morgan Glen. "Two farms, one on either side of the road. One belongs to the Creeches, the other to the Taylors. Good people, but if someone tried to home-invade either of them, they'd probably get their heads blown off.

"Besides," he added. "Cell service is still good there. If the phone was there, we'd know it."

"I know this one," Sticks said, pointing to the road heading east. "It borders Daniel Boone for about ten miles and connects up with Jacksonburg Road."

Jo traced the line of the road as it skirted the edges of Daniel Boone National Forest. "Are there any entrances to the forest off of it?"

"Not that I know of," Sticks said. "Not car entrances anyway. Plenty of hiking and ATV trails, though. Closest car entrance is right after you turn on Jacksonburg."

"There's a place a few miles up with rental cabins," one of the deputies said. "Mostly hunters and fishermen used to stay there. It's been out of business for a while. Owner died and the wife put it up for sale. She left the electric turned on so potential buyers could get a good look at it. I've seen pretty good-sized ads for it in the paper, and the realtor's got a flyer for it in the window of his office. Wouldn't be too hard for your guys to find out about it.

"And," he added. " Most of the cabins sit far enough back in the trees that they aren't visible from the road. Any one of them would be a real good place to hold a hostage."

***

The porcelain tank lid made enough noise to wake the dead as it bounced off Wendell Halsey's face and hit the floor. Wendell Halsey, however, made no sound after his initial yelp of surprise when he saw the lid coming at him.

Kate stepped out of the bathroom and stopped, looking down at him. He had fallen on his side, eyes shut, his nose at an odd angle, blood running from it and his lip. She glanced at the door, knowing she should get out while she had the chance, but instead she knelt beside him and put her fingers to his throat. After a second, she felt a pulse. He was still alive. She could only hope she hadn't caused him permanent brain damage.

She had planned on swinging the toilet lid hard at Halsey, but at the last second, she couldn't bring herself to do it. He was a criminal, yes, and had helped hold her captive, yes, but he didn't seem evil—more like a silly boy who had gotten in over his head. She wanted to get away, but she didn't want to kill him, so instead of swinging with all her force, she had thrown the lid at him, striking him in the face.

She stood and headed for the door. Throwing it open, she ran out and stopped in surprise. Gabriella Halsey was walking toward the cabin, a scant fifty feet from her. Gabby's yell shocked Kate back into movement. She turned and ran around the side of the cabin and into the woods.

The light was dim outside the cabins, but with only a sliver of moon, the light under cover of the trees was practically nonexistent. A few feet in, Kate had to stop for a second to let her eyes adjust. Behind her, she heard Gabby yell for Wendell and then the sound of running footsteps heading toward the woods. Kate had hoped Gabby would see Wendell on the floor and be more worried about him than about catching Kate, but it sounded like Gabby had never gone into the cabin.

Kate moved through the woods as fast as she could. There was little undergrowth thanks to the thick canopy overhead, but branches slapped at her face and arms, stinging the existing cuts and making scratches of their own. She began swinging her arms in front of her to let them take the blows instead of her face. Fifty yards or so in, she stepped in a depression under dried leaves, lost her balance and fell hard. A stab of pain shot through her neck. She lay on the ground until the pain subsided to a bearable level, hoping there were no copperheads or rattlesnakes coiled in the leaves. Catching her breath, she stood, testing her ankles. They seemed to still be in good working order.

Behind her, she heard Gabby cursing as she fought her way through the darkened woods. The thick covering of dried leaves made it impossible to be quiet and still make any speed through the forest. Gabby had homed in on the sounds Kate had made and was heading straight toward her. Kate looked around and up, trying to gauge which direction to go.

When she had exited the cabin, she thought she recognized the place. It was what used to be called the Forest Glen Cabins. The back of the property butted up against Daniel Boone National Forest land. If she was right, that's where she was now—in the national forest. She not only had to worry about Gabby catching her, she had to worry about getting lost. Public roads bordered Daniel Boone this close to its edge and forest service roads crisscrossed it, leading to campgrounds, boat docks, and private land located inside the forest. If she could circle around and come out on one of those roads, she might be able to make it to a house or flag down a car. She started moving again, angling to what she hoped was left of where she had entered the trees. It seemed to be her best chance of coming out on the road leading to the Forest Glen. Gabby cursed again, sounding closer. Kate picked up her speed.

She had just ducked in time to avoid a low branch when she heard a man shout for Gabby, and Gabby answer back. Wendell Halsey was apparently up and joining the hunt. A part of Kate— the stupid part, she thought—was relieved to know he was still able to move and call for his wife, but now she had two hunters on her trail. She started to run, ignoring the blows the forest was delivering to her already battered body. She tripped again, this time over a log, breaking her fall with her hands, and stoving her right index finger in the process. Less than a minute later, she was down again. When she stood, her left ankle screamed a protest when she put weight on it. Ignoring it as best she could, she kept moving, hoping that the forest was giving Wendell and Gabby the beating it was giving her.

Suddenly she saw light ahead. The headlights of a car were penetrating the gloom, letting her see that the trees were thinning. She'd been afraid she was running in circles, but she must have made it to the road leading to the Forest Glen Cabins. Hope spurred her on and she swatted at the branches and undergrowth, forcing her way through them, until she was standing clear along the side of the road. Less than a hundred yards away a car had just rounded a curve and was moving toward her. She started waving her arms, resisting the urge to shout. It would only clue Gabby and Wendell in to her position, and the driver wouldn't be able to hear her anyway.

For a few miserable seconds, she thought the driver wasn't going to stop, but then the motion of the car slowed. It came to a stop in the middle of the road. She relaxed, almost collapsing with relief. She could get a ride away from here now. The driver of the car likely had a cell phone—didn't everyone these days? She would call the police and tell them to protect Jackson. He would be safe. Then she would ask the driver to take her to Eden General, and she could see her mother. She was going to get out of this alive after all.

"Thank God," she said, starting toward the car as a man stepped from the driver's side. He was stocky, with brown hair that was receding and a concerned look on his face. "I need help. There are people after me. They want to kill me."

The man reacted quickly. He came forward, grabbing her arm and supporting her weight as she limped to the passenger side of the car. He closed the door behind her and came around to the driver's side. He paused for several seconds, looking back at the woods before getting in and pulling away.

Kate leaned back against the passenger headrest and nearly groaned at the welcome relief it provided to her sore neck. She realized that she was trembling and wrapped her arms around herself, trying to calm down. She was safe now, thanks to this man being willing to stop for a stranger. She looked over at him. He was leaning forward in his seat, his body tense, staring through the windshield. Probably wondering what he's gotten himself into, she thought.

"Thank you," she said. "I owe my life to you."

He glanced at her and back at the road.

"My name is Katherine Rawlings." Her voice trembled. She took a deep breath and continued. "I teach at Raven University. I was abducted earlier this evening, but I managed to escape. If you hadn't come along, I'm not sure I would have gotten away."

Still the man didn't respond. Odd. She would have expected him to be peppering her with questions by now. She felt the first flicker of misgivings.

"Can I borrow your phone? I need to call the authorities."

"No service out here," the man said without looking away from the road.

Kate saw the sign for the Forest Glen Cabins up ahead just as she felt the car begin to slow. She sat forward, her body suddenly tense as she realized the man was preparing to turn into the cabins.

"What are you doing?" she yelled at him. "Don't go in there! That's where they are!"

She grabbed at the wheel, trying to wrench it back toward the road, and the man swung his right arm at her, backhanding her across the face. Her head bounced off the passenger side window, pain shooting through her neck. Doing her best to ignore it, she started toward him again but stopped when she saw the gun. Belatedly, she realized she should have heeded the advice given to her as a child—never get in a car with a stranger. She collapsed against the passenger door and began to cry.

Chapter 32

The cabins that could be seen from the road were dark, no cars parked near any of them. The deputies had told them that the cabins spread out in both directions and extended several hundred yards back into the woods. A graveled drive circled the perimeter of the property and was intersected at three points by other drives leading past rows of cabins. They had arranged to split up, Jo, Cal and Lou taking the right side of the perimeter drive, while the deputies and Sticks took the left. The deputies thought they would be able to see lights from the interior cabins from the perimeter.

They moved slowly, headlights off, the gravel crunching under the tires sounding as loud as gunfire to Jo's ears. The Forest Glen Cabins sat in a mixture of old hardwood and evergreen trees. Light from the crescent moon penetrated the tree cover enough to make the gravel visible, which was good since it was the only navigation guide they had, but everything else around them was in almost total darkness. Jo hoped Lou could see enough of their cruiser to avoid rear-ending them if they had to stop suddenly.

They had been moving at a crawl for what seemed like hours, occasionally seeing the vague shape of a cabin, when Jo sensed the lane curving to the left. They had reached the rear of the property. As they came around the turn and straightened out, Cal leaned forward.

"Look," he whispered. "Lights."

On their right the outlines of buildings were more visible now, thanks to light emanating from the windows of the cabin a hundred or so yards down. Two cars were parked at the side of the small structure, but they were too far back to tell if either vehicle belonged to Jones.

The radio came to life.

"Lights and cars," the deputy said. "No one's supposed to be in any of the cabins, so it might be your guys. How do you want to handle this?"

"How far back are you?" Jo asked.

"Just come around the turn," the deputy said.

"Stop there and come the rest of the way on foot. You two and Cal move around to the back. Spread out so you can see the sides as well. Sticks, take the front left corner, Lou, take the right front. I'm going to try to get a look in the windows before we go in."

The deputy confirmed. Jo turned the cruiser off, and she and Cal got out, leaving the doors standing open rather than make noise shutting them. Cruisers had their dome lights turned off as a matter of routine, so light wasn't a concern. Lou had her personal car, so she shut her door as quietly and quickly as she could to douse the light. The three of them began advancing toward the cabin.

As they drew nearer, they could determine the makes and models of the cars. One was an Impala, the other was a tan Focus. Neither fit the description of Jones's car. Maybe he's not involved after all, Jo thought. Maybe the illegal entry was for nothing.

The deputies and Sticks appeared out of the dark. Sticks gave her a wave and took position at an angle from the corner, gun held at his side. The deputies disappeared around the far side of the cabin, Cal moved down the right side of the building, and Lou took position at the right corner.

The cabin sat high from the ground, a crawlspace underneath, steps leading to a railed stoop and the front door. To the right of the stoop a window sat several feet off the ground, the sill just below her eye level. As she moved quietly toward it, she thought that for once her lack of height was a blessing. She could see in the window but wouldn't have to crouch down to avoid being seen.

As her eyes adjusted to the light in the room, she saw Rawlings. She was tied to a chair in the center of the room. She looked bad, her face swollen and bleeding, the eye on the side toward Jo beginning to turn black. Her shoulders were shaking, and Jo knew she was crying.

She recognized one of the men and the woman as Wendell and Gabriella Halsey. They were standing at the foot of the bed and appeared to be arguing with a stocky man in jeans and a tan polo shirt. Halsey looked as bad as Rawlings. He had a golf-ball-sized goose egg on his left temple, his nose was twisted to the right in an unnatural position, and his face was covered in blood and the beginnings of bruising. At first Jo thought the other man must have done the damage, but his clothes and hands didn't look like the clothes and hands of a man who'd been in a fistfight. No guns were visible, but she didn't doubt they had them.

She motioned to Lou and Sticks to join her at the front. She went up the steps and turned the knob slowly. The door was unlocked. Flinging it open, she charged into the room, Lou and Sticks behind her, guns drawn.

"Police!" she yelled. "Get your hands where I can see them! On your head! Now!"

The Halseys and the stocky man froze for a second in shock and then did as told. While Jo and Lou kept them covered, Sticks went forward and searched each one, removing a gun from an ankle holster on the stocky man's left leg, and cuffed them behind their backs. He retrieved another gun from under a pillow on the bed.

As the last cuff clicked in place, Lou holstered her weapon and moved quickly to Rawlings.

"Oh, girlfriend, look what they did to you!" she said as she cut Rawlings loose. She helped her friend to her feet, and Rawlings fell into Lou's arms, sobbing. Lou held her, murmuring assurances that everything was going to be all right.

Jo radioed to the deputies and Cal that the building was secured. A few seconds later, she heard footsteps on the stoop, and the deputies entered the room, followed by Cal.

"We'd like to keep the prisoners separated," she said to the deputies. "Can you transport one for us?"

The deputies nodded and moved forward. As the bodies in the room shifted, the stocky man turned.

"What the hell…" Cal said. "Andy?"

***

Cal had gotten more exercise in the last fifteen minutes pacing back and forth outside of the Eden P.D.'s interrogation room than he'd gotten in the last year. He stopped, surprised, when the door opened. As Jo and Sticks shut the door, he saw that son-of-a-bitch who had once called himself a cop sitting stone-faced, his cuffed hands folded in front of him on the table.

"He's not talking, is he." It was a statement, not a question. He knew the detectives would not have left the room so quickly had Andy been answering their questions. "Lawyered up?"

"You got it." Jo rubbed her reddened eyes and stifled a yawn. "Acknowledged his name, asked for a lawyer, and that was that. We offered a public defender, but he refused. Said he'd get one with his phone call."

"Let me guess. He wants to call Chicago."

"Right again." She looked at him with those eyes. "How well do you know this guy?"

"We didn't hang together, but I've known him for years. Or thought I did. We both worked District Four for a few years after I got out of the academy. He made detective first then transferred to organized crime." Cal clenched his fists. "The son-of-a-bitch! He was probably in Duda's pocket back then. No wonder the department's never been able to take Baby down."

"How'd you both end up working for Gallagher?"

"Mutual friend—Mike Watson. He retired first, went to work for Gallagher and started recruiting other guys who were close to retirement. Andy and I weren't the only ones, but we were the only ones who took the job."

"Do you think he's capable of murder?" Jo said.

"You think he did Mabry?"

"I don't think anything for sure at this point. But papers in your friend's car show he rented it just after 9AM in Chicago the day Mabry was killed. It's less than an eight-hour drive from Chicago to Eden, and a gas receipt shows he filled up at a Lexington station early in the evening. The gun he had on him is a .38 and it's loaded with hollow points—the same kind of ammo that killed Mabry. So I ask you again—do you think he's capable of murder?"

Cal stepped to the tiny window in the door of the interrogation room and looked through it at Andy. He was still sitting with his hands clasped on the table, his face unreadable. Was he capable of murder, Cal wondered? If a man was willing to help kidnap and beat a woman for the Star, was it that much of a stretch to imagine he might kill for it? Fifteen million and a gangster calling the shots would have been powerful motivation to kill Mabry. As far as Cal was concerned, the only question was whether the man he'd worked alongside these last couple of years had also killed Sam.

"Yeah, I think he's probably capable," Cal said. "Not that my opinion matters much without hard evidence."

"Which we don't have—yet." Jo yawned, not trying to stifle it this time. "The Ashland forensics people will try to match the bullet that killed Mabry to Miles's gun, but it'll take a while and it might not prove anything. Hollow-points don't leave a lot to work with when it comes to matching."

"Can I talk to him?"

"I'm afraid not, Mr. Becker," Jo said.

It was the answer Cal expected, but he was still disappointed. He turned back to the window. Andy had changed position and was now curled over the table, his head resting on his folded arms, his face turned away from the window. Had he been involved with the Drayer heist from the beginning, Cal wondered. For that matter, had he been part of the crew that did the actual robbery? Cal wasn't sure if Sam and Andy even knew each other, but it was possible. Sam could have recognized Andy. If he had, there would have been no choice but to kill him.

But even if Andy wasn't guilty of pulling the trigger himself, he was in bed with those who were. That made him responsible for Sam's death, whether before or after the fact. Cal turned away from the door and mentally added another name to the payback list he carried in his head.

Chapter 33

It was only Steven's insistence that she would frighten their mother half to death if she didn't get her cuts and other wounds addressed first that kept Kate in the emergency room instead of rushing to her mother's bedside. Bette had had a mild stroke, what the doctors called a TIA. They wanted to keep her at least one more day for observation, but she would be okay—at least as okay as she had been before the stroke.

The nagging worry that her mother would die before she could see her had been at the back of Kate's mind throughout her ordeal with Leonard and the Halseys. It shared mind space with the worry that *she* would die before her mother could see her. Now it looked like they both had a little more time.

Wendell Halsey was two cubicles down from her in the emergency room, handcuffed to the gurney and guarded by a uniformed Eden officer. Lou had wormed his diagnosis out of the nurses and assured Kate he was going to recover from the blow she had dealt him without "any more brain damage than what he was born with."

The Halseys had apparently seen her get in the car with the stocky man—Lou told her his name was Andy Miles and that he was an investigator at the firm where Cal Becker worked—and headed back to the cabin. They were just coming out of the woods when Miles pulled her from the car. She had given up then, knowing she had lost her last chance to escape. The man called Leonard had had enough time to get to Mayfield and realize she'd lied to him. When he returned, he would kill her and then go after Jackson. Even now, under the bright lights of the ER, surrounded by doctors, nurses and other patients, she still found it hard to believe she was safe. When someone called out in a loud voice or banged into something, she could not keep from flinching and breaking out in a cold sweat.

After what seemed like an endless night in the emergency room, Kate was transferred to a room on the same floor as her mother for another day of observation. She endured the questions the admitting nurse had to ask for her paperwork and the taking of her vital signs for what seemed like the hundredth time. Lou hugged her and left for the Eden P.D. to make a statement for the record.

Sunlight was just starting to show behind the outlines of buildings outside Kate's eastern-facing window. Fatigue was beginning to replace anxiety, but she wanted to see her mother more than she wanted sleep. Steven helped her slip an extra hospital gown on backward so her bottom wouldn't hang out, and together they headed down the hall to their mother's room, Kate shuffling in hospital booties, her body protesting every step with spasms of pain from her abused muscles.

The door to Bette's room stood open only a few inches. Kate slipped in quietly, not wanting to disturb her mother if she was sleeping, and was surprised to see her father there. Steven had told her that he was in Bette's room when she was admitted to the ER. Because the man called Leonard was still at large, her father had been warned against returning to the house in Mayfield, but she had expected him to have left for Steven's. It wasn't like him to stick around where he was needed.

He didn't hear her come in. Sitting in a chair pulled close to the side of the bed, he was holding Bette's right hand in both of his, head bent, talking to his wife in a low voice. Bette didn't seem to hear him, her eyes closed, apparently sleeping. Kate moved closer, catching a few words of what her father was saying, and realized he wasn't talking to her mother after all. He was praying.

She started to back out of the room but bumped up against the edge of the door, making a noise. He turned, tears glistening in his eyes.

"Thank God!" His voice breaking on the words, he jumped from his chair and pulled her to him, hugging her hard. "Thank God!"

"It's okay, Daddy. I'm okay." She hugged him back, trying not to wince. The hug hurt her sore body, but she needed it, craved it even. She wasn't going to let a little pain interfere. "We're all okay."

He began to sob then, his body spasming against hers. She was surprised at how thin and frail he felt and flashed back to the night she had seen him through the window of their old house. Too many years had passed since she'd been held by the strong, solid man her father had been. Now that man was gone, replaced by a weak old man who had forgotten how to connect with his family. But maybe, just maybe, he was starting to remember. She hugged him tighter and began to cry.

***

"We solved a kidnapping," Sticks said. "But have we solved a murder?"

"I wish I knew." Jo rubbed her eyes and groaned. "Damn, I'm tired."

Between the conflict with Nick and all that had been going on at work, she'd been short on sleep for the last couple of weeks, but the all-nighter she'd just pulled had put her over the edge. Every inch of her body ached and her eyes felt like she'd used an emery board on them. She wanted to go home and crawl in bed, but she was too tired to get up from her desk chair.

On the way back to the station with their prisoners, she had asked dispatch to call out Lewis and Samuels. She had also requested a marked unit pick up Johnny Crouch. She wasn't buying he didn't know where his son was, and she wasn't buying his claim that it wasn't his truck at Hanover Hall the night Mabry was killed.

The four detectives had spent what was left of the night interrogating everybody they had locked up and still they didn't have any answers. Gabriella Halsey hadn't said much, but she told them William Jones's real name—or at least the name she knew him by—was Leonard Nowles. Leonard Nowles had a driver's license and a couple of credit cards in his name, but that was as far as the paper trail went. No social security number, no birth certificate, and no clue to his whereabouts. Sticks was of the opinion that Nowles was hightailing it back to Chicago, but Jo wasn't sure she agreed with him. The Star was still in play, and she couldn't see a man as ruthless as Nowles leaving without it.

When they questioned Wendell Halsey at the hospital, he swore he didn't know Nowles by any other name then asked for a lawyer. The Applegates denied—again—having anything to do with Mabry's murder. Johnny Crouch refused to confirm or deny his involvement, just sat silent and still like a damn Sphinx, a smug look on his face. He didn't even seem upset that they had pulled him in again for questioning. He continued to deny knowledge of his son's whereabouts.

"I'd say Nowles is a good bet for Mabry's murder, wouldn't you?" Sticks said.

"He's capable of it," Jo said. "So is Miles. But it doesn't make sense either of them would kill Mabry before getting the Star. Nowles kidnaps Rawlings and tortures her, trying to get her to tell him where it is. Wouldn't he have done the same to Mabry? Why shoot him before he got what he wanted?"

"Maybe it wasn't planned. Maybe he tried to snatch Mabry, and Mabry fought back."

"That's possible," Jo admitted. "I could see it happening that way, whether it was Nowles or Miles. Trouble is, I can also see Johnny Crouch avenging his daughter or the Applegates getting caught ripping off the car. And I'm not ready to write Rawlings off as a suspect either."

"Are you serious? Do you really believe hell hath no fury like a woman scorned? After thirty years?"

Jo shrugged. "Their relationship didn't end back then, remember. They could have gotten into a lover's quarrel. He was a no-good, cheating bastard back then. Maybe he still was. Or maybe she decided she didn't want to share the Star."

"So you definitely think she was in on the Drayer thing?"

"I'm too tired to definitely think anything." Jo forced herself to stand up. "I'm going to bed."

Chapter 34

The doctors discharged Kate shortly before noon on Monday with instructions to take it easy for a couple of days, and in particular, to rest her strained neck muscles and tendons. Her entire body ached, but much of the swelling had gone out of her face, leaving minor cuts and heavy bruising. She tried to cover some of the damage with makeup but quickly gave up. The cuts had to kept clean, and the bruising was so dark that makeup didn't conceal it. She looked like hell, and there wasn't much she could do about it except wait for time to heal her wounds.

She had spent most of the morning in her mother's room. Bette was awake and in good spirits, although confused about what had happened. Her doctor decided to keep her a few more days so she could undergo physical therapy to help her regain her strength.

Harry Rawlings had spent the night in Bette's room. The staff had finagled him a breakfast tray, and he invited Kate to eat with them. Bette was cheerful, Harry was atypically talkative, and Kate quickly came to the conclusion that breakfast had done more for her recovery than any treatment she'd received.

Kate had promised Lou she'd call her for a ride when she was released, but Lou showed up early. When they left the hospital, the sun was shining, the temperature warm, but not hot, and birds were singing in the redbud trees that bordered the parking lot. Kate felt her spirits lift. The man who had kidnapped and beaten her was still out there somewhere, but her mother was going to recover and her father was beginning to act like his old self. Life might not be quite perfect yet, but it was getting better.

On the way to Holly House, they talked about the events of Saturday night, about Bette, about Jackson, and they laughed and joked. They avoided the topic of Michael. One day soon they would have to sit down and face that issue. Kate didn't know if she could make Lou understand why she had continued to see Michael and why she'd kept it from her. Truth be told, Kate wasn't sure she understood it herself, although she was beginning to suspect Michael had been a crutch, a way to keep a serious relationship at bay. They were in each other's lives, but they didn't have to put a lot of effort into what they had. She was sure a shrink would blame her father's remoteness, and maybe that was so. But while it might be an explanation for her choice in men, it wasn't a good excuse. It was time she started acting like a grownup instead of a damaged child.

It was going on one by the time Lou dropped her off at Holly House and headed back to work. Edna had apparently been watching for Lou's car because she opened the front door as Kate came up the porch steps.

"Honey! It is *so* good to see you out of a hospital gown!"

Edna hugged her, but gently, holding back the strength Kate knew she had. Taking Kate's arm, she led her through the foyer and into the dining room. Pulling out a chair at a window table, she motioned Kate into it.

"I'll be right back with a nice cup of tea." She bustled out of the room just as Ann and Ginger came in from the direction of the kitchen.

"Lady, you live a life every bit as exciting as your books—and your face shows it!" Ginger's eyes were sparkling.

Kate burst out laughing and then groaned at the spasm of pain that shot through her neck.

"Oh, honey, I'm sorry," Ginger said, as Ann glared at her. "I was just trying to cheer you up. We've been so worried about you."

"It's okay," Kate said. "Laughter is good medicine, right?"

"Right, but you probably should take it in small doses for a while." Ginger scowled. "That damn Jones! I knew he was a no-good from the minute I saw him!"

"You did not. You just thought he was creepy." Ann gave Kate's hand a quick squeeze. "Hello, Kate. It's good to have you back home."

"Creepy is the same thing as no-good. Cal was suspicious of him, too, you know that. That's why we got his prints."

"Cal? Prints?" Kate was confused.

"Let her tell it," Ann gestured to Ginger.

Edna arrived with tea for them all. While they drank, Ginger filled Kate in on the real reason Cal Becker was in town and the clever—she pointed out, while glaring at Ann—way she'd gotten Leonard Nowles's prints for Becker. Ann rolled her eyes when Ginger told them Cal thought she'd make a good detective. Although she didn't voice her opinion, Kate decided she agreed with Becker.

Jackson entered the room just as Ginger finished her story. Kate met him halfway to the table and hugged him. He hugged her back and then held her at arm's length, tears in his eyes.

"I am so sorry, Katherine," he said. "For everything you've been through. I wish I had done things differently."

"Why, Jackson? What could you have done to change things?" Kate was surprised. Jackson appeared to think what had happened was his fault.

"If I had given Michael the money he wanted, he would have left Eden. The monsters that were following him would not have hurt you like they did."

"Jackson! Michael had no right asking you for money. And you had no way of knowing that the rest of this would happen. Do not blame yourself!"

Jackson stared at her, his mouth working, as if he wanted to say something, but finally he just shook his head and looked away. Kate saw a tear trickle from the corner of his eye.

"Here, sit down." She pulled a chair out from the table. "Have some tea."

"No, no." Jackson waved his hand. "I have some errands to run on my way home so I need to get going."

"On your way home?"

"I'm moving back in today. Now that those thugs have been locked up, there's no reason for me to stay away any longer."

"Jackson, they aren't all locked up! The one we knew as Jones—his real name is Leonard Nowles, by the way—is still out there. It's not safe for you yet."

"Katherine, I seriously doubt that Neanderthal is still in Eden. His cohorts are behind bars, and the police are looking for him. I don't think we'll see him again in our lifetimes—thank goodness!"

"You're probably right," she said. "But still…"

"I cannot hide out here for the rest of my life." Jackson took a deep breath. "I'm going back to my home."

"I'll come with you then," Kate said. "I'm sure there's still some work that needs to be done."

"You most certainly will not come with me! Not after what you've been through." Jackson shook his head. "My house may not be tidy, but it's livable."

"Jackson…" Kate started to protest, but a look from him stopped her. She felt like she should help him, but a part of her was relieved. She was afraid if she spent time alone with him, she might break down and tell him how much danger he'd been in. She wasn't sure he could handle that on top of Michael's murder, the break-in at his house, and the worry her kidnapping had caused him.

He left shortly after. Ann and Edna were going to visit Bette, and Ginger excused herself to tend to the house's laundry and cleaning. Kate went to her room, grateful for the chance to be alone. She showered, dried her hair, and stretched out on the bed. Between the normal hospital noises and thinking about the hours spent in the cabin, she hadn't slept well the night before. She was trying to get her sore body in a comfortable position for napping when Ginger knocked at the door.

"You've got a call," she said when Kate opened the door.

Kate took the handset from Ginger and thanked her.

"I just heard what happened," Chris Irons said without preamble. "I ran into Lou. Jesus, Kate, are you okay?"

"Hello to you, too, Chris," she said.

"Hey, I'm sorry." He laughed. "Let's start over. Hello. Heard about you being kidnapped over the weekend and wanted to see what you thought of the experience."

Kate laughed and then winced. "Ouch," she said. "Don't make me laugh. I'm still sore."

"But you're okay?"

"Nothing that time won't fix. A few cuts, some bruises, and my neck still hasn't recovered from the incident at my office, but I'll heal."

"I tried your cell first, but it rolled to voice mail."

"Apparently I lost it. Lou thinks it fell out of my pocket in the trunk of the car I was kidnapped in. Lou tells me that's how the police found me."

"I'll never complain about technology again!"

Kate laughed. "Me either. Unfortunately, the phone must have died because the police can't get a location on it now. It would been nice if they could have found Nowles—that's the man who kidnapped me—like they found me."

"Is there anything I can do to help? I could bring whatever you might need from your office, even cover a class if it's okay with Jackson."

"No, but thanks." Kate hesitated. "And thank you for being so concerned."

"Of course I'm concerned. I like you, Kate. A lot, in case you haven't figured that out. I hope we can get to know each other better. But whether we do or not, I will always want the best for you."

"I don't know what to say," Kate started, but Chris interrupted.

"Don't say anything right now. I'm not pressing you for anything, not even a 'yes' to dinner or a drink sometime. I know you need time to get over everything that's happened. Just know that if and when you're ready for that dinner and drink, I'm ready."

"Well…" Kate stopped, not sure what to say.

"I know, I know. I should play hard to get, but I never learned how."

Kate laughed. They talked a few minutes longer about her ordeal, Jackson and his retirement, and what an ass Paul Holland was. After they disconnected, Kate sat for a few minutes, the phone in her hand, replaying the conversation. She liked Chris, and he seemed to like her. Why was she hesitating? She had accepted dates from men at other places she'd worked, so why not here? Was it because Eden was forever connected to Michael and what they'd had? Lordy, she hoped she wasn't that far gone!

She stretched out on the bed and closed her eyes, but after a few minutes, she gave up. She was tired, but she was too keyed up to sleep. She crossed to the desk and turned on the laptop. She hadn't checked email in a couple of days. Might as well clear out her Inbox while she waited for her body to settle down for the sleep she knew it needed.

As expected, she had about a hundred unread messages. Hitting the Delete key rapidly, she passed on winnings from a Nigerian lottery, the chance to enlarge her penis, and email flyers from several department stores and online shopping sites. She read a couple of messages from friends in Nebraska and one from Dolly giving her an update on *Flee's* sales to date.

She almost deleted the message from an online greeting card company but stopped with her finger on the key. It was a notification telling her she'd received a card from someone named Michael. She racked her brain trying to think of anyone else she knew named Michael, but she only knew one and he was dead. He must have set this card up before he was killed but for what reason? It wasn't her birthday, and it certainly wasn't Christmas.

Then she remembered *Flee*. Michael had probably sent an atta-boy card to congratulate her on the book's publication, maybe setting it up before he'd decided to give her the pat on the back in person. She smiled, suddenly glad to have this one last message from him. She clicked on the link, and her browser opened a screen displaying an envelope on a background of flowers and butterflies. She followed the instructions to click on the envelope, and a white note card slid up out of the envelope. "Find the treasure in our special place," it said, followed by "Always, Michael."

She felt her heart speed up. "Our special place" was what they had called the roof of Hanover Hall. Had Michael hidden the Star in the same place they'd stashed wine, candles, and their sleeping bag all those years ago? For that matter, was the old corrugated shed still there? Should she call the police? Or maybe Cal Becker? He was just down the hall. His company had insured the Star. Maybe he should know before the police—or at least, at the same time.

But what could she tell them? That she'd gotten a cryptic message from her dead lover? She'd have to explain about the roof and how they used to go there to drink wine and make love under the stars. Even if they took the message seriously—and they probably would—and searched the roof, who knows what they might find? It would be like Michael to simply leave her a gift. He would expect her to think it romantic. He had sent roses after her first book. Maybe he'd left a bouquet of artificial flowers on the roof to congratulate her on this one. It would be like him to think that might entice her to go up to the roof with him for old times sake.

She stood and began dressing. Better to check it out first. She didn't want to be embarrassed if it turned out to be a personal gift. And the more she thought about it, the more she doubted it was the Star. Surely even Michael wouldn't be reckless enough to hide jewels worth fifteen million dollars on the roof of a public building!

***

Cal watched from the door of his room as Rawlings took the stairs two at a time and rushed out the door. Curious, he thought. He'd been reading the Lexington paper in the parlor when Rawlings arrived home from the hospital. She'd looked tired. He'd heard her half-hearted offer to help Price at his house and watched her climb the stairs to her room. He'd have guessed she would spend the afternoon sleeping, not running out of the house like it was on fire. Maybe her mother had taken a turn for the worse? Ah, well, none of it was his concern. Not anymore.

He closed the door to his room and returned to his packing. The consensus in Chicago was that Mabry had done something with the Star on his way to Eden, and there was no point in wasting any more time in Kentucky. Two shirts, some socks, and a handful of briefs later, he stopped. The house was quiet; Rawlings was gone. It was the only chance he'd have to take another look in her room. Maybe he'd missed something the first time around, or maybe she'd brought something—a clue, maybe, the Star would be too much to ask for—in since his last search.

Taking his lock picks, he slipped quietly out the door, down the hall, and into Rawlings's room. The blankets were pulled back on the bed, as if Rawlings's plan had been to get some shuteye before she'd decided to jump up and run out of the house. Cal quickly checked the drawers, closet and bathroom, finding nothing new since his last visit. Groaning, he got down on his protesting knees on the side Rawlings had been lying on, checked under the bed, and ran his hands under the mattress. Nothing. He got to his feet, went around to the other side of the bed, and repeated the search under the bed and mattress. Still nothing.

On the desk, Rawlings laptop sat open, the geometric shapes of a screensaver floating across the screen. He sat down in the desk chair and tapped the touch pad, bringing the screen to life. An electronic greeting card was open on the screen. Although there could be other Michaels in her life, Cal was willing to bet the card was from the one lying in the county morgue. He read the message and felt his heart speed up. The "treasure" referred to in the card could only mean the Star, and Rawlings was on her way to retrieve it. He had been right. She'd been in cahoots with her old lover all this time. In Cal's eyes, that made her as guilty of Sam's death as Mabry. He would see to it that she paid for that guilt.

Chapter 35

A late afternoon quiet hung over the hall outside Kate's office. She could hear the voice of a lecturer coming from an open door at the far end, and a phone ringing in the English office, but the doors of offices belonging to professors were all closed. She passed two students on her way to the maintenance closet, neither of whom looked up from their smart phones.

She had expected the closet door to be locked, and it was. The ancient doorknob and lock looked to be the same one she and Michael had breached all those years ago. If she hadn't lost her touch with a credit card, she could be inside in less than thirty seconds. She pulled the American Express card from her wallet, checked the hall to be sure no one was in sight and slipped the card into the gap between the door and the frame just above the latch. She wiggled and bent the card, but the latch stayed firm. Down the hall, she heard the lecturer's voice rise above the noise of students gathering their belongings as he gave them instructions on their next assignment. In less than a minute, the class would be dismissed.

She forced herself to relax. "Feel it," she heard Michael say from across the years, "feel the card touch the latch and then give it a little shove to the left." Following instructions she'd thought she'd forgotten, she finally felt the latch move and heard the click as it disengaged from the strike plate. She opened the closet door and slipped inside just as the first student exited the lecture hall.

A sense of deja vu washed over her. The maintenance closet looked and smelled the same as she remembered. Why she had expected it to be different, she didn't know. Mops, buckets, vacuum cleaners, and floor polishers were timeless tools that seldom required updating.

She crossed to the door leading to the roof. A floor polisher blocked it. She moved two buckets and a gallon jug of cleaner to make room for the polisher and pushed it out of the way. The roof door was locked, but she quickly worked her magic with the credit card, confident and sure now that she didn't have to worry about someone seeing her. She pulled the door shut behind her with its lock disengaged. She didn't want to take a chance on not being able to unlock it so easily on her way out, but she also didn't want to leave the door standing open in case one of the maintenance staff needed something from the closet.

Just as when she and Michael had come to the roof, the metal door at the top of the stairs wasn't locked. Apparently the maintenance crew thought the locks on the other doors were enough. Opening the door, she stepped out into the late afternoon sunshine, blinking while her eyes adjusted, and looked to her right where the corrugated metal shed had once stood.

It was still there. More rust covered the metal than she remembered, but it still looked strong and stable. She crossed to it and gave the door a tug. It swung open more easily than she'd expected, and she wondered if Michael had oiled the hinges. Inside, in the corner to the right of the door, stood a metal box that looked new, the kind of box sold at Walmart to protect valuable documents in the event of a fire. The shine proved it hadn't been sitting in the shed for three decades. Michael must have bought it to use as his "treasure chest."

She kneeled in front of it, feeling grit pressing into her knees. For a few seconds she hesitated to open the box. Inside would be the Star, proof that the man she had loved had ceased to exist even before the bullet took his life. Then she squeezed the latch, only a little surprised to find it unlocked, and raised the lid. Inside was a plastic grocery bag. She lifted it out. It felt like papers. She laid it aside and checked the box. There was nothing else.

Confused, she pulled the stack of papers from the bag. It was a manuscript, an old one. The pages were yellowed, and the type looked like it had been done on a typewriter. She fanned the edges, thinking maybe they were hollowed out and concealed the Star in the middle, but they were solid. She got to her feet, brushed the dirt off her knees, and moved to the door where there was more light. She skimmed the first page and the second, but by the time she got to the third, she slowed down. Leaning against the door frame, she read through several pages and then flipped ahead in the manuscript and read some more, feeling her world tilt on its axis as she realized what she was holding.

***

"You did what?"

It wasn't often that someone walked up to an Eden detective's desk and admitted to a crime. But Cal Becker had done exactly that and didn't look the least bit worried about it.

"Well," Cal said. "It's not like I haven't done it before. As you well know."

Jo felt her face grow hot. Damn it, she thought. I should have known better than to go along with that little escapade. Yes, Rawlings's life had been in danger, but it was still a mistake, and it hadn't helped a damn bit in finding her.

"There was a woman's life at stake then," she said between gritted teeth. "Last time I checked, she was just fine."

"Okay, okay." Cal held his hands up in surrender. "Arrest me if you want, but first hear me out."

He told her what he'd found on Rawlings's email and saw her expression change from anger to interest.

"Treasure," she said. "In their 'special place.' Any idea where that might be?"

"None," Cal said. "But I was thinking that Chief Pelfrey might know."

"She probably does," Jo said. "Whether she'll tell me if she knows why I'm asking is another story."

"So don't tell her why you're asking. Tell her one of the Halseys told you Mabry was always talking about a special place he and Rawlings used to go and you think he might have hidden the Star there."

Jo stared at him for a second before pulling the phone to her and hitting a speed dial number.

"Hey, Lou," she said. "Got a question you might know the answer to."

***

"It's empty." Cal held up the metal box, its lid open. "Rawlings has been here, and now she has the Star."

"You don't know that." Lou glared at him. "Michael used to leave flowers and other gifts for her up here, and he called it 'treasure.' You're jumping to conclusions based on something that scumbag Halsey told you."

"How we got the tip isn't important," Jo said. "What's important now is finding your friend. In case you've forgotten, Leonard Nowles is still out there."

"I haven't forgotten, but I'm beginning to think you've forgotten who the villain is here. It's damn sure not Kate!"

"Then call her. Tell her to come in and talk to us about what was in that box."

Lou looked uncomfortable. "I can't," she said. "She hasn't replaced her phone yet."

"Convenient," Cal muttered.

Lou glared at him.

***

Jackson's garage stood open. Kate crossed to the door leading into the house and found it unlocked. She let herself in without bothering to knock, something she never would have done before. Considering the reason she was here, the niceties of civilized society no longer seemed to apply.

She heard music coming from Jackson's study at the rear of the house and moved that way. The door was open, a piano sonata—Mozart, she thought—playing on the stereo. Jackson was seated behind his desk, a half empty bottle of Scotch in front of him and a glass in his hand. He was still dressed in the pants, shirt and sport coat he'd been wearing when he left Holly House. As she stepped into the room, she saw that he was crying, tears trickling down his face, but he made no sound. He looked up, startled, and wiped his face just as the CD ended.

"Katherine. What are you doing here?" His voice sounded unnaturally loud in the sudden silence. "I told you I didn't need any help…"

His voice trailed off as he saw her expression.

"I read Michael's book, Jackson. Enough of it to know what you did."

He stared at her, the drink forgotten in his hand. For what seemed like an eternity, they were frozen like that, his guilt-tortured eyes looking at her out of an old man's face. She felt paralyzed, unable to pull her gaze away from his, trying to work up the courage to ask the question she knew she had to ask.

"Did you..." Her voice shook and she started over. "Did you kill Michael?"

He shuddered and closed his eyes, shoulders slumping. For several minutes, the only sounds were traffic passing on the street and a dog barking at a neighbor's. Kate held her breath, waiting for the answer to the question she was already wishing she hadn't asked. Finally, Jackson opened his eyes, looked straight into hers, and Kate caught a glimpse of the hell that lurked behind them.

"Yes," he said.

"Oh, my God! Why? For God's sake, Jackson, why?" Kate heard her voice wavering on the edge of hysteria and fought to get herself under control.

"It was an accident, Katherine! I swear it! I only meant to frighten him. I never intended to kill him. Never."

Jackson's eyes filled with tears, and he blinked them away. He sighed deeply.

"If only I had given him what he wanted," he murmured the words she had heard him say more than once over the past few days. Suddenly she understood.

"He was blackmailing you."

Jackson nodded. "He gave me the manuscript to hold as collateral for the loan I made him over thirty years ago. I think I was the only person who knew he was working on it. I knew how good it was, Katherine, how valuable. I was sure he would repay the money and go on to publish."

He leaned forward, setting his glass clumsily on the desk. Whiskey sloshed onto the desk pad, but he didn't seem to notice.

"I wanted to see him succeed. You have to believe that. You and Michael were my own personal stars, bright talents I felt proud to have guided." His lips twisted into a bitter smile. "My own talent was something of a shooting star itself, wouldn't you say? Not as valuable as the one Michael stole, unfortunately. One bright burst and then nothing but a fizzle. But if you two succeeded, I could at least be proud of my contribution as mentor."

"But Michael never repaid the money and never came back for his manuscript." Kate took a deep breath. "When did you decide to put your name on it, Jackson? When did you decide to steal it?"

He winced at her harsh words. "It wasn't like that, Katherine. I lived with *Dogwood Days* day in and day out, knowing how good it was, how beautiful. I hadn't heard from Michael in years. For all I knew, he was dead. I wanted that beautiful book to be read by others. It deserved that."

He stood up and began to pace behind his desk, a slight stagger evident. Kate wondered how much he'd drunk in the short time he'd been home.

"I worked on it over the years, cleaning it up here and there. I sent it to my agent for him to look over. I didn't say it was mine." His expression was pleading. "I didn't. I said the author was a friend who wanted an honest opinion."

"So how did your name end up on the cover?"

"My agent loved it," Jackson said, as if he hadn't heard her question. "The funny thing was, he didn't believe me when I said it wasn't mine. Then I realized it *was* mine. At least, partly. I had input from the beginning. I guided Michael from the first word to the last. We collaborated on it, Katherine."

His voice took on a whine. "That's what I finally came to realize. It was as much mine as his. Why, you wouldn't believe how much I had to clean it up in order to submit it. That qualified me as a collaborator even if I hadn't worked on the original draft."

"I believe that's called editing, Jackson. Not creating." She marveled that this intelligent man was finding it so easy to rationalize plagiarism. Maybe that was how he rationalized murder as well.

"Damn you!" His face reddened with anger. "Damn you for your smugness! What would you know about creating? Pulp fiction is all you're good at!"

"At least I only write about murder." She lifted her chin and stared at the man she'd called a friend, the man who had been like a father to her at one time, wondering if she'd ever really known him.

"Michael was a filthy thief and a blackmailer, Katherine!" Jackson slammed his fist against the wall, and she jumped. "I would think you of all people would know the kind of man he was."

"He didn't deserve to be murdered so you could steal his book."

"I told you, it was an accident!" Jackson's voice had grown shrill. He stopped for a moment, taking a deep breath in an attempt to regain control of his emotions. "He needed money to get out of the country. He didn't tell me why, just that he was in a lot of trouble, and he needed to disappear. He asked me for an inordinate sum, Katherine. I could have gotten it, of course, but I was afraid he wouldn't stop there. I didn't know what to do."

Tears filled his eyes again. "You don't understand how difficult it's been for me. To be a success as young as I was and not be able to repeat it. It's eaten at me, day in and day out, and the more it ate at me, the less able I was to write—I mean, *really* write. I needed a success, Katherine. To be able to go out in a blaze of glory like Georgia said. To be remembered as a talent, not a has-been."

"You killed him so you could retire in a blaze of glory?" Kate could hardly believe her ears.

"It was an accident! I thought if I could frighten Michael enough, he'd leave and that would be the end of it. I knew he was being pursued by someone. I thought it was the police. I knew he couldn't afford to stay in Eden long."

"What happened?" Kate forced herself to ask the question.

"I told him to meet me at Hanover after the party was over. I told him we would work things out. I think he thought I had the money there. I waited for him in the parking lot. With a gun."

Jackson shook his head, as if in wonderment at his own foolishness. "I abhor guns, but this one belonged to my father. I always meant to sell it, but I never got around to it. I thought I could scare Michael. I threatened to kill him if he didn't leave me alone. I told him I'd already given him all the money he was ever going to get, that he owed me the book in exchange for the loan he'd never paid back. I told him he couldn't prove the book was his."

"What did he say?"

"He told me there was another copy of the manuscript that he had hidden in a safe place. I didn't believe him. How could I? How could anyone possess that beautiful story for three decades and not do anything with it? I called him a liar."

"And then you killed him."

"No! Not like that! He laughed at me. Can you believe that? He laughed at me! I told him to shut up, but he just kept laughing. Looking back, I suppose he did it to distract me, but at the time I didn't see that. All I know is, he laughed at me, and then he grabbed for the gun." Jackson shook his head. "Michael was used to such drama. I wasn't. I panicked. I was afraid he was going to kill me if he got control of the gun. I fought him for it, and the next thing I knew, it went off."

He sank back into the desk chair and buried his face in his hands. "I watched him die, Katherine. God forgive me, I didn't even try to save him."

Katherine stared at him. His shoulders shook, but no sound came from him as he cried. Outside, she heard a car horn honk as it went by on the street in front of Jackson's house and marveled that the world was careening on as if nothing had happened. She stood waiting, for what she didn't know. A miracle, maybe? A miracle that would bring back the Jackson she had known and loved to replace the plagiaristic murderer who sat before her.

After what seemed an eternity, Jackson raised his head. She sucked her breath in, startled at the change in him. His tears had stopped. He was smiling, but the smile didn't extend to his eyes. This wasn't the Jackson she knew, and she suddenly realized she'd been a fool to come here and confront him alone.

Chapter 36

"What are you doing?" Kate stared at the gun Jackson had pulled from his jacket pocket. "Are you going to kill me, too?"

Kate felt like she was in a nightmare, a crazy mishmash of the ordinary and the unthinkable. She loved Jackson like a father, and he loved her like a daughter. Fathers didn't kill daughters. They just didn't.

He looked at her for what seemed like an eternity and then lowered his eyes to the gun in his hand. His shoulders slumped, and he sighed, a long and tortured sound.

"I suppose that would be the smart thing to do," he said. "As the old saying goes, in for a penny, in for a pound. Better than admitting to stealing that beautiful book and living with the shame. Better than admitting to murder and spending what's left of my life in a prison cell."

"How are you going to explain shooting me in your own house?" Logic. Maybe he would respond to logic. If she could just make him realize there was no way he could get away with another murder....

Jackson laughed and hiccuped, swaying on his feet, and she realized she wasn't facing a rational man. She was facing a man too drunk and desperate to realize there were no good options. When he sobered up, he might regret what he'd done, but that wouldn't help her if she were dead.

"I wouldn't have to leave you lying on my study floor," he said. "My car has a large trunk, and there's a convenient river close by. I could drop your body there and throw the gun in with it. Even if you both were found, there would be no way to trace the gun to me. My father bought it from a private seller back in the fifties. I doubt there was ever a record of the sale."

"The police will find Michael's manuscript. They'll figure it out, just like I did."

"You came here from Holly House, fresh with your discovery of the truth. If the manuscript isn't in your car, it's in your room. I could get it before your body is discovered. When you're found, the authorities would assume another of Michael's cronies did the deed. No one would suspect me. I'm just an old man."

"Jackson, please—don't do this."

He smiled again. This time the smile reached his eyes, and Kate saw the Jackson she loved.

"Don't worry, Katherine," he said, his voice low. "I couldn't kill you any more than I could kill Michael intentionally. What I did to him has been eating me alive."

He motioned to the door. "Go now," he said. "I don't want you here when I do what I have to do."

All thoughts of her own safety vanished as she realized he was going to kill himself. "No, Jackson, no! You can't! The police will understand. Michael's death was an accident."

"Even though I had one of the best possible motives for his murder? I don't think so. I'd rather go out in a blaze of glory, even if that glory does fade once the truth comes out. At least I won't have to be here to face it."

"I'll be with you." She started toward him, hoping to get close enough to take the gun. "You won't be alone. Jackson, please, don't do this!"

"I agree. Please don't," said a voice she recognized. "At least not just yet."

She whirled around as Leonard Nowles stepped into the room. He was holding a gun in his hand, and it was pointed directly at her.

"I'm glad I got here in time to hear the whole story. Shame on you, Dr. Price. Stealing the Professor's book like that." He chuckled. "You just never know about the most respectable types, do you?"

He moved around the edge of the room, his gun swinging past Katherine and coming to bear on Jackson.

"Put it down, old man," he said.

"Or what?" Jackson straightened. "You're going to shoot me? Save me the trouble of doing it myself?"

Nowles shrugged.

"Probably," he said. "But not until after I shoot this lovely lady here."

"No!" Jackson's hand began to shake. After a few seconds, he laid the gun on the desk. "Let her go!"

"Maybe I'll let you both go if you tell me where the Star is. And maybe I won't. But it's the only chance you've got."

"We don't *know* where it is!" Kate clenched her fists, surprised to feel herself growing angry. This no-good SOB had tortured her, and he still didn't believe her when she said she knew nothing about the Star's whereabouts.

"What about you, Dr. Price? I never had a chance to question you as thoroughly as I questioned this lady. You have a secret you want to share—I mean, besides the fact that you stole the Professor's book?"

"If I knew where that damnable thing was, I'd have turned it over to the authorities long ago."

"Well, we'll see what you say after spending some quality time with me," Nowles said. He gestured with his gun. "Move away from the desk."

Kate moved back toward the window, while Jackson started around the desk on the side closest to where Nowles stood. As he reached the corner of the desk, he grabbed the whiskey bottle by its neck and swung it at Nowles.

"No!" Kate screamed as Nowles stumbled backward, and a shot rang out.

The momentum of Jackson's swing caused him to pitch forward as the bullet struck him, knocking Nowles back against the wall of the study. Nowles cursed and shoved him away. He was still holding the gun pointed at Jackson as the old man fell to the floor.

"Dumb ass." He pointed the gun at the back of Jackson's head and pulled the trigger again. Jackson's body jerked and then went still.

"I hope you're going to be more cooperative."

He raised his eyes and the gun toward Kate, as she pulled the trigger of Jackson's revolver again and again, and continued pulling as it clicked on the empty cylinder.

Chapter 37

"Hey," Jo said when Nick answered.

He'd left messages over the weekend, messages she had ignored. She'd given herself the excuse that she was busy with the kidnapping, but the truth was, she hadn't wanted to talk to him. They'd parted on good enough terms, but after he'd driven away Saturday morning, she'd felt the resentment begin to build again.

"You finally decided to get back to me, I see."

"Yeah. I'm sorry. Can you talk, or am I interrupting something?"

"Just eating Chinese and reading all the stuff they gave me today. How about you? How's the case going?"

"We're calling it done although we haven't found the Star." She filled him in, starting with the kidnapping and ending with the double shooting at Price's house.

"Wow!" he said when she finished. "I see why you didn't have time to call."

Was that sarcasm in his voice, she wondered. Or am I just too tired and too paranoid?

"Yeah, it did get kinda busy." She felt the beginnings of a headache and massaged the area between her eyebrows. "So how's the new job looking?"

"Good. It looks great, actually. Lot to learn, though."

"Then I'd better let you get back to it." She stood. "I've still got paperwork to do before I head home."

"Maybe you could get a flight up here next weekend? We could look for an apartment or a house together?"

What would be the point of that, she thought, but didn't say. She knew Nick was hoping to get her involved in selecting a place to live. He hoped she'd get enthused about it, and, by extension, about D.C. and the move.

"Yeah, maybe," she said. "Depends on what's going on here. Love you."

"Love you, too," he said.

As she headed back to the detective section, she thought about that. She did love Nick and probably always would. How could you not love someone who'd been a part of your life for so many years, someone you'd created a living, breathing human being with? He'd said he loved her, too, and she believed him. The question was, would it be enough?

Sticks was slumped in his chair, eyes shut. When he heard her at her desk, he opened them and yawned. "Are we about done here?" he said.

"I guess so."

"You don't sound convinced."

"I'm not."

"Rawlings's story checks out. I mean, it'd be nice if we had a video of the event, but everything points to her telling the truth."

Rawlings had told them she hadn't been able to rest and had decided to help Price with what still needed to be done at his house. According to her, Price had been in his study when she arrived, shredding an early draft of his novel while drinking whiskey and listening to music. They were talking when Nowles stepped into the room. He had a gun and began demanding they tell him where the Star was. When he threatened to hurt Kate to get answers, Jackson grabbed the closest weapon at hand—the whiskey bottle. He swung it at Nowles who shot him. Jackson fell into him, and the two of them hit the floor. When Nowles went down, another gun fell out of the back of his pants and slid across the floor. Nowles had pushed Jackson off, got to his feet and shot Jackson in the head, just as Kate emptied the gun that she had grabbed off the floor into Nowles.

Lena and Bob had finished processing the crime scene. The physical evidence supported Rawlings story about how it went down. No reason to think it was anything other than what it appeared to be. So why, Jo wondered, did she have the feeling that she hadn't heard the whole story?

"The Star's still missing," Jo said.

"Yeah, it is." Sticks yawned again. "Maybe the lady author's got it, maybe she don't. But we searched her car, remember?"

Rawlings had readily agreed to the search. Jo had told her they'd learned that she and Mabry spent time on the roof of Hanover Hall in their younger days. She seemed to accept it as natural that the police would search the roof in the hope of finding the Star or clues to Michael's killer. She claimed she hadn't been on the roof since graduate school.

"For all we know," Sticks said. "Some student took his girlfriend up on the roof like Mabry used to do and found it."

"Yeah, right."

"Coulda happened."

Jo's desk phone rang.

"A Mr. Applegate is here to see you," Vera said.

Since the younger Applegates were locked up, it had to be Hanover Hall's maintenance man. He probably wanted to talk about his son and grandson. She was tempted to have Vera tell him she'd already left, but at the last second, her conscience wouldn't let her. According to what everyone said, Robbie Applegate was a really nice man. Thanks to his son and grandson, he'd had enough disappointment in his life. She didn't need to add to it.

"Send him back." She hung up and turned to Sticks. "Robbie Applegate wants to talk to us."

Sticks groaned.

The old man stopped inside the door and looked around as if he wasn't sure he was in the right place. He had a cardboard box in his hand. It was about the size of a boot box with the logo of a snack company on the side. It appeared to be wrapped with packing tape.

"Mr. Applegate?" Jo stepped forward. "I'm Detective Valentine. You wanted to see me?"

"I guess so," he said. "If you're the detective that's investigating Mike's murder."

Jo glanced at Sticks. He looked as surprised as she felt.

"This is Detective Mullins," she said, gesturing to Sticks. "We've both been working the Michael Mabry case."

Sticks held out his hand. Robbie shifted the box to his left arm and shook, and then sat down in the chair Jo indicated for him. He set the box on the desk.

"So what can we do for you, Mr. Applegate?" Jo said.

"It's this here," he said, nodding his head toward the box. "When Mike first got to town, he brought it by Hanover. Asked me to hang onto it for him for a few days. Said it was important to him, and he didn't trust it not to get stolen if he left it in his motel room."

You've got to be kidding, Jo thought.

"After I heard about him getting killed, I didn't know what I should do with it. I hung onto it, thinking maybe I would hear something about his family, but then this weekend, I heard a rumor that the police think Mike was part of that bunch that robbed the museum up in Chicago. That jewel they stole is still missing, right? I got to thinking, what if it's in this box? I don't like thinking Mike would do something like that, but if there's one thing I've learned with my own boys, you can never tell about a person. Figured it was best to bring it here."

Jo lifted the box. It's about the right weight, she thought. She removed a letter opener from her desk drawer and sliced through the packing tape holding the two sides of the lid together. The inside was stuffed with wadded up newspaper. As she laid it aside, she noticed it was the Lexington Herald-Leader. Mabry had packed the box after he'd gotten to town.

Under the paper was a maroon velvet bag. As she lifted it out, she felt a solid object inside. It was slightly larger than her hand, oblong on three sides, the fourth rising to a point about two inches above the rest. She laid it on her desk blotter. The bag was secured with a gold drawstring cord, but the knot yielded to her fingers easily. Inside, the object was wrapped in a white cloth that felt like silk. She unwrapped it slowly to expose the object that had caused the deaths of five people.

It was beautiful, no doubt about that. The gold and the diamonds glistened in the light, but it was the massive ruby that stole the show. Jo estimated the gem to be three inches in diameter. The light above her desk didn't reflect off the surface of the gem but instead was absorbed into it, warming the blood red color until it seemed to be a living thing. She moved it back and forth and caught a glimpse of the "star" inside. The piece was heavy, and she marveled that a long-dead woman had been able to carry the weight of it and the headdress it had graced on her head.

She looked at Sticks. He was standing behind Robbie, staring at the Star, his mouth hanging open. He raised his eyes and looked back at her.

"Well." He closed his mouth and swallowed hard. "Sure didn't see that one coming."

Chapter 38

Jackson's memorial service was a media event. Thanks to a slow news week, the story of a bestselling author whose book was soon to be a movie being killed by one of the villains involved in the Drayer Museum heist played on the national news five days in a row, leading the broadcast for three of them. Organized crime involvement and the villain having been killed by a mystery novelist who was the former lover of the villain's partner didn't hurt the story any.

Dolly reported that a well-known true crime writer and two Hollywood producers were already sniffing around. She had fielded several requests for Kate to go on talk shows, but Kate refused. Dolly understood her reluctance but suggested it might stop the calls and sell some books at the same time. But no matter how persuasive Dolly might become, Kate was never going to tell the story to anyone in the media. The police had accepted her version, particularly after the Star surfaced. She wasn't going to push her luck by telling it to a reporter.

The memorial service was held in the Raven University auditorium. All eight hundred seats were filled, most with friends, co-workers, students, and former students who had come to pay their respects to Jackson. The director and producers of the movie being made of *Dogwood Days* allegedly came to pay homage to a great writer, but Kate suspected it was more for the publicity than out of respect. A well-known actor, rumored to be the likely choice to play the leading role, attended with his wife. The Hollywood presence naturally fueled the media frenzy even further, but Raven University restricted cameras to the outside of the building.

She sat center right in the front row, Chris on her right. Roger and Lou sat on her left, providing a barrier between Kate and the

Hollywood contingent who filled most of the seats on the left side of the front row. Ann, Edna, Ginger, Cal Becker, and Mary Dunn sat on the other side of Chris. Members of the English faculty and university administrators occupied the remainder of the first row and the second. Jackson had had no heirs. Respected and well liked by the university leaders before his death, he became their idol after it was learned he had left his entire estate to the university, including any future proceeds from his books.

The shuffling and murmuring stopped as the service began with a video that Kate and Lou had compiled of photos taken throughout Jackson's life. As she watched, Kate thought back to the events of that day, replaying them in her mind as she had many times over the last two weeks.

She didn't know how long she had pulled the trigger after all the bullets were fired into the body of Leonard Nowles, but eventually she realized the hammer was clicking on empty chambers and stopped. Minutes passed as she stood staring at the body of her friend, unable to move or even think. Eventually a small voice in her brain began chittering. "Call 9-1-1," it said, "call 9-1-1."

She punched in the first two numbers on Jackson's phone but stopped as, in her mind's eye, she saw the future as it would unfold if she told the truth. Jackson would go from being a beloved professor and famous writer, mourned by all who knew him, to a plagiaristic has-been. Jokes would be made at his expense in late night monologues, the movie production would likely shut down, enrollment at Raven—especially the English department—would be adversely affected. And for what purpose? To give Michael, a man who had wasted his life and his talents, not to mention having hurt a lot of people, the credit and recognition that was due him? What good would it do him in the grave? Maybe Jackson didn't deserve to have his secret kept, but there was more than just his reputation at stake. It was at that moment she decided the story needed a major revision.

She wiped Jackson's gun clean of prints and then pressed Leonard Nowles's dead fingers around it. Removing it from the dead man's grasp, she held it in her right hand and pressed the trigger repeatedly, just as she had when there were bullets still in the cylinder. If the police could match the bullet that killed

Michael to the gun, the only fingerprints they would find would be Nowles and her own. When she finished with the gun, she hurried to her car and retrieved Michael's manuscript. It didn't take long to run it through Jackson's shredder.

When she finished, she placed the 9-1-1 call. The revision had been simple. Delete a little backstory, add a little text, and the ending was changed forever. With those few changes, the sordid truth became a story of heroism. If Michael was watching from the afterlife, she thought even he might appreciate her creativity.

As the video ended and a local minister stepped to the podium to begin the service, Kate took Chris's hand. He squeezed it and gave her an encouraging smile. I'm here for you, the smile seemed to say. I don't intend on going anywhere.

And neither do I, Kate thought. The search committee had graciously accepted her withdrawal from the pool of candidates for the chair, trying unsuccessfully to hide their relief. Publicity about a criminal ex-lover and fatal shootings might be great for selling novels, but it didn't help parents of students sleep well at night. She doubted she would be asked to continue as a part-time professor, but that was fine with her. It was time to walk away from the ivory tower.

As the minister adjusted the microphone and placed the paper containing his eulogy on the podium, Lou nudged her. "What did Johnny Crouch want with you?" she whispered.

"Who?" Kate didn't know any Johnny Crouch.

"The old guy in the blue suit who shook your hand when you were coming up the walk outside. I saw him stop you. What did he want?"

Kate remembered now. The man had stopped her, extended his hand, and she had shaken it. He'd held her hand in both of his for a moment before turning away and entering the building with the rest of the crowd attending the service. He hadn't said a word during the entire encounter.

"What did he want?" Lou whispered again.

"I have no idea," Kate whispered back, as the minister began to speak.

###

About the Author

I live with my husband, three dogs, and two cats inside Daniel Boone National Forest in Kentucky. I divide my time between writing mysteries and writing romances (as Lolli Powell). I love to hear from readers and can be found at: www.laurelheidtman.com.

If you enjoyed this book, please leave a review at your favorite online retailer. Readers depend on reviews to guide them to books they might enjoy, and authors depend on them to spread the word to readers.

Thank you.

Laurel Heidtman

~~~ Books By This Author ~~~

As Laurel Heidtman:

Whiteout (thriller)

Eden series (mystery):

    Catch A Falling Star

    Bad Girls

    A Convenient Death

    Murder in Eden boxed set (contains the first three Eden books)

As Lolli Powell:

The Boy Next Door (contemporary romance)

The Wrong Kind of Man (romantic suspense)

The Gift: a novella (holiday romance)

Top Shelf Mysteries (cozy mystery):

    The Body on the Barstool

    Whiskey Kills

    Name Your Poison (coming late summer 2019)

www.ingramcontent.com/pod-product-compliance
Lightning Source LLC
Chambersburg PA
CBHW031949240626
47153CB00003B/916